THE SLEEPOVER

KERI BEEVIS

B

Boldwood

First published in Great Britain in 2022 by Boldwood Books Ltd.

A CIP catalogue record for this book is available from the British Library.

Paperback ISBN 978-1-80415-123-5

Large Print ISBN 978-1-80415-119-8

Hardback ISBN 978-1-80415-118-1

Ebook ISBN 978-1-80415-116-7

Kindle ISBN 978-1-80415-117-4

Audio CD ISBN 978-1-80415-124-2

MP3 CD ISBN 978-1-80415-121-1

Digital audio download ISBN 978-1-80415-115-0

Boldwood Books Ltd
23 Bowerdean Street
London SW6 3TN
www.boldwoodbooks.com

PROLOGUE

When she looked back to the summer it happened, it hadn't been all bad.

There were six of them that year, the Americans having moved to the village after Christmas. Generally, they were a tight-knit group and seldom let anyone else into their circle, but curiosity had been piqued by the different accents and cool clothes, and barriers had dropped. And for the first time, they had allowed a boy into their fold.

The country had been gripped by a heatwave and when school finally finished for the summer holidays, they made the most of it, meeting up early in the mornings, keen to show their new friends around. Lazy days were spent cycling along country lanes, playing games of hide-and-seek, climbing strawbales and daring each other to ignore the 'DANGER, KEEP OUT' notice and venture onto the train track.

When it became too hot, they went swimming in the river to cool off, and made future plans over lazy picnics of crisps, melted chocolate bars, and warm cans of Coke.

The days were hot but the nights were unbearable, and open windows had been a necessity. Heads had tossed and turned, finding no cold side to the pillow, and legs had dangled out of sheets; the need to escape the sticky heat overriding any fears of monsters under the bed.

It had been a blessed relief when they were allowed the occasional outdoor sleepovers. They were entering their teenage years and had excitedly talked about crushes, while spooking each other with urban legends, before falling asleep under a clear sky of stars, the only sounds coming from the intermittent hooting of an owl and the chugging of the last train as it passed through the edge of the village on its way from Marks Tey to Sudbury.

The memories were vivid and should have been innocent. And she guessed they mostly were.

Before the monster. Before her.

Everything had changed that summer, and in the aftermath, the last years of childhood had been robbed as they were forced under a media spotlight, now members of the newly coined Hixton Five, unable to escape what had happened, and having to relive the horrors again and again.

The monster had said that as they were children, no one would believe them. But she had been wrong. The adults had listened and they had believed. And the monster had been taken away.

That was twenty years ago.

When she allowed herself to think back to the sound of the lid closing, the darkness suffocating, that sharp and sweaty scent of fear, it was overwhelming and all too real.

So she tried not to remember. It was easier that way. She had built a good life and she tried to replace the bad memories with happy ones.

For a long time, it had worked.

But now, try as she might to leave the past behind her, the events of that summer were starting to plague her dreams again. Even creeping into her everyday thoughts.

Because the monster had been freed.

And she couldn't help but worry that a storm was brewing.

1

As she stood on the beach watching the three dogs tussle over a frisbee, Hannah Cole reminded herself that moving to the North Norfolk coast was the best decision she had ever made.

Sometimes it was easy to forget that.

Yes, it was an hour's drive from Norwich, where she had been living before, and the flat she had inherited after her beloved nan passed came with its share of problems. It was in the attic of an old four-storey building that had leaks and draughts and dodgy plumbing, and a lift that groaned loudly when working, which wasn't often. But the trade-off was the flat's location in the port town of Wells-next-the-Sea. The flat was in a cosy back street, but just a five-minute walk to the quayside and if she craned her head far enough out of her bedroom window, she could see the crabber and angling vessels moored in the harbour, and the creeks cutting a winding path through the salt marsh beyond.

Early each day, before the holidaymakers descended, she headed away from the bustle of the quayside, down the mile-long path that led to the beach. It was like entering a different world, especially when the tide was out, as it was this morning, and with miles of unspoilt golden sand before her, the crash of the waves in the distance, her mood always lifted.

The dogs loved it as much as she did and when they had tired of playing with the frisbee, she would take them into the pine woods that served as a backdrop to the prettily painted beach huts, before returning them to their homes.

Her Pawsome Pet Services was something she had started up earlier in the year, keen to cut back on her copywriting commitments and find a job she really loved. She got to work with animals and it was also more active, getting her out from behind her desk.

Rufus, Cookie, and Spot. They were her regular charges and she took them out most weekdays. The three of them were the best of friends, despite differing in looks and personality. Rufus the giant black poodle towered over Cookie the Tibetan terrier and scruffy little mongrel, Spot. Rufus was the youngster. Big and bouncy, with boundless energy, but gentle too. Cookie was highly strung, but also a diva, the pretty little princess who didn't like to get her feet wet, while Spot was the most laid-back, taking everything in his stride. Hannah watched them as they played, enjoying the early-morning warmth of the September sun, the sky an almost cloudless deep blue.

She whistled to the dogs, rewarding Cookie and Spot, who came running immediately, with a dog biscuit each from the stash she kept in her bag. Rufus was always the stubborn one, initially ignoring her as he charged along the water's edge with the frisbee in his mouth. He soon came bounding over when he realised he was missing out on treats.

As Hannah clipped on their leads and headed into the woods, the curtain of trees blocked out the sun, the temperature becoming cooler. This was one of her favourite parts of the walk, as she drew in the scent of the pine cones, the crunch of twigs underfoot overriding the thrash of the waves. She often had the woods to herself at this time of the morning, though never felt unsafe, the dogs alerting her if they heard anyone coming. Out here was a good place to be alone with her thoughts and make decisions. And right now, she needed to figure out what she was going to do about her mother and stepfather's silver wedding anniversary party.

In two weeks' time, she would have to return home to the sleepy village of Hixton in Suffolk, where she had grown up. As it was for a special occasion, her mother wanted her to stay for the weekend, while Hannah had plans to drive home after the party. It had been a bone of contention the last few times they spoke and Hannah was beginning to realise that unless she could find a compromise, she might have to give in.

She had left Hixton when she was nineteen, glad to put the place with all its bad memories behind her, and she avoided returning home for visits unless it was necessary. She never stayed the night, not even at Christmas, preferring to make the two-hour drive home, but on this occasion her mother was putting her foot down. The idea made her queasy.

Hannah was still searching for a solution when her pocket started vibrating, the sound reverberating through the woods. She reached for her phone, frowning when she saw the face of her best friend, Rosie, on the screen. It wasn't yet 8 a.m. Rosie was never awake before 8 a.m.

'Hey, you're up early.'

'Hannah?' Rosie's voice was a panicked whisper. 'I need you to come and get me.'

'Why? Where are you?'

'There's this guy and I'm at his house. We're in the middle of nowhere. I want to go home.'

Hannah's heart started thudding. 'What do you mean there's a guy? What happened? Did he force you to go against your will? Where's your car?'

'It's back in the city. Please, Hannah. You have to help me before he wakes up.'

'I'll call the police.'

'No! No, don't call them.'

'Has he hurt you?'

'Just come and get me, please! I'll explain when you get here.'

Hannah clicked onto Rosie's Snapchat locator. 'You're in Bawdeswell?' She knew of the village. It was about twenty miles from Wells. 'I'm out with the dogs. It's going to take me a while to drop them off and get to where you are.'

She waited for Rosie to respond, but there was just silence.

'Rosie?'

Still nothing.

'ROSIE?'

'What? Yes, I'm here. I thought he had woken up.'

'Rosie, if you're in danger, I need to call the police.'

'No police! Promise me, Hannah.' Rosie sounded on the verge of tears and Hannah's gut twisted, wondering what the hell kind of trouble she was in.

'Okay, I won't call them. I'll be as quick as I can.'

'Just hurry, okay? Message me when you get here and I'll sneak out.'

All three dogs were looking at Hannah as the call ended and she hurried them homewards, grateful that they belonged to neighbours who were on her route. Normally she would stop to chat, but Rosie's call had spooked her. Who the hell was she with and what had happened to her?

Wondering how wise an idea it was to show up at this man's house alone, she called her ex-husband on the way to Bawdeswell.

She could hear the exasperation in Josh's voice the moment Rosie's name was mentioned.

'You know this is going to be another case of cry wolf, don't you, Han?'

'She sounded really upset.'

'Of course she did. She plays you like a fiddle every time.'

There had never been any love lost between Rosie and Josh, even though they were two of the closest people in Hannah's life. Josh thought Rosie was a drama queen, while Rosie couldn't understand why Hannah kept him around. 'Ex should mean ex, as in good riddance,' she had said on more than one occasion.

Truth was, Hannah and Josh worked better as friends than as husband and wife. Their marriage had been short-lived, over when they were still in their mid-twenties, and it wasn't until they were divorced that they really started to understand one another. Hannah still loved him, but she wasn't in love with him, and this last eight years as friends, Josh Cole had become more like the brother she had never had.

He might have had his doubts about Rosie's emergency, but he still insisted Hannah call him when she arrived at the address. As she pulled off the road and into the driveway of the house that she had nearly missed due to the high hedgerows of the narrow twisting country lane, she was glad he had. Part of her wondered as she tapped his name into her phone whether she should be ignoring Rosie's wishes and calling the police anyway.

'Are you there yet?'

'I've just arrived. Josh, this place is in the middle of nowhere. What if she really is in trouble?'

'Then call the police.'

'I can't. She made me promise I wouldn't.'

There was silence on the line and then she heard him sigh. 'I think you have your answer. If Rosie was really in trouble, she wouldn't stop you calling them. In fact, she would have called them herself instead of dragging you out there.'

Hannah wanted to stick up for her friend, but deep down she knew Josh had a point. She agreed she would call him back again, once she knew Rosie was okay.

'And promise me you won't get out of the car.'

Hannah bit down on the urge to tell him he was an idiot for thinking she would even consider it. Honestly, though, it was comforting to know he had her back. Instead, she assured him she would stay in the car, then ended the call before firing a quick message to Rosie.

I'm here.

She decided it was safest to leave the engine running and tapped her fingers nervously on the steering wheel, eyes on the house, watching for Rosie. The walls had been rendered in a creamy yellow. It looked well maintained and to the side of the property was a black BMW.

Nice house, nice car, but really it meant nothing. Bad people could own nice things.

She glanced at her phone, saw her message had been read, but there was still no sign of her friend.

Rosie had said she would be waiting for her to make contact. So where the hell was she?

2

A couple more minutes passed and Hannah was on the verge of calling the police when Rosie finally appeared.

She was dressed in a tight-fitting, black dress, one that barely covered her arse and showed off her slender legs, and her dark hair was pulled back in a messy knot. A typical Rosie party outfit.

Hannah wound the window down. 'Are you okay?'

She had expected Rosie to be distressed, but she didn't appear concerned. The only sign of her anxiety came after she carefully shut the door behind her.

It had barely closed when it swung open again and a tall, chiselled man stepped out, wearing just a pair of joggers and a confused frown on his face as he followed her to the car. 'Rosie? Are you leaving?'

Rosie glanced at Hannah, shooting her a panicked look that warned her to play along, and Hannah's hackles rose as her friend turned back to the man and reached up for a kiss.

That distracted him momentarily, but his attention was soon on Hannah. 'Who's this?'

'This is my friend, Hannah. Hannah, meet Doug.'

Hannah couldn't bring herself to speak. Instead she nodded curtly.

'Hi.' Doug still looked confused, understandably so. 'How did you know Rosie was here?'

'I forgot, Hannah has a... thing we have to go to,' Rosie answered quickly, before Hannah could tell him the truth.

'A thing?' As he glanced between the pair of them, his eyes narrowed in suspicion. He seemed pleasant enough, but Hannah could hear the edge in his tone.

'Yeah.'

'But—'

'So it was lovely meeting you and thank you for last night, but we need to go.'

'I was going to make you breakfast.'

'We can do that another time. Call me.'

Rosie was already hurrying around the car and climbing into the passenger seat.

'You never gave me your numb—'

The door slammed shut, cutting off the end of Doug's sentence.

'Seriously, Rosie?' Hannah hissed as she wound her window up. 'I thought you were in danger.'

'Go. I'll explain on the way back.'

Josh had warned her, but Hannah hadn't listened. She slammed the gearstick into reverse, knowing she only had herself to blame.

'You're mad at me,' Rosie said, as Hannah backed out of the drive. Doug was standing on the front step watching them, a frown now on his face.

'I thought you were in trouble. I nearly called the police.'

'I never said I was in trouble. You assumed I was.'

'Are you surprised? You let me think you were. I thought it was an emergency.'

'Well it was.' Rosie's tone was turning petulant. 'I didn't want to be there. I should never have gone home with him.'

'So why did you?' Hannah asked, exasperated.

'Last night, it seemed like a good idea, but then I woke up in his bed this morning and I panicked. You know what I'm like when I've had a few drinks. My judgement goes out of the window and I can't help myself.'

'Maybe you should give the alcohol a break then.'

'Crikey, Hannah. You're not my mother.'

'I'm not trying to be.' Hannah bit her tongue, resisting the urge to point out that she had just come and picked Rosie up at her insistence. Exactly the sort of thing a mother would do.

'Well, can you stop laying into me please. My head is pounding.'

Serves you right. She didn't say the words aloud, knowing what Rosie was like when she was in one of these moods. There would be no rationalising with her. Her friend could be the sweetest, kindest, and most thoughtful person, but she also had a self-destruct button.

Not good when there were a lot of people out there willing to take advantage of her.

She didn't even bother to ask where Rosie had met Doug or why she was out drinking heavily on a Sunday night. It was a regular occurrence with Rosie and the bars in Norwich were a home away from home for her. The only thing that ever differed were the men she hooked up with.

'Are you working today?' she asked instead, assuming she was taking Rosie back to Norwich.

She used the word 'working' loosely. As an only child who had lost both parents, Rosie didn't want for money. Her father had invested wisely, while her grandmother, who had died a few years later, had been stinking rich. The money Rosie had inherited had left her more than comfortable.

Still, she liked to keep herself busy and it was hard to keep up with her schedule as the jobs she did weren't regular. Her résumé listed her first and foremost as an actress, though most of the projects she had worked on had never been released. Of the ones that had, she had played a dead body, had a cameo role in *Hollyoaks*, plus a couple of one-line parts in low-budget films. Then there was the modelling, and her YouTube channel, which was probably her biggest success. She endorsed beauty products, tested out the latest fads, and preached a healthy lifestyle to her subscribers that Hannah knew she didn't follow herself. Rosie was good at persuading people. She had the gift of the gab when it came to getting companies to send her freebies and her bubbly personality shone through, ensuring she came across as likeable to her many followers.

She also knew how to work the circuit, flitting back and forth between Norfolk and London, getting to know every other Z-list celebrity, blogger, and vlogger out there, as well as a few bigger hitters.

Her life was a world away from Hannah's, and Hannah had zero interest in the parties and events Rosie tried to lure her to. On paper, the two women were opposites, but their childhood ties were strong and Hannah was one of very few people Rosie could be her true self with.

'Nothing in the diary, thank God. Do you fancy grabbing an early lunch? We could try that new burger place that's opened and maybe go for a facial afterwards.'

'Sorry, I have work to do.'

Rosie pouted. 'You're no fun.'

'You're welcome to come over. The job I'm working on shouldn't take too long to finish.'

'I think I'm just going to slob around my flat, order in junk food, and watch movies,' Rosie decided. 'And I am never drinking again.'

'Of course not,' Hannah agreed dryly. It was only Monday, but there was no waiting for the weekend for Rosie, and they both knew she would open a bottle of wine early evening, and that she would probably end up heading out again into Norwich to one of the bars. She couldn't seem to help herself.

And once Rosie was drunk, her guard lowered and she made herself vulnerable. She had no pause button when it came to alcohol and drugs. Doug had seemed like an okay guy, but one day Rosie was going to go home with the wrong person. That scared Hannah half to death and she tried again to persuade Rosie to stay with her.

'You can slob at mine. Have a bath or a nap. Make yourself feel human again. Then when I've finished, we can order takeout and have a catch up.'

Rosie mulled the idea over, a slight frown on her pretty face, and Hannah thought she was going to say no. 'I guess that would be nice. You'll need to lend me some slob-out clothes.'

'Of course.'

As Hannah turned the car around and headed back towards the coast, her phone started ringing.

Rosie rolled her eyes as Josh's name flashed up on the dashboard. 'What does he want?'

Damn it. Hannah had promised to call him back. 'He was worried about you.'

'You told him? Seriously, Hannah. What you do, and definitely what I do, it's none of his business.'

'You're too harsh on him. He's a good guy. And he cares.'

'Guess you'd better answer it then,' Rosie huffed.

'I'll call him back,' Hannah said, as the phone cut to voicemail. If she took the call now, it would have to be on loudspeaker and she didn't want Rosie and Josh to start sniping at each other.

Rosie was a little subdued the rest of the drive home, giving mostly monosyllabic answers, and Hannah suspected she was still stewing over the call to Josh, though she looked pale, so maybe her hangover had really kicked in.

After they arrived back at Hannah's building, she marched ahead, going straight for the lift.

'It's not working,' Hannah informed her.

That was met with a sigh. 'Again? I don't know why you insist on keeping this place. You know it's probably worth a fortune because of the location. You could move back to Norwich and buy something newer and at least twice the size. You'd probably have money left over too.'

Yes, okay, she could, and it was something she had briefly considered, but the location was important. Hannah loved living in Wells and she would never be able to afford anywhere else here, even if she got top whack for her flat. 'I like it here,' she said simply, following Rosie up the stairs.

'I'm sure you'd like it somewhere else too if you'd stop being so stubborn.'

'This place has its charms.'

'Of course it does. Like the quirky broken lift and the temperamental heating.' Rosie kicked off her heels as they reached the top landing, scooping them up in one hand, while she used the other to rub at the ball of her foot. 'I can't wait to have a bath. My feet are killing me.' She frowned. 'The hot water is working, right?'

She was facing the stairs so hadn't spotted the man outside Hannah's front door. Having heard their voices, he had turned to watch them, a faintly amused expression on his face as they approached.

Hannah's spine stiffened as she pushed past Rosie, her keys ready. She didn't know him and he didn't look like he was delivering anything. He had no reason to be here. Unless he had the wrong address.

'Can I help you?'

'You're Hannah Cole, right? Used to be Hannah Freemont?'

Her spine stiffened. He knew her maiden name? Something she wanted to leave firmly in the past. 'What do you want?'

The man smiled. She suspected he was trying to put her at ease, to let her know he meant her no trouble. Unfortunately, it had the opposite effect. She knew that smile too well.

'My name's Liam Quinn. I'm hoping you can spare me fifteen minutes.'

'Why?'

If he was taken aback by her coolness, he wasn't letting on. She was aware of Rosie moving to stand beside her, knew from her silence that she was equally wary.

Quinn rocked back on his heels, studying them both. 'I'm a writer and I'd really like to talk to you about a book I'm working on.'

He waited a beat, staring directly at Hannah and, when he finally dropped his bombshell, she realised too late, her mouth dropping open in shock, that it had been to gauge her reaction.

'It's about Eileen Wickham.'

3

They had deserved it. When it all became too much, Eileen tried to remember that.

At times, it was difficult. The press had painted her as a monster, the judge had called her remorseless, cruel, and evil, stipulating that she would serve her full sentence, and her fellow inmates at HMP New Hall had viewed her with disgust from the start.

Eileen Wickham, or Eileen Wicked if you took notice of the headlines, had quickly understood that she wouldn't change popular opinion, the press had seen to that, so she had kept her head down, tried her best to stay out of trouble, and served her time. People had already made up their mind about her, so there was little point in trying to sway them.

And did she really care what they thought anyway? She had no regrets about the things she had done and had enjoyed scaring the hell out of those spoilt and entitled kids. They had no idea how lucky they were and it had done them good to get a taste of the dark side.

She only wished she hadn't been caught. Those little bitches had a lot to answer for. Because of them, she had lost everything.

The need for atonement, for revenge, had burned bright and strong, but she had swallowed it down, tried to be the model prisoner, and by the time her release came around, she understood it was all about playing a game, about telling those in charge what they wanted to hear.

She had been anxious and her belly jittery with nerves the day she was released, unsure of what might be waiting for her on the outside, but Bill had taken care of everything. Her boy had been there the day she was released, taking her to the house he was renting for them. She was on licence and would have to regularly meet with a probation officer, but finally, after twenty years, the freedom she had craved was hers.

Unfortunately, she quickly learnt that it came with a price.

It had taken less than forty-eight hours for word to spread around her neighbourhood and for people to realise who she was, and they weren't happy. And then there were the journalists wanting her side of the story. Well, they could just fuck off. She remembered how they had ganged up on her before and she had nothing to say to any of them now.

Bill saw them off. Every last one of them.

The threats though, they weren't so easy to dismiss. The first warning was graffiti on the front door. The second had been delivered on a brick through the front window. She wasn't welcome here and she should leave before things became worse.

Eileen had grown up in foster care and had endured her fair share of bullying and abuse, but she wasn't as tough as she used to be. She was a sixty-three-year-old woman and no match for the group of men who tried to intimidate her as she was making her way to the corner shop to buy cigarettes.

Bill was furious, but although she gave him a description of the men, he wasn't able to track them down.

He tried his best to take care of her, but Eileen became afraid to leave the house and that wasn't good when her boy worked away during the week.

Admitting to weakness and living in fear was tough for her to handle. From humble beginnings, she had worked her way up to top dog and then it had been stolen from her. Bitterness and rage warred with self-pity as she mourned the woman she had been and loathed the one she had become.

She couldn't live like this and something had to give.

When Bill finally witnessed her explode one weekend, he realised it too.

Before he returned to work the following week, he made her a promise. 'I have a plan. I'm going to fix this. Just give me a few days.'

And so she waited.

4

Hannah told him he was a vulture. That was a new name for the list.

Liam Quinn had been called callous, intrusive, overly persistent, and an insensitive bastard before, but never a vulture. He had also never had a door slammed shut in his face quite as quickly as when Hannah Cole had told him to get lost. He was obviously losing his touch. Which was why he was up early the following morning and had parked his car a short distance down the road from her block of flats, waiting for her to make an appearance.

He wasn't callous or a vulture, at least he didn't think he was, and he tried not to be too intrusive. An insensitive bastard? Okay, maybe on occasion, but he was working on that. Persistent though? Yeah, that was him spot on. And Hannah was about to find out just how persistent he could be.

She hadn't been quite as he had imagined. Yes, she was blonde, like in the picture on her website, and of course her face was the same, but the woman he had encountered yesterday had a tougher exterior and frown lines that had deepened when he had told her who he was. And what the online image hadn't captured was just how startling her wide green eyes were when you were caught in their gaze. He suspected she didn't suffer fools easily and wasn't going to be quite the pushover he had hoped.

One bonus was she hadn't been alone. Liam had recognised Rosie Emerson immediately and had for a moment thought his job was going to be easy with the pair of them in one place. Two birds, one stone and all that. Of course, that had been before the vulture calling and the door slamming.

He got it. Of course he did. And perhaps in hindsight, given what they had been through, showing up on Hannah's doorstep hadn't been the smartest move. This wasn't his first non-fiction book and he should have known better.

Hannah and Rosie had been scarred by experiences no thirteen-year-old should have to face, and now here he was, some bloke wanting to dredge it all up for a book he was writing. It was understandable they were going to be wary. They thought he was doing it to make money out of their tragedy. And okay, yes, he had bills to pay, but it wasn't the only reason.

He had been wanting to tell this story for a long time and the need to do so was personal.

Not that he would ever reveal that to Hannah Cole or Rosie Emerson. At least not until it was time.

While he waited for Hannah to appear, he filled his belly with a breakfast bap and coffee purchased from one of the local cafes, ignoring the doleful eyes of his passenger, Tank, who was going to leave a puddle of drool all over the seat if he didn't put his tongue away.

In the past, Liam would have been tempted to buy Tank a bap of his own, but during his last check-up, the vet had warned that the dog was overweight and told Liam he needed to stop overfeeding him. Easier said than done when you had 93lbs of slobbering fur trying to guilt you into sharing every mouthful of food, just like he was doing right now.

Tank had already eaten breakfast, but seemed to have forgotten that and the staring was now being accompanied by lip licking and agitated whining, guilting Liam into feeding him the last piece of sausage. He was too bloody soft for his own good where his dog was concerned.

Breakfast polished off, Liam was just about to get out of the car to find a bin to dispose of the rubbish when the main door to the flats opened and Hannah emerged, hair tied back in a ponytail and her eyes hidden behind a pair of oversized sunglasses.

Tossing the cardboard cup and breakfast bap wrapper into the back of the car, he turned to Tank.

'Okay, you're up, pal. I need you to be your most charming self.'

Liam had studied Hannah's Pawsome Pet Services website, where she spoke about her love of animals, especially dogs, so he was certain she would soon fall for Tank. Part Bernese mountain dog, part poodle, he was an oversized teddy bear. What was not to love?

Hannah had already disappeared round the corner, but he had seen the direction she had gone and he clipped on Tank's lead, coaxing him from the car. This was the tricky bit. The giant bundle of fur would have happily stayed on stakeout all day if he had his way, letting out what sounded like a reluctant huff as he plonked his arse down on the pavement.

'Come on, mate. We need to go.'

By the time he had persuaded Tank to get up, Hannah had a considerable lead, but the seaside town was small. She couldn't have gone far without a car.

Or so he thought. Minutes later, Liam found himself on the quayside with no idea where she was.

He glanced around for her. Ahead was the harbour, dotted with colourful fishing boats, and beyond that was the salt marsh, the sun highlighting the glittering paths of the creeks that wound from the quay down to the sea. The main quayside road stretched in both directions, lined with gift shops and restaurants, and although it was early morning, it was still alive with the bustle of activity from those getting ready for another day of trade.

It was a beautiful morning, the sky a cloudless blue, and it was going to be another warm day, likely to bring with it a last flurry of tourists wanting to make the most of the end-of-season weather.

A handful of side streets led off the road and Hannah could have disappeared up any one of them. As Liam cursed under his breath, the dog gave him a bored look, as if to say, 'Ready to call it a day?' Breakfast baps and stakeouts Tank was all for, walking and exercise not so much.

'It's your fault we lost her. Now we're going to have to find out where she went.'

Tank's response to that was to squat down on the pavement and go to the toilet.

'Nice,' Liam muttered, glad he had remembered to bring poo bags.

As he cleared up the offending mess and deposited it in a nearby bin, Hannah appeared again from one of the side roads, this time accompanied by a pretty little black and white terrier.

'Now you're interested,' he commented, as Tank's head shot up.

This time, Liam had no trouble getting the dog to his feet as they followed after Hannah, keeping a safe distance away.

Here on the quayside was not the place to have a confrontation, and remembering how she had been the previous day, Liam had no doubt their next encounter would be heated. He planned on getting Hannah to talk, but knew it wasn't going to be easy.

He soon learnt they were heading down to the sea, though it seemed she had other charges to pick up en route. By the time they were on the beach road, she had three of them in tow, the terrier joined by a black poodle and a scruffy little dog.

Her love for animals was how Liam planned to try and break her. Tank was big and stubborn and lazy, but he was also a handsome son of a bitch. When Hannah met him, then when she realised how much Liam adored him, he hoped she might start to thaw.

The beach was some distance from the quayside and Tank was tiring as they approached the tiny roundabout leading to the car park and toilets, whining and sulking to let Liam know he'd had enough. It took a mix of intrigue at the dogs in front, Liam encouraging and tugging on his lead, plus sheer willpower, to get him up the pathway and down onto the sand. The tide was out, the beach stretching for miles, and spotting the other three dogs in the distance, off the lead and playing near the sea, Tank suddenly found a new lease of life. He almost dragged Liam along behind him, as he raced across to join them.

That was the point at which Hannah spotted them, pushing her sunglasses up on her head, her green eyes widening at the beast lumbering towards her, then narrowing again, a scowl settling on her face when she recognised his owner.

'Are you following me?' she demanded, as Liam somehow managed to put the brakes on Tank.

'Just walking my dog. But fancy running into you here.'

'Looked more like he was walking you. And yes, what a coincidence.' Her tone was ice.

'Are those three all your dogs?'

Of course he knew they weren't, but he needed a conversation opener that didn't cut straight to Eileen.

For a moment, he didn't think she was going to answer him, as she turned her back on him and whistled to the poodle, who was getting a little over enthusiastic in his playtime and upsetting the terrier. 'Rufus! No!'

She had better command over him than Liam had over Tank, as the dog backed off immediately. Meanwhile, his own dog was getting petulant and threatening to pull his arm out of its socket.

'No,' Hannah repeated, this time to Liam, her tone less friendly than when she was telling Rufus off. 'Look, I don't mean to be a bitch, but I have no interest in talking to you or having anything to do with your book, so can you just bugger off and leave me alone please?'

Her arms were folded and her expression stony.

Liam gave her what he hoped was his most charming smile. 'Of course. As I said, I'm just here walking my dog.'

He had expected this reaction, so wasn't disappointed. Time for Tank to work his magic and win her over, he decided, unclipping the dog's lead.

And that was when all hell broke loose.

5

If she wasn't so angry, it might have been comical. The giant ball of fur bounding across the beach with the current source of Hannah's irritation hot on his tail, yelling at him to stop. Of course the dog didn't take a blind bit of notice. It had been obvious who was in charge in that relationship the moment she had laid eyes on the pair of them.

The dog, Tank she learnt from the yelling, was heading straight for the sea, making a beeline for Rufus, Cookie, and Spot, which wasn't particularly a problem. All three were well socialised and Tank might be the size of his namesake, and disobedient too, but he didn't appear to be vicious. Despite his size, he was still a youngster and probably just wanted to play.

Still, she edged towards the water, wanting to be close by in case she had judged it wrong.

Delighted to see the newcomer, Rufus and Spot ran in circles around him, while Cookie kept her distance. Unfortunately, it seemed she was the one Tank was keenest to meet and seeing Liam Quinn hopelessly chasing and failing to catch his dog, Hannah sped up her pace.

'It's okay, sweetheart,' she coaxed, stepping into the foray and reaching for the terrier.

As she lifted her out of Tank's reach, Quinn managed to clip the lead on his collar.

'Sorry,' he apologised, turning to scold Tank. 'I didn't realise he would take off like that.'

'He needs training.'

'Sorry?'

'You're telling him off, but it's not his fault.'

'You've lost me.'

'There are no bad dogs, just bad owners. You need to take him to training classes if you can't control him.'

'I see.' From the faint smirk on his face, he didn't *see*, or care, what she meant at all. 'I'll bear that in mind.'

Of course you will. Hannah kept her thoughts to herself, not wanting to get into an argument, not wanting to get into anything with Liam Quinn that would give him an excuse to keep up conversation. The sooner he left, the better.

She turned her back on him, stroking Cookie behind the ears as she stepped away, and hoping he would respect her privacy and go. Instead, she heard him yell, 'TANK', and didn't have time to react as the disobedient fluffy monster charged in front of her, trying to get to Cookie, his lead tangling around Hannah's legs.

It all happened at once. Liam trying to control his dog while Hannah did her best to keep Cookie away from Tank. The lead tightened further and the next thing she knew, she had lost her balance, Cookie scrambling out of her arms as she fell, and she was flat on her back in the sand.

For the briefest moment, there was silence, then she was aware of the dogs barking and Liam was crouched down beside her, a hand on her shoulder.

'Shit! Are you okay?'

Anger and embarrassment heated her cheeks as she tried to sit up, shaking him away. 'I'm fine. Get off me.'

'Are you sure? You hit the ground pretty hard.'

'We're on sand.'

Sand or no sand, he was right and she was pretty sure she was going to have a lovely bruise on her bum later. She tried to get up, mildly panicked when her left leg didn't cooperate.

Seeing her struggling, Liam offered his hand.

She ignored it at first, determined to refuse any help. He had done more than enough. The sharp stabbing pain in her ankle had her stumbling though, as soon as she put weight on it, and without thinking, she grabbed onto his arm to stop herself from falling.

Dammit. She must have twisted it or something. This was not good.

'You need to get that checked out. I can take you to the hospital.'

'No!' There was no way in hell she was getting in a car with Liam Quinn.

'Home then?'

'I'm fine,' she muttered through gritted teeth, tentatively letting go of him and testing her balance. Standing was one thing. Her ankle hurt like a bitch, but as long as she kept the bulk of her weight on her right foot, it was bearable. Walking was going to hurt like hell, though.

'Look, just stop being stubborn and let me help you, okay? I feel kind of responsible.'

'Kind of?' Hannah stared at him. 'This is *all* your fault. If you hadn't been stalking me—'

Her comment was met with a derisive snort of laughter. 'I wasn't *stalking* you.'

'You were following me after I asked you to leave me alone.'

'Look, we can argue about this all day, but while we do, the dogs are going to get bored and— Tank! Jesus, TANK. LEAVE HER ALONE!'

In the panic after her fall, Hannah hadn't realised that Liam had let go of his dog's lead and she looked around in alarm to see the giant beast sniffing after Cookie again. The little dog didn't seem too stressed by it, having assessed and dismissed him as a threat.

'They're okay. He's not bothering her.'

It did highlight the problem of how she was going to get the dogs home. She was responsible for her charges, and while she might be able to limp back to her flat alone, she would struggle to do it with the three of them on leads. She couldn't leave them here.

Rosie was still in the flat. Hannah had left her asleep on the sofa. Would she answer her phone?

'So what do you want to do? Tempting as you're making it to leave you here, I won't.'

Liam chanced a smile and Hannah scowled at him. They weren't friends and she refused to play nice with him.

'It's fine. You can go. I'll call my friend.'

She reached into her pocket for her phone and dialled Rosie's number, annoyed when there was no answer and irritated that Liam was lingering instead of leaving as instructed.

And dammit. If Rosie didn't pick up, Hannah didn't see that she had a choice. She was going to have to accept his offer of help.

'Look, I get it, okay. You don't like me; you don't want to be interviewed by me. But I don't see how you're safely going to get three dogs home unless you let me help you.'

When she stared at him but didn't argue, he continued.

'How about a compromise? I'll get you home and I promise I won't mention a word about my book or what happened back then.'

She was silent for a moment as she digested that. 'And what is the compromise?'

'I'm writing this story, Hannah, with or without your help, and I'm sorry you don't like that.'

Of course she didn't like it and she knew the others in the Hixton Five would feel the same. Lauren, Jill, and Tash had all moved on with their lives, but Hannah knew they were guarded about their past, and Rosie would never cope with having everything dug up.

As for poor Miles, he wasn't even here to defend himself.

'It's not okay, you know. Using what happened to us to try to make money for yourself.'

She swore she saw a flash of temper in his blue eyes at her accusation, but his tone when he spoke was even. 'Is that what I'm doing?'

'You know it is.'

'Look, all I ask is that you take my card and you consider talking to me. You don't have to, but I'm staying locally for the next couple of weeks, so please at least think about it.'

He raised his eyebrows slightly in question as Hannah pretended to ponder his offer.

Of course she wasn't going to talk to him and she didn't plan on giving him any consideration at all. The card he gave her would go straight in the bin. But she was going to need his help getting Rufus, Cookie, and Spot to their homes, then back to her flat, so she supposed she should at least pretend to go along with his proposal.

'So if I think about it, you promise you'll leave me alone?'

'I promise.'

'And my friend, Rosie. You won't bother her either?'

It was Liam's turn to hesitate and she could tell from the slight twitch as his cheek dimpled that he didn't like the extra clause.

'It was worse for her. Please leave her alone.'

If he already knew that, and she guessed he did, he didn't say.

'Okay,' he agreed eventually. 'So do we have a deal?'

Hannah was going to break that deal and she couldn't help but suspect Liam might go back on his word too, but for the next half an hour, or however long it took them to get back into town, drop the dogs off, then back to her flat, they had an uneasy alliance.

She nodded. 'We have a deal.'

6

Rosie hadn't long been awake and, spotting she had a missed call from Hannah, had immediately phoned her back, worried when it when to voicemail. Hannah would be out with the dogs, so why was she not picking up? Had something happened?

She had been glancing out of the window, anxiety twisting her gut and wondering what to do, when she spotted the two figures with the big dog heading down the street. Relief skittered through her as she spotted her friend, but it quickly turned to anger when she realised who Hannah was with.

Flinging on a hoodie Rosie found in the wardrobe and still wearing checked pyjama bottoms, she charged out of the flat and down the stairs, just as Hannah and the man who had his arm around her, arrived at the main entrance of the building. She had recognised his rangy build, tawny-coloured hair and dark bomber jacket, and her heart was racing.

Liam Quinn. The man who had given her a restless night's sleep.

'What the hell are you doing with him?' Rosie was aware her voice was raised, but she couldn't help it.

'I was walking the dogs and—'

'You don't walk *that* dog,' she snapped. 'And not with *him*!' She pointed a finger at Quinn. 'I had a missed call and I've been trying to get hold of you. I was worried.'

'I'm sorry,' Hannah sounded apologetic. 'I had the dogs and couldn't answer. I—'

'Why are you walking funny?' Rosie demanded, finally noticing Hannah was limping. 'Have you hurt her?' Her second question was aimed at Quinn, who seemed more amused than concerned, which just added to her fury.

'Of course not. Well... not intentionally.'

As Rosie's cheeks heated with rage, Hannah tried to placate her. 'I fell over and I've hurt my ankle. I think I've probably twisted it. Liam happened to be down on the beach with his dog. He helped me get home.'

'Liam? You're on first-name terms with him?'

'Do you need a hand getting upstairs?' Quinn offered, ignoring Rosie.

'I can manage, but thank you.'

As Hannah turned to go, he stopped her.

'Wait. My card.'

'Umm, okay.' She avoided Rosie's pointed look as she took the card, quickly pocketing it.

'Hannah? What the hell?'

'It's not what it looks like,' Hannah assured her as they left Quinn on the pavement and walked into her building.

'You just took his card!' Rosie dropped her arm, taking a step back. 'Please tell me you're not considering talking to him?'

'Of course I'm not. Look, can you help me get upstairs please? My ankle is killing me. I need to get some ice on it. Let me sit down and I promise I will tell you everything.'

7

Hannah Freemont and Rosie Emerson.

I wasn't sure how I would react, seeing them again after all of this time. They are no longer children, but they are still recognisable. Blonde Hannah and dark-haired Rosie, one much taller than the other, their mannerisms still the same. Rosie has lost her spark, but I can see she is trying so desperately hard to pretend she still has it. She is, and always was, the more animated of the two. Hannah is calmer, more reserved, but there is an edge to her that didn't exist before. And, of course, she is no longer Freemont, having taken and kept her ex-husband's name.

Hannah Cole.

I had wondered briefly if it was because she was trying to escape her past, to shed her skin, but that didn't explain her actions now. I watched her and Rosie walk into the building and I don't have to be a genius to know they will be upstairs right now talking about me. Talking and plotting their next move, which makes me sick to my stomach, realising that even after all this time, they can't just move on.

Haven't they already done enough damage? Destroyed enough lives?

Anger heats the blood coursing through my veins. Both of them have caused so much trouble, though Hannah is the one I still mostly hold *responsible. She ignored our threats and, by doing so, she ruined our games. She is the one I want to even the score with most.*

Now I've seen first-hand what a scheming bitch she is, and realise that she won't let things drop, I am going to make her pay.

It is time that someone holds these women accountable for their actions, shows them the consequences of what they have done, and I look forward to teaching them a lesson.

8

The plan had been for Tank to charm Hannah Cole, not literally knock her off her feet, but while the move hadn't been ideal and Liam still felt shitty about it, at least it had given him a little time to work on her.

He had kept to his promise, not mentioning Mrs W or the book he was researching on the walk back to her flat, though that had as much to do with concentrating on walking four dogs and trying to support Hannah so she didn't fall again as it did with gaining her trust.

She had taken his card, the one he had written the address where he was staying on the back of, though he suspected it might end up in the bin, but she had also agreed to at least consider talking to him. He didn't know if she would get in touch, but at least it was a start.

She had been cool but civil with him on the walk back, which was definitely a step up from slamming the door in his face, but there was still a long way to go and he didn't have much time.

The Airbnb was his for another couple of weeks and while he

had agreed he wouldn't pursue her for an interview, it didn't mean he couldn't bump into her again. Wells was a small town.

She would talk to him one way or another. He just needed to be creative and perhaps a little sneaky about it.

Right now, he was thinking he should do something as an apology, nudge that door open a little wider, and he was googling local florists as he enjoyed a late-afternoon beer on the deck, Tank snoozing and snoring contentedly in the patch of sun at the top of the steps.

A bouquet of flowers might thaw Hannah. Definitely not roses. He didn't want to give her the wrong idea. Something bright and cheerful. A 'sorry I knocked you on your arse' gift, not one that suggested he was interested in her romantically. She was already mad at him, and he didn't want to upset her further.

He was beginning to wonder if flowers were the right way to go when his phone started ringing. He glanced at the screen, saw 'Mum' flashing up, and hesitated before answering it, wondering why she was calling.

She knew he was out of town. Had something happened?

Their relationship had never been the easiest and she had been absent for a large part of his life, but still she was his responsibility, his own flesh and blood, and he had promised he would take care of her.

'Hello?'

'Oh, Liam. There you are.'

'What's up, Mum?'

'I just wanted to hear your voice. We haven't spoken for a few days.'

'I told you I had to go away for a bit.'

'Do you know when you will be back?' she asked. 'I miss you.'

'I don't know. It depends how long the job takes. Maybe next week. Maybe longer.'

'Oh.' He could hear her disappointment and knew she was just trying to guilt him.

Of course it worked. It always bloody did.

'Look, I'll see you when I'm back, okay, and we can catch up then.'

'Do you promise?'

'I promise.'

It was a charade they went through, both knowing she would call again in a couple of days and ask the same questions. He got it. She hated being on her own.

'I miss you, Liam. I love you, son.'

'I love you too, Mum, and I'll see you soon.'

Disconnecting the call, he threw his phone down on the table and scrubbed his hands over his face. She no longer acted like the woman he remembered as a child. These days, she was more needy and, dare he say it, fragile.

Tank lifted his head and looked at him with huge, sympathetic, brown eyes.

Taking another drink of beer, he turned back to his MacBook. Time to return his attention to the far more important matter of Hannah Cole.

9

Hannah had offered for her to stay again, but truth was, Rosie was too agitated.

Hannah had explained about her encounter with Liam Quinn, but it was all so convenient.

Rosie believed Hannah's story, but didn't like how Quinn was trying to worm his way in. And his ploy seemed to be working. Hannah might say she was having nothing to do with him, but she was already on first-name terms with him.

It was messing with Rosie's head and putting her in a bad mood. She needed to get back home and blow off some steam. Ensuring Hannah had everything she needed, she caught a taxi to Fakenham, then a bus back home to Norwich.

Her favourite solution to her problems was alcohol, and the first thing she did when she returned to her flat was pour a large gin and tonic. The second was to go through her phone book for potential drinking buddies.

After making half a dozen calls, she finally struck gold with 'Action Man Austin'. Everyone in her phone book had a nickname, from Hannah Banana to Jerk Face Josh. Action Man Austin was

Rosie's old gym instructor and, at six foot four with rock-solid biceps, he more than deserved the moniker she had given him.

They took advantage of the late-afternoon warmth, picking an outside table at Rosie's favourite bistro and laughing and chatting over cocktails, which had been exactly what she had needed, finally able to shut off that dark and unpleasant part of her life, and just enjoy herself.

As the afternoon wore into evening, she decided she was open to losing herself in a night of good sex. Unfortunately, it wouldn't be with Austin. Although she flirted outrageously with him, she knew she would never turn his head. Their preferences were too similar and there had been more than one occasion that they had competed for the attention of the same man.

While Austin lifted her mood, with it just being the two of them, it made it more difficult to pull. Everyone assumed they were a couple.

With no prospective shag in sight and Austin needing to head home, they finally called it a night.

Given how mild it was, and the fact it had already cost her nearly thirty quid to get back from Wells, Rosie decided to walk home, the alcohol making her struggle to focus on the road ahead. The sky that had earlier been a vivid blue was now inky black, a reminder that darker days would soon be on the way.

In a couple of months, it would be winter, and Rosie found it harder to keep her perky party girl mask up in shadow-filled dreary days that offered little in the way of light. It was ironic perhaps, as her worst nightmare had happened to her during the warmest of summers, but the blackness and the misery she had experienced then always seemed to surface when the sun was furthest away, reminding her that she could hide and pretend that the summer of 2002 hadn't scarred her, but deep down, everyone knew it was a lie.

The others had moved on. Even Hannah to an extent. But not

Rosie. During the day, she painted her fake-as-fuck smile onto her face and tried to fool everybody. But at night, she drank herself stupid or took sleeping pills, occasionally did both together, to try to block out the memories. Mostly it worked, but sometimes it didn't.

That self-destruct button of hers was just waiting to be pushed.

By the time she turned off the main road, heading up the twisting sloped driveway to the building where she lived, her mood had plummeted and she was indulging in one of her self-pity parties.

The sound of rustling in the bushes pulled her out of it, halting her in her tracks, her anxious eyes looking for the source of the noise.

She hadn't heard any footsteps, but was someone hiding on the path up ahead?

The thought had her hesitating and unsure if she should continue as she watched the bushes, waiting for another sound.

Maybe it had been her imagination.

It was the bravado of the alcohol running through her veins that spurred her on. That, and the fact her bladder was close to bursting. She hurried up the driveway, passing the spot where she thought that she'd heard a noise. There was nothing there, no one tried to grab her.

But then the rustling came again, this time from closer to the building, and her heart hammered.

'Who's there?'

She had aimed for strong and assertive, but her voice sounded weak and pathetic, the slurred words telling whoever was tormenting her that she was drunk and vulnerable.

Of course no one answered and she reached into her bag for her keys, gripping the one for the main door tightly between her fingers.

She was just about to take another step forward when, with no warning, a shape ran out of the bushes at her.

Screaming, Rosie dropped her keys.

As she stared at her neighbour's cat, her legs shook and it took her a moment to steady her breathing.

'You little shit,' she managed eventually. 'You scared the crap out of me.'

Lucien blinked at her with bright yellow eyes and circled her legs in response, but when Rosie bent down to make a fuss of him, he darted back into the bushes.

It was just the cat. *For fuck's sake, Rosie.* She had almost lost her shit over nothing.

Scooping up her keys, she headed for the main door, formulating a plan in her head: boots off, wee, glass of wine, hot shower.

Her flat was on the first floor and as always she had left the table lamp on, its warm glow welcoming her. Kicking off her boots, her feet silently groaned in relief.

After peeing, she padded across the open-plan living room cum kitchen to her bedroom, hitting the switch. Light spilled onto the room and her attention was immediately drawn to the wall behind her bed, the pretty silver wallpaper that she had paid a small fortune for now covered in crude red paint.

At least she assumed it was paint, the word had dripped down the paper and onto her pillow before drying.

BITCH

Her hand flew to her mouth, partly muffling the sob that escaped.

Someone had been inside her flat.

Were they still inside her flat?

Her legs were shaking, threatening to collapse as she unsteadily backed away, crouching slightly so she could see under the bed. No one was there and the only other place they could hide was the wardrobe. She grabbed the can of hairspray from her dressing table, the nearest thing she had to hand, and approached the mirrored doors, her trembling finger poised over the nozzle.

Breathe, Rosie.

She pulled open the door, a little of the tension ebbing out of her when the interior light came on showing nothing but clothes.

The front door? Had she locked it?

A fresh wave of fear gripped her as she rushed from the bedroom to check, choking out a relieved sob as she realised she had.

She was safe for now.

But how did whoever broke in get inside in the first place?

She glanced at the balcony door, saw it was very slightly ajar. There was no way she had left it like that.

Even as she locked it again, she questioned how safe she was and the sudden panic that whoever had been in her flat might come back threatened to overwhelm her.

Think, Rosie. She needed to call the police. Or Hannah. She would know what to do.

As she reached for her phone, it started ringing. Seeing the unknown number flashing up on the screen, she nearly dropped it. No way was she answering when she didn't know who it was.

She watched it ring, scared to move her hand in case she accidentally hit answer.

Eventually it stopped and she went to pull up Hannah's number. Before she could press call, the unknown number started to ring again.

Go away!

She was about to hit decline when it crossed her mind that it could be something important. There were few people Rosie truly cared about, but she held them close. If something had happened to one of them and she hadn't answered the call...

That made up her mind.

'Hello?'

When she was met with silence, her heart began to thump.

'Hello?'

She could hear breathing so knew someone was there.

'Who is this?' She snapped out the question, the hand holding her phone trembling.

Still nothing.

'I can hear you, so I know you're there. I'm going to hang up now. This isn't funny.'

As she went to end the call, a sound like a clock being wound up chilled her bones. Metal grinding against metal, the cogs winding tighter with each turn. She waited for that familiar click, the last twist of the key, and when it came, in the moment before the music began, a stray tear slid down her cheek.

The jewellery box tune pulled her back in time to that summer when she had just turned thirteen, sucking her into the nightmare from which she had never really escaped.

She threw the phone down, her hand covering her mouth. And in that moment she understood it wasn't over. The woman who haunted her dreams was coming for her again.

10

'Rosie, you're scaring me. What the hell is wrong?'

As she waited for her friend to answer, Hannah was struggling into her jeans, the phone jammed between her right ear and shoulder, and the foot she had bandaged refusing to comply.

'She's found me. I knew it wasn't over.'

Rosie's voice was barely a whisper, making it even harder to understand her now than when she had been sobbing hysterically.

'Who has found you?'

'She has. Mrs W.'

It was no secret Eileen Wickham was out of prison, but Hannah doubted she would be stupid enough to track Rosie down. She would surely know she would be the first person the police would look to.

'Mrs W was in your flat?' she asked, trying her best not to sound sceptical.

'I heard her music box.'

'Her music box?' Hannah repeated. Was she talking about the one that Mrs W had owned?

'Yes! She called me. I heard it playing.'

Had she imagined it? It was possible. Rosie still struggled with the past.

'Where are you now?'

'In the bathroom. I locked the door.'

'What? Why have you locked the door?' When her question was met with silence, her panic rose. 'Rosie? Answer me. Is she there now?'

'I don't know. I don't think so. But what if she comes back?' Rosie's question was almost whispered and Hannah could hear the fear behind her words. 'I can't do this any more, Hannah.'

'Rosie? Listen to me. I'm coming over, I'll be there as soon as I can. I'm calling the police too. Stay in the bathroom, keep the door locked. I promise I'm on my way.'

'I can't,' she sobbed.

'What do you mean, you can't?'

'I just can't do this. I'm sorry.'

'Rosie? Rosie?'

It was too late. Rosie had disconnected.

Frantically, Hannah called her back, swearing when it went straight to voicemail.

Hoping this wasn't another situation where her friend was crying wolf, she called the police.

'She's going to have a lot of explaining to do if this is another false alarm,' Josh commented, his tone amicable as he pulled into the driveway of the block of flats where Rosie lived, parking alongside the two police cars. Hannah could see a uniformed officer outside, and some of the residents from the other flats had come out, curious to know what was going on.

His nonchalant attitude, convinced that this was simply another blown-up drama, had actually helped keep Hannah calm on the hour ride to Norwich, but now she was here, her heart was pounding. She didn't care if this was a wasted trip, she just needed to know that Rosie was okay.

To give Josh his dues, he had come over as soon as she had called him. There was no way Hannah could drive on her twisted ankle and, to be honest, she was so jittery, worrying about Rosie and what she might find at her flat, she would have been a liability on the road.

'She's going to be okay, Han,' he told her now as he turned off the engine. 'You know that right? We've been here before and no doubt we will be here again.'

He didn't know that, couldn't know that, but deep down she knew that he was probably right.

'You can wait here if you want.'

'And miss out on smugly telling you I told you so?' Josh's tone was dry as he unclipped his seat belt, following Hannah out of the car.

'I'm Rosie Emerson's friend, Hannah Cole. I called the police,' Hannah said as she part hopped, part stumbled towards the young uniform standing by the main door. 'Where is she?'

Before he could answer, another officer was ushering her and Josh up the stairs and into Rosie's flat.

'Where is she?' she repeated, trying to push past him. 'Let me through. Rosie, where are you?'

Rosie had always been the vulnerable one, the youngest and the smallest in their group, and Hannah had tried her best to protect her.

'She's not here.'

What? Had she misheard him? 'Of course she's here. She locked herself in the bathroom.'

'Well she's not in there now.'

'She must be. Have you checked properly?'

Even as she asked the question, she realised how stupid it sounded. Rosie's bathroom was tiny and there was no place to hide.

The constable gave a smile that she guessed was supposed to be sympathetic, but it looked more pitying, which only served to wind her up further.

'So where the hell is she?'

'We don't know. Her flat was empty when we arrived.'

Hannah gasped in panic. 'She took her.'

That had the PC's eyes narrowing. 'Who do you mean "she"?'

'She said Eileen Wickham had found her. That's what I said when I made the call!'

'Someone has been here, yes, but they would have been gone long before Miss Emerson called you. The paint on the bedroom wall is already dry.'

'What paint?'

Hannah didn't wait for him to answer, pushing past him into Rosie's bedroom. The crudely written word had her catching her breath.

'You mentioned Eileen Wickham. Why did Rosie think she was responsible?'

'She said she was scared Mrs Wickham would come back.'

But had Rosie jumped to conclusions that it was Mrs W? Had this been a random break-in? She had been jittery when the news came in that the woman had been released. They all had been.

Mrs W's words after she had been sentenced, shouting out, 'One day you'll pay for this, you little bitches,' were less frightening as time passed, but still, Hannah had wondered whether the woman held a grudge.

Was the word 'bitch' just an unfortunate coincidence?

'You need to find Rosie,' she told the constable. 'Whether it was

Eileen Wickham or not, someone broke in here and she could be in danger.'

'We think Miss Emerson left of her own free will.'

'Sorry? No, she wouldn't do that. She was upset and scared. When she called me, she was too frightened to leave the bathroom.'

'One of the neighbours saw her leave.' The PC's tone was gentle. 'There wasn't anyone else with her.'

'What? No! She wouldn't just go.'

'Hannah.' Josh had remained silent as she spoke with the PC, but now he spoke her name with a weary patience. 'Listen to reason. Yes, it's worrying that someone's broken into her flat, but we both know Rosie spooks easily. It's quite possible she just took off.'

He was wrong. She wouldn't. She just wouldn't.

Even as she argued with herself, Hannah knew it was a lie.

Coming home and finding that someone had broken into your flat, that would freak the hell out of anyone, but no one more so than Rosie. It wouldn't be the first time she had gone into flight mode, wanting to get away from everyone just to forget.

'We still need to find her and make sure she's okay,' Hannah urged.

'And we will.' Josh's tone was gentle. 'You've left a message for her and we'll keep trying her. In the meantime, there's nothing we can do here, so let's leave the police to do their job.'

Frustratingly, he was right. Hannah had no choice but to wait for Rosie to make contact.

* * *

After answering the questions that the PC had for her and leaving their contact details in case anything further was needed, Hannah followed Josh back to his car, wincing in pain as her sprained foot throbbed from where she had been putting too much pressure on it.

'Are you going to be okay?' he asked, dropping her outside her building an hour later. 'I can help you up to your flat if you want.'

'It's fine. I've got it.' Hannah hesitated. 'But thank you for taking me tonight.'

'Will you let me know when she shows up? I know I get annoyed with her sometimes, but I'd like to know she's okay.'

Hannah nodded, pressing a quick kiss against his cheek. As far as ex-husbands went, she was pretty bloody lucky.

'And try to get some rest!' his voice echoed after her as she climbed from the car.

She made it up the stairs through sheer stubbornness, muttering a number of cuss words about the broken lift as she went, and wishing she had accepted Josh's offer to help her. Tomorrow she would make an effort to rest her foot, conscious that while she was unable to walk comfortably, she couldn't take the dogs out, losing precious income. She had scaled back on her copywriting work and what she was earning from that barely covered her bills.

Liam Quinn had a lot to answer for.

The bouquet of brightly coloured flowers resting against her front door immediately caught her attention as she reached the top landing and she hobbled over, both curious and a little wary as to who had left them.

No one she could think of would send her flowers. Unless, of course, it was one of her clients.

The bouquet was simply wrapped in brown paper, with no label to indicate where it had come from. A plain envelope poked out of the top and she plucked it out as she let herself into her flat, kicking off her shoes and heading straight for the kitchen.

She really needed to take the weight off her ankle, but curiosity over the flowers was taking precedence.

Setting the bouquet down on the counter, she opened the envelope, pulling out the card and blinking as she read the words.

It had to be a joke.

Remember, Hannah. Tears don't wash with me.

Bile rose in her throat and she dropped the card on the counter, angry that her hand was shaking.

Only one person had ever said those words to her, but it wasn't possible... was it?

Tears don't wash with me.

I'm going to give you something to cry about.

No one will ever believe you.

She couldn't have these flowers in her flat. Getting a bin liner, she dumped the bouquet inside, knotting the bag and opening the front door, shoving it out in the hallway.

She glanced cautiously around the landing, realising they been hand-delivered.

Had Mrs W been here? Did she know where Hannah lived?

The very thought made her shudder and she quickly shut the door, locking it and sliding the latch across. Rosie was convinced Mrs W had been in her flat and now Hannah had received these flowers. Was Mrs W playing some kind of game with them?

She thought of the others – Lauren, Jill, and Tash. Had anything happened to them? Tash maybe, as she still lived in Norfolk. But Jill was in Croydon now and Lauren in Sevenoaks.

Should she check in with them or would they think she was being paranoid?

She decided to WhatsApp them anyway, creating a new group that didn't include Rosie, not wanting to scare her any further.

Hi all. A couple of unsettling things have happened tonight. There was a break-in at Rosie's flat and I've just received some anonymous flowers with a message: *Remember, Hannah. Tears don't wash with me.* There's only one person I know who's said that, so not gonna lie, it's put me a little on edge. Are you all okay? Xx

She quickly followed the message up with a second one.

Oh, and there's no Rosie on this chat. She's gone AWOL (spooked by the break-in), so doesn't know about the flowers. If she contacts anyone, can you let me know please? Xx

She reread the messages. They didn't make her sound too crazy. She was just checking in with her friends after a couple of odd things had happened. And she had left out the bit about the vandalism, not wanting to be too specific. The music box too. Hannah wasn't sure if Rosie had heard it or imagined it, so she decided to err on the side of caution.

Lauren was the first to reply.

Sorry to hear what's happened. Everything is okay here, but thanks for the warning. Make sure you keep your door locked. Just in case. X

Tash was next.

Shit, Hannah. Are you okay? Do you want me to come over?

Then finally Jill.

Just trying to play devil's advocate. Are you sure both things are connected?

Jill had lost her brother and it often surprised Hannah that she was the one who offered most resistance to anything Mrs W related. Tash had once suggested that perhaps it was too painful for her to revisit, which was why she had tried to distance herself. These days, the only one she was still really close to was Lauren.

The chat thread continued, Hannah pointing out that it was a pretty unique phrase. Who else would know Mrs W had said those words to her? Tash and Lauren were both taking her more seriously than Jill though, who told Hannah to stay safe before wishing them all goodnight.

Hannah declined Tash's offer for company. It was late and Tash didn't need the drive up to the coast. She thanked her, promising she would stay barricaded inside her flat.

She tried Rosie again, leaving another voicemail urging her to call, then, her nerves shot, she fished in the cupboard for the bottle of brandy she knew was in there and poured a generous measure into a glass.

She wasn't a huge drinker, but tonight, as painful memories surfaced, she had a feeling she was going to need it.

11

2002

If Tash hadn't insisted on adding the extra bricks, chances are she would have made the jump and there would have been no need for them to go to the farmhouse.

It was easy to look back and see how things should have played out. Thirteen-year-old Natasha Hogan was not easy to reason with once her mind was made up. Her parents had bought her a BMX for her birthday and in typical daredevil Tash style, the challenges she set herself had become bigger and bolder.

It had just been Hannah and Rosie with her when the accident had happened. The Americans, Jill and Miles, were away for the weekend with their father and step-monster and Lauren had left early as her grandparents were coming to visit.

Hannah suspected Lauren was glad to get away, bored of the day being about Tash and her new bike. Her two friends were polar opposites; Tash the tomboy who liked adventures and didn't mind getting dirt on her clothes, and prim and proper Lauren who was happiest reading fashion magazines or talking about boys.

It was mid-afternoon and they had been playing on the construction site of new houses that were being built on the outskirts of the village. It was somewhere they weren't supposed to go, but the builders didn't work on a Sunday and what they didn't know wouldn't hurt them.

After exploring the shells of the new homes with their part-built walls and scaffolding, they had taken materials to create jumps for Tash to do on her new bike, the plank of wood balancing against the bricks gradually creeping higher and higher.

Hannah had tried to talk her out of making the final jump, but Tash was determined to do it.

As her BMX left the ramp, the angle was all wrong and watching the girl and her bike fly through the air, Hannah held her breath, seeing the accident unfold.

When Tash finally landed, it was on her bum and the bike was on top of her.

Rosie started crying at that point, while Hannah rushed over, terrified that Tash had badly hurt herself. Her friend's face was pale and her knee bloody, but she managed to give Rosie and Hannah the thumbs up.

Although she was limping as she wheeled her broken BMX out of the building site, Tash was more concerned about the telling-off she was going to get from her parents than the fact she had hurt herself.

'My dad's going to kill me. He's probably going to make me stay home for the rest of the summer.'

'I'm sure he won't,' Hannah reasoned. 'Not when he sees you've hurt yourself.'

'You don't know my dad.' Tash rolled her eyes dramatically.

Hannah did and she knew that Mr Hogan could be strict. But not about something like this, surely? 'Don't tell him we were on the building site. You can pretend you were just riding your bike down the road and fell off. We'll cover for you, won't we, Rosie?'

Still sniffing away tears, Rosie nodded. 'I won't say where we were.'

She was the youngest of the group and tended to go along with what the others wanted. When she had first started hanging around with Hannah, Tash, and Lauren, she had grated on their nerves, but over time, Hannah and Tash had softened towards her. Lauren still had her moments, but mostly they protected her like a sister.

'Thanks, but he's still going to kill me for being clumsy enough to fall off my bike.' Tash was determined this wasn't going to end positively and started citing examples of how unreasonable her dad could be. She was interrupted by the sound of an engine approaching from behind and the three girls stepped to the side of the road to let the vehicle pass.

Instead it slowed, pulling up alongside them.

The window was already down, probably because of the warm afternoon, a face they all recognised smiling at them from the driver's seat.

Hannah knew Eileen Wickham. They all did. She had moved to the area a couple of years back with her son, Bill, who was two years above the girls at school, and she was a familiar face around the village.

'Hello, Mrs Wickham,' Hannah greeted her, smiling shyly at Bill, who was sitting in the passenger seat of the pick-up. He was one of the more popular kids at school and their paths rarely crossed. Truth was, she was a little intimidated by him.

He didn't smile back. If anything, seeming a little annoyed that his mother had stopped.

'Are you girls okay? Natasha, I noticed you're limping?' Mrs Wickham was frowning as Hannah stepped back so she could see Tash, her eyes widening as she spotted the drying blood on her knee. 'You've hurt yourself. You poor love.'

'It's nothing, Mrs Wickham. I fell off my bike, but it's just a little graze.'

'You can't walk home like that, my girl. Come on. Let's get you in the truck. I'll take you up to the farmhouse and get that wound dressed for you.' When Tash looked like she was about to protest, Mrs Wickham added, 'I have some Cornettos in the freezer if you'd all like one.'

Rosie's eyes were widening. 'Strawberry?'

'Yes, I have strawberry. Chocolate too.'

Both Rosie and Hannah were sold, but Tash still dragged her heels.

'It's very kind of you, Mrs Wickham, but I should really go straight home. My dad is going to be mad when he sees what's happened to my bike.'

'Have you badly damaged it?' Mrs Wickham was climbing out of the truck now, taking Tash's bike by the handlebars and studying the front wheel. 'You know,' she said conspiratorially, 'I reckon my Bill could take a look at this, get it looking brand new again.'

Tash's eyes widened. 'Really?'

'And your dad need never know.'

'You promise you won't ever tell him?'

'I promise. It can be our little secret. So what do you say, girls? Shall we go back to the farm and have some ice cream? I can clean up Natasha's leg while Bill takes a look at her bike.'

Tash looked at Hannah and Rosie, smiling for the first time since her accident.

'Okay, let's go.'

12

Hannah was still asleep when her doorbell rang, starting awake, disgusted with herself when she realised she was still fully dressed and had fallen asleep on the sofa, the almost empty bottle of brandy on the floor beside her.

She knew it was morning from the daylight streaming through her window, but didn't realise quite how late it was until she looked at her watch: 10:06.

What the hell?

She never slept that late.

But, then again, she never usually knocked back a dozen shots of brandy.

The doorbell rang again, this time followed by knocking. She wasn't quite sure which sound was worse, both hammering at the pain in her head.

'Hold on! I'm coming.'

Who the hell needed to speak to her so urgently?

And then she remembered the events of the previous evening – Rosie's break-in and subsequent disappearance.

She was back.

Moving faster than was advisable for her pounding head, and remembering her twisted ankle the moment her foot touched the floor, she stumbled to the door, not even bothering to check the peephole before she flung it open, ready to lay into Rosie for scaring the crap out of her.

Instead, she found herself face to face with Liam Quinn. Something that shocked her into silence. It quickly wore off as he pushed past her, stepping inside her flat and closing the door.

'What the hell do you think you're doing? I never invited you in. In fact, I remember you very clearly agreeing that you would leave me alone.'

Even as the words left her mouth, the missing piece of her evening came back to her. Josh dropping her back at her flat just before 10 p.m., the bouquet of flowers that had been left for her, and the phone call she had made before she had passed out drunk.

* * *

'You piece of shit. You promised you would leave me alone.'

'Hannah?' Liam's voice was slow with confusion and sleep.

'You know it's me and you know exactly why I'm calling.' Hannah clutched her phone to her ear, the brandy she had been drinking fuelling her temper. 'You didn't really think I would be stupid enough to fall for your bullshit move, did you?'

There was a brief silence before Liam answered. 'What move?'

'Seriously? You're going to pretend you don't know what I'm talking about?'

'Honestly, I have no idea. But I've got to say you're worrying me a little. Are you okay?'

'Am I okay? Oh, I see what you're angling here. You're trying to make me question myself. That's your plan, is it? Make me wonder if I'm going mad or if Eileen Wickham is really coming after me.'

'Sorry?'

'I'm not going to fall for it. You've picked the wrong person to fuck with, Liam Quinn.'

'Wait a minute. Backtrack. Why do you think Eileen is coming for you?'

'You know why!'

'Hannah, can you shut the hell up for a minute and listen to me. Why would you think Eileen is coming for you?'

The steeliness in his tone momentarily shocked her into silence.

'Hannah, are you still there? Hannah?'

'The flowers that you sent me, pretending to be her.'

The last four words were said with less conviction. She had managed to convince herself that it wasn't Mrs W. The timing of Liam showing up and the flowers arriving was too coincidental. He had to be behind sending them, right?

'I never sent you any flowers.'

'You did. They were outside my flat.'

'Nope. Nothing to do with me.'

Her drunken brain tried to process that. For some reason, she had thought by accusing him he would own up, but she supposed if he was playing some kind of game with her, trying to trick her into letting him interview her for his stupid book, then of course he wouldn't admit to sending them. That realisation brought with it fresh fury.

If Liam Quinn thought he could mess with her, then she would show him he had made a mistake.

* * *

Hannah didn't recall much past that point. She knew she had shouted at him, not just about the whole flower trickery game he was playing, but also about the beach and how he was an irresponsible dog owner, that it was his fault she had twisted her ankle, which was now losing her income. And she was fairly certain the call had ended with her disconnecting when he tried to reason with her. That might explain why he was now standing in her living room, hands on hips and a scowl on his face.

Okay, scowl might be pushing it, but he didn't look happy to see her, even if he was the one who had come to her.

'You look like shit.'

'Pardon me?' Apparently, he was full of compliments too.

He glanced at the sofa and the creased cushions, then at the bottle lying on the floor.

'Have you even been to bed?'

Hannah ran a self-conscious hand over her hair as he looked back at her. 'That's actually none of your business.'

'It is when you call me up and start ranting at me at gone 11 p.m.'

Colour heated her cheeks. Now sober and in the cold light of day, she could see that she had been jumping to conclusions.

She had briefly googled him last night before calling, saw that as well as writing true crime, he was a successful fiction author. Would he really resort to playing mind games?

While she was beginning to regret what she had done, she couldn't muster the energy to explain her actions. Right now, checking on Rosie was more important, and she grabbed her phone from where it was poking out between the sofa cushions, apprehension knotting her stomach when she saw that Rosie still hadn't made contact. Hannah's WhatsApp messages had been read, but there was no response to them or the voicemails, and a quick check of Snapchat showed that Rosie's locator was switched off.

Ignoring Liam, she tried calling her friend again, dismayed when it continued to go to voicemail.

'Do you seriously have nothing to say?' he asked, as she ended the call.

Christ, would he just drop it? Her head was pounding and her mouth too dry. She just wanted him to go so she could drink a gallon of water, feed her empty belly, and crawl into bed while she waited for Rosie to make contact.

'Look, about last night. Maybe I was a little quick to accuse you, but you can surely understand why I did?'

'Is that supposed to be an apology?'

'Will you leave if it is?'

Her answer seemed to both frustrate and amuse him as he studied her and Hannah squirmed a little, aware she hadn't even looked in a mirror yet, so had no idea how rough she looked after her night on the sofa.

It didn't help that Liam looked fresh as a daisy, his blue eyes alert, no dark smudges or bags in sight and a healthy colour in his cheeks. Even his hair, which she would ordinarily describe as a bit of a scruffy mess, seemed to be more tamed today.

'Look, I get why you don't like me, and yes, I guess I can understand a little how you jumped to conclusions over the flowers. I didn't send them though. You'll just have to take my word on that. I'm not going to keep arguing with you. It's not why I came here.'

'It's not?' Hannah was immediately wary. She narrowed her eyes. 'Why *are* you here?'

'To try to make amends.'

What? She hadn't expected that.

'You were right about the beach. It was my fault... okay, well Tank's fault, that you fell over. Same thing though. He's my dog, my responsibility. And I didn't really think about how you twisting your ankle would affect you doing your job.'

This was a turn-up for the books. Was he actually apologising? 'Go on.'

'So I'll do your dog walks for you.'

'Sorry?' That wasn't what Hannah had been expecting either and she wondered for a moment if she had misheard him.

'I'm in town for a bit, so I'll take care of it until you're back on your feet.'

'No, you can't do that.'

'Why can't I? Don't you trust me?'

It wasn't a trust thing, though, to be fair, Liam had already proven he wasn't great at walking dogs. She didn't point that out, suspecting it would just cause another argument.

'You can't do it because I've already reassigned the walks for the rest of the week. I'm friendly with another dog walker and we cover each other's shifts now and again. She's taking the bulk of them and the ones she can't do, I've already cancelled.'

Liam considered that, nodding. 'Okay, so what else can I do to try to make things right?'

You could leave, Hannah was tempted to suggest, but she suspected he had no intention of going anywhere. Besides, she had another idea.

'You really want to make amends?'

'I do.'

'Tell me why you're writing this book.'

He looked frustrated. 'I'm a true crime writer, Hannah. It's my job.'

'But why Eileen Wickham? Why this story?'

'Why not this story? I remembered the case from when I was a kid and it resonated. It could have been any of us, right?'

His answer sounded a little rehearsed. Was it really that simple?

'So there's no other reason?'

He shook his head, held eye contact. 'Why would there be?'

'She's been out, what? Six weeks? Do you know where she is? Is she back in Suffolk?'

Liam's eyes narrowed. 'She's in Suffolk, but not Hixton. Where are you going with this, Hannah?'

'I want you to take me to see her.'

She could see that had thrown him, as she expected it would, and he took a moment to consider her request.

'Why?'

'Because you didn't send those flowers, she did, and I want to tell her to leave me alone.'

'Why do you think Eileen sent them?'

This time, it was Hannah's turn to hesitate. She guessed if she wanted Liam to take her, she had to give him the truth. He listened as she told him about the note with the flowers, though his expression gave nothing away.

'So will you take me to see her?' Liam Quinn wouldn't be her first choice of travelling companion, but he was the most logical, because he knew where she was. Plus, he did owe her.

He gave her a measured look. 'You're sure you want to go?'

No, of course she didn't want to. She had to though. Mrs W needed to stop and what clearer way to send that message than by turning up on her doorstep?

'Yes.'

And I don't want to go alone.

Hannah didn't admit to that. The idea of coming face to face with Mrs W after all of these years had dread knotting her belly. She needed someone with her for support.

'We can go to her house, but I can't promise she will speak to you.'

'You don't have to promise me anything. Just take me there.'

'Okay. When?'

She looked him straight in the eye. Hoped her nerves didn't show.

'Do you have any plans today?'

13

While Hannah showered and put on clean clothes, Liam familiarised himself with her kitchen, putting on the kettle before hunting in the cupboards for a frying pan and ingredients. By the time, she reappeared, the omelette he was making was turning a golden brown, the air filled with the aroma of cheese and bacon.

Hannah paused in the doorway, the frown on her face suggesting she was a little annoyed at him taking over her flat. 'What are you doing?'

'Making you some breakfast.'

'I never told you that you could use my kitchen.'

'No, you didn't. But you look like crap and you need to eat.'

'I can tell you're a writer. You have such a lovely way with words,' she muttered sarcastically, though she didn't protest too much and he suspected her belly might have something to do with that. If she was anything like him, drinking too much alcohol would have made her hungry.

Her call last night had been unexpected, and the request to see Eileen was yet another surprise. Liam had expected any truce to be more difficult to achieve, though he was grateful for the way in and determined to make the most of it.

She took the mug of coffee he had poured her, mumbling something that he thought was supposed to be a thank you, and dumped in both milk and sugar before stirring it rigorously, then she sat herself down at her small dining table to wait.

After putting the plate of food in front of her, he left her to eat while he cleared up the kitchen, pleased to note she was wolfing it down.

He had already tried the charming and hapless approach and it hadn't worked. Perhaps being more direct with her would work better.

Whatever approach was needed, he would adapt. Hannah played a key role in his story and he would not back off until she had given him everything he needed.

* * *

She was quiet on the ride down to Suffolk and he left her to brood.

They had stopped by the Airbnb after leaving Hannah's, picking up an excitable Tank, and after spending the first twenty minutes restless at being relegated to the back seat of the car, the dog had finally settled, and was now snoring away.

Liam was aware Hannah was caught up in the past, but he also picked up on her nerves. She had tried her best to hide them, but failed, and he knew she was nervous at the thought of seeing Eileen.

One of the conditions of the woman's release was that she didn't return to Hixton. Instead, Bill had rented a house in Sudbury, which she had moved in to, and that was where they were headed.

He purposely took a different route, so they wouldn't go near the farm.

The place was no longer inhabitable. Despite talks with developers about buying the land for new housing, it had never happened and the farmhouse that had long ago been the family home was now a dilapidated mess. Vandals and squatters had abused it over time. The windows broken, the wallpaper peeling, and the torn carpet reeking of piss. Both inside and out were covered in graffiti, much of it with reference to the woman and her crimes. Liam had already spent time in the farmhouse and it was difficult to comprehend that it had once been a deceptively inviting and cosy place. The kind that lured you in, unaware of the cruelty lurking within the walls.

Hannah's mother and stepfather still lived locally and he wondered how it was for Hannah each time she visited home. He imagined Eileen was never far from her thoughts, and probably more so now she was out of prison.

'Do you think she's gone back there at all... since she got out?'

Hannah's words cut through his thoughts and he glanced over at her.

'To the farm,' she elaborated, though he knew what she meant.

'She's not allowed to. It was one of the terms of her release.'

'I know that, but do you think she's gone back there anyway?'

Liam drummed his fingers on the steering wheel as he considered her question. 'I have no idea. Have you been to the farm since?' He threw the question back at her, curious to know the answer.

He had automatically assumed no, but then Hannah had already surprised him more than once.

He thought back to the pictures he had seen of her online. She was softer in print, but actually more attractive in the flesh. Those green eyes of hers so expressive, showing every emotion she experienced. Mostly, in Liam's case, it had been annoyance. Right now, they looked haunted and it was distracting enough, that he had to force his attention back to the road.

'No!' When she eventually answered, she snapped out the word and he assumed that was it, she was going to close down again, so she surprised him when, after a moment, she continued. 'I've wanted to. There have been a couple of times I've tried to go back there.'

Liam didn't respond, hoping she would fill the silence.

'It's not a masochistic thing. I'm not trying to torment myself. I guess it's a fear I want to try to conquer. It's been twenty years and it annoys me that a stupid farm still has such a hold over me.' He could hear the mix of vulnerability and annoyance in her voice.

'So you're scared to go to the farm, but you want to go and see Eileen?' The question wasn't judgmental or scornful. He simply wanted to understand.

'It's different. You wouldn't get it.'

'You don't know that. Try me.'

From the little huff she gave, he suspected she couldn't be bothered to explain, but he didn't push and eventually she spoke.

'Eileen Wickham is just a person and she's got to be in her sixties now. The farm, that was the place where it happened. I know it sounds ridiculous, because surely I should be more afraid of the woman who did those horrible things, but this place haunts my nightmares more than her.' Hannah gave a humourless laugh. 'Don't get me wrong. I'm not looking forward to seeing the woman. I would rather leave her in the past.'

'So why are we going to see her? Is it really just because of the flowers?'

'I have to. I need to ask why she's doing this to us.'

'Us?'

Hannah's silence had him glancing in her direction and he could tell from her expression of annoyance that she had slipped up.

'What do you mean "us"? What else has happened?'

'Nothing. Just the flowers.'

'Us is plural.'

'Nothing else has happened. It was a slip of the tongue.'

Liam gave her a measured look, but decided not to push it, fearful she would shut down again.

She was lying. Of that he was certain. He just had to figure out what she was lying about.

14

———————

'Are you still sure you want to do this?'

Hannah nodded; aware Liam was looking at her. Her focus though was on the grey-painted terrace house across the road, with its black front door and window box filled with half-dead flowers. It was unremarkable, both the house and the street, and there were no doubt dozens, if not hundreds, of almost identical roads and properties dotted around the country. This one was different though. It was where Mrs W lived. The woman who had misshaped their lives.

Okay, so maybe not so much Tash and Lauren's, they hadn't been scarred quite so badly. But Jill had lost her brother, while Rosie's personal life was a mess. And Hannah had put up a wall, warier now of who she could trust.

Things were always scarier as a child. By confronting Mrs W and taking away her power, would she finally be able to move on?

Liam had switched off the engine, Tank waking up from his snooze and clambering around on the back seat, toenails scrapping against the leather and letting out a few unsubtle whines. As he poked his head through the seats, Hannah made a fuss of him, scratching behind his ears and burying her face in the soft fur of his neck. They couldn't bring Tank all this way without letting him have a walk and she made a deal with herself that once she had spoken to Mrs W, they would find somewhere nice to take him.

After a moment, she heard the click as Liam released his seat belt. Was he planning on coming with her?

'You can wait in the car,' she told him, reluctantly releasing Tank.

Was Liam disappointed at that? They had driven all this way. It was difficult to tell from his expression.

'Are you sure?'

She suspected he already knew she was hiding something, thanks to her slip-up that Eileen may have done more than send flowers, and she was under no illusions that he would be trying to figure out what she was holding back from him. At some point, he might find out what had happened at Rosie's flat, but Hannah didn't intend to lead him there. It was better, easier, if he didn't know. The last thing Rosie needed was him harassing her. It was better if Liam's attention stayed focused on Hannah.

At least for now.

Rosie still hadn't surfaced. Hannah had checked her phone half a dozen times during the drive down and although it wouldn't be the first time Rosie had pulled a stunt like this, it was still a worry.

'I'm sure,' she told him.

Under different circumstances, she would have welcomed the support, but Liam Quinn wasn't her friend. She had to keep reminding herself of that. It was difficult when he kept showing up, leaving her no choice but to get to know him a little better. It was easier to dislike him when she knew nothing about him.

In fact, she knew he was an author, but that was pretty much it. Perhaps she shouldn't have been so willing to get in a car with him and let him drive her out of the county. Truth was, they may not be friends, but she did trust him that he wouldn't hurt her. She wasn't completely stupid though, and as a precaution, she had messaged Josh and told him where she was going and who she was with.

Besides, it had been her own stupid fault that Liam had shown up this morning and she was kicking herself for opening the brandy last night. If she hadn't been drunk, she wouldn't have called him, and if she hadn't have called him, he wouldn't have rocked up at her flat.

But then she also wouldn't now be here outside Mrs W's house, ready to confront the woman.

Was she ready?

That was a loaded question; Hannah wasn't sure she would ever be ready for this meeting.

She had to go through with this though.

As she got out of the car, crossing the road to the terrace house, she wondered how the woman would react. Would she even recognise Hannah? It had been twenty years and Hannah had only been thirteen at the time. Her hair was still blonde, but her face had matured and she had grown several inches.

If Mrs W didn't recognise her, would Hannah need to have an awkward conversation to remind her? And if she did, would Mrs W scream and shout at her or try to slam the door in her face?

Liam would be watching her, of that she was sure, and the temptation to go back to the car and ask him to come with her was overwhelming. Instead, Hannah put one foot in front of the other. She had already let her guard down around him more than she was comfortable with and she refused to start leaning on him for support or allowing him to see how vulnerable she really was.

You are stronger than you think, Hannah. You can do this.

Despite repeating the mantra, it took all of her courage to knock on the front door.

This close, she could see the remnants of red paint, possibly graffiti. She could only imagine the words that might have been written there.

Liam had been able to track Mrs W down, so how many others knew she lived here?

Was it just graffiti or had she endured worse?

Hannah refused to feel any sympathy for the woman. She had brought it on herself.

Dirty little bitch.

My house. My rules.

I'm going to teach you a lesson you won't forget.

As she waited for the door to open, her gut churned and her legs trembled.

Come on. She just wanted this to be over with.

Face her fear, tell the bitch to leave her alone, go home, never come back.

Would it be that easy?

A door opened, but it wasn't Mrs W's.

'She's not there.'

Hannah glanced over to the neighbouring property and the man who was talking to her. He had a scowl on his face.

'She won't answer because she's not there.'

Hannah's relief was tinged with disappointment. She didn't have to face her, but she had come all this way for nothing. Was it worth waiting? Would her nerves handle it?

'Okay, thank you.' She tried smiling at the neighbour, but his scowl remained in place. 'I'll perhaps try again later.'

'No point,' he muttered. 'She's gone.'

'What do you mean she's gone? She lives here.'

'Not for the last few days. I'm guessing our message got through to her in the end. This is a nice place. We don't want her type here. And if you're anything to do with her, you're not welcome here either.'

'Are you threatening me?'

'Consider it a polite warning.'

Before she could respond to that, the man stepped back into his house and slammed the door.

Hannah looked at Mrs W's house again, then back across the road to where Liam was watching. She shrugged and watched him get out of the car in response.

'She's not here,' she told him as he jogged over to join her. 'The neighbour says she left a few days ago.'

'Are you sure?'

'He seemed certain. When did you last see her?'

'About a week ago.' He gave a wry smile. 'She told me to piss off.'

'Really? I thought she was on board with this whole book thing.'

That was interesting news. So Mrs W wasn't a Liam Quinn fan either.

'I'm not exactly painting her as a hero.'

'I see.' Perhaps Hannah had been wrong to jump to conclusions about the book without at least asking. She had assumed it was being written with Mrs W's blessing.

'It's about the crime she committed, what drove her to do what she did, how she was caught and put away, and the long-lasting effect it had on everyone. That's why I wanted your input, to be certain I am portraying your version of events as accurately as possible.'

And still making money out of it. Hannah kept that thought to herself.

While she was still uncomfortable with the idea of a book, though, how it was being written did change things. And it had happened over twenty years ago. Perhaps, despite her reservations, it was a story that was ready to be told.

That was something for her to put away and absorb later. It wasn't just her story after all. There were others involved too. The rest of the

Hixton Five deserved a say, as did the family of Scott Copeland, Eileen's first victim. Right now, Mrs W's whereabouts were of more interest and Liam was peering through cupped hands into the front window.

'Can you see anything?'

'The furniture is still there, but I'm guessing it came with the rental.'

'What about personal stuff? Pictures, mugs, maybe a coat or shoes.'

'Nothing I can see. I'll check round the back.'

'Should you do that? Won't it be locked?'

Liam didn't answer, already disappearing down the alleyway that linked the properties, and Hannah glanced around the empty street before following after him. She was still limping, but the pain in her ankle had definitely eased a little.

There was a latch to open the gate to the rear of the house, but no lock, and they were easily able to access the small patioed garden. It was sparce, lacking in colour and personality, with just a couple of empty potting tubs stacked up and a rusted watering can.

Liam looked into the kitchen window. 'There's a kettle, but nothing else on the worktop.' He tried the back door.

'What are you doing? You can't break in.'

'Relax. It's locked. I was just checking.'

Was that all he was really doing? Hannah couldn't help wondering what he would have done if the door had been open. All this snooping around was making her uncomfortable, especially given whose house it was.

'She's obviously not here, so we should go.'

To her relief, he agreed. 'Yeah, Tank will be having a shit fit at being left in the car.'

As they turned to leave, Mrs W's neighbour glared at them across the low fence.

'You have no business being back here,' he snapped at Hannah, before turning his attention to Liam, his eyes narrowing. 'You again!'

'Good to see you, Mr Towler.'

'You've already been told you're not welcome. Now she's gone, there's no need for you to be loitering around, so bugger off before I make you regret it!'

The smirk on Liam's face suggested he wasn't overly bothered by Towler's threat. Still, he guided Hannah back towards the alley-way. 'We're just going, but I'm sure I'll see you again. You have my card.'

The comment was met with a number of expletives. Mr Towler clearly wasn't a fan of Liam Quinn either.

'You want to interview him?' she asked, waiting for Liam to unlock the car. On the back seat, Tank was already barking in excitement at their return.

'Yeah, if I can get him to stop being so aggressive. He's been living next door to her. I want to know how that has worked out for him and for her. Not so well, I'm guessing.'

He clicked his keys and they got in, Hannah making a fuss of Tank while trying to stop him from climbing between the seats.

'So that was a wasted trip. Do you have any idea where she might be?'

'No, but I'm going to call a friend in the police. I'm sure her probation officer already knows she's no longer here, but I'll let him know, just in case.'

Hannah nodded. 'Can you please not mention I am with you?'

'Sure. If that's what you want.'

She did. In fact, the last thing she wanted was anyone thinking she had gone looking for Mrs W.

She wondered again where the woman could be. Was it possible she was violating the terms of her release? That sat uneasily with Hannah.

If Mrs W was prepared to break the law, just how far was she willing to go?

Hannah was silent while Liam made the call, her thoughts returning again to the summer of 2002. Mostly she tried to block it out, but with everything that had happened over the last couple of days, it was inevitable she was remembering.

'What did he say?' she demanded, as soon as Liam ended the call.

'He's going to call me back when he's spoken with Eileen's probation officer.'

Hannah sighed in frustration, even though she knew it wasn't Liam's fault they couldn't immediately locate Mrs W. 'Do you mind if we make a slight detour on the way back?' she asked. She was determined this trip wouldn't be a total waste of time.

His eyebrows shot up in curiosity, but he nodded. 'Where did you have in mind?'

'Well, this one deserves to stretch his legs.' She rubbed Tank affectionately on the head. 'So I was thinking we could go to the farmhouse.'

Liam was silent for a moment. 'Really? Are you sure you want to go there?'

No, not at all, Hannah's brain screamed. It had been a fruitless journey though, and while they were so close, she should try to conquer her fears.

She forced her tone to sound decisive. 'I'm sure.'

15

When things got really bad, Rosie tended to jump on a train to London. Once there, if she couldn't find a friend whose sofa she could crash on, she would lose herself in the anonymity of the bars and clubs, and find a willing stranger who was prepared to take her home. A binge of alcohol, drugs, and hot sex always helped to numb her anxiety.

The problem was, she always eventually had to resurface. Sometimes her binges lasted a day or two, at her worst it was over a week. This time, the numbing part hadn't happened. She had tried the drinking, the pill popping and flirted her arse off, but the sweet release from her problems hadn't come and she had ended up a sobbing mess on a sticky nightclub floor as she frantically searched through her phone for someone to take pity on her.

Eventually, she had been given a bed, but as she had tossed and turned, sleep had refused to come, leaving her exhausted as she thought about what was waiting back home for her.

The crazy bitch had broken into her flat.

Because the break-in and the phone call had to be connected, surely? And who else would know about the music box?

She knew she should call Hannah back. Her friend was worried about her and had left countless messages and voicemails. She had told Rosie to stay in the bathroom, but of course, Rosie hadn't listened. Being trapped in that tiny room had made her claustrophobic. She had needed out of her flat, out of Norwich for a bit. Unable to deal with the real world until she had found some relief, though, in truth, that relief had not arrived.

Giving up on sleep, she had felt in an even worse state.

Everything was falling apart and she wasn't sure if she could piece herself back together again this time. If Mrs W could see her now, she would laugh at how pathetic Rosie had become.

To make things worse, London was supposed to be her escape, her respite, but even that wasn't going to plan, and after a terrible morning she tried to pick herself up with some retail therapy. It was while wandering along Regent Street with armfuls of bags that she ran into her footballer ex, Gavin.

Their relationship had lasted a couple of years, though had been tempestuous and peppered with arguments and break-ups. Both of them were hot-headed and could be a little insecure, so they were probably not the best match, but there was no denying that between the sheets their chemistry was off the chart.

An afternoon of filthy sex finally helped to clear her head and for a short, sweet while, her worries disappeared.

Later, when she was on the train, dread at the idea of returning home to her flat returned. She couldn't stop thinking about the graffiti or that creepy bloody music box tune. It was playing on a loop in her head.

Hannah would say she was crazy, and okay, perhaps Rosie was a little messed up. Could anyone blame her? Hannah hadn't been there. She hadn't heard the music box. If she had, she would know Rosie was telling the truth and that she was right to be afraid.

16

I have her attention now. She sees me.

The flowers I sent her were an inspired move, one to make her remember, to remind her what she has done, and to let her know this isn't over.

I had hoped she would panic, that it would scare her, but never once did I dream it would make her want to confront her past.

If I hadn't been there at the time, I wouldn't have believed it. First Mum's house, then the farm.

I wonder what Hannah planned to say if Mum had answered the door.

Sorry for ruining your life?

Sorry I couldn't just shut up and take the punishment I deserved?

Sorry I was in your home and forgot that a mother always knows best?

Of course it would be none of those things. That is just wishful thinking. No, she had gone there to attack and accuse. Still taking the righteous and almighty stance that she is the victim.

Her visit was a waste of time of course. Mum is no longer at the house and she won't be coming back. Thanks to Hannah and her friends, she has been judged and sentenced, and the finger of blame will never go away.

They need to pay for that, particularly Hannah and Rosie.

Their evidence is the reason Mum went to prison. It is because of them that I ended up in a young offender's home.

I have worked hard over the years to build myself back up, to create a respectable life for myself, knowing that when Mum was released, it would be my job to look after her.

Just as it is my job to atone her.

All I have ever wanted is to prove myself to my mother, to have her tell me she is proud.

I know people say she was cruel, but they don't understand. She was only trying to educate me, to make me into the perfect son. One she could love and be proud of.

It won't take much to tip Rosie over the edge. A simple phone call and a little bit of graffiti have already proven how easy it is to scare her.

As for Hannah, I am just getting warmed up. If an innocent gesture like flowers prompts this kind of reaction, I can't wait to see how she responds to the other things I have planned.

I am going to enjoy every moment of watching her unravel. And when she is finally at her weakest, that is when I plan to finally reveal myself to her.

Hannah hated showing any sign of weakness and she had been kicking herself for telling Liam she wanted to go to the farm.

Yet, it would be easier with someone else there, she had surmised. They would go inside together and she would manage to remain calm and detached as she viewed the place of her childhood nightmares, finally putting them behind her once and for all.

Perhaps the band of tightness across her chest as the farm came into sight should have been a warning, at which point she should have told Liam to stay on the main road and not take the turn-off, but she was too stubborn.

She could work past the fear. She would do this, she had told herself.

Except it turned out she couldn't, and now she was back at home, beating herself up because she had tried and failed, and she had humiliated herself in the process, showing Liam Quinn that she wasn't quite as tough as she tried to make out.

To give the man some credit, he hadn't pushed her, playing down what was essentially a panic attack as if it wasn't a big deal, understanding she was embarrassed and didn't want any fuss. And he had been quietly supportive, letting her work through the episode as she tried to pluck up courage to get out of the car, before deciding it was perhaps a step too far. Instead, they drove on, stopping a little further away so Tank could have his walk.

Hannah was beginning to understand that she had misjudged Liam. She still wasn't happy that he was writing a book about what had happened, hoping to profit from the tragedy, but he had been good to her today and if she was being completely honest with herself, she quite liked his company. She liked his dog too.

Still, she was uncomfortable that he had seen the chink in her armour and when he had dropped her back at her flat, she had decided against inviting him in for coffee, turning down his offer again to help with the dog walking.

Yes, he was okay, but they were on opposing sides over the book. Besides, he would be moving on soon. There was no need for them to form any kind of relationship. Today had simply been about Mrs W and trying to find out what was going on.

Liam had eventually heard back from his friend who confirmed the woman was missing. Hannah didn't like that one bit, and it only served to exacerbate her worries.

Settled on the sofa with a mug of tea, her twisted ankle raised on cushions, she checked her phone, saw that Rosie still hadn't been in touch, and tried her again, leaving yet another message.

Then she let Josh know she was home safe.

It had been the right call, telling him where she was going, even if he had tried to talk her out of it. He didn't understand that she had needed to do this. Plus, he was immediately suspicious of Liam. Hannah had purposely kept the details a little vague, not wanting him to know about Liam's book. She didn't need a lecture about that.

Liam on her mind, she typed his name into Google again, curious to know more about the man she had just spent the day with. She gave his Amazon biography another glance, this time taking a closer look at the books.

He had only written one other book in the true crime genre, which had been about the Steve Noakes murder spree, and it had been well-received, both critically and commercially, with reviewers praising his straightforward yet sensitive style of relaying the facts.

Hannah clicked onto a recent YouTube interview with him, trying to reconcile that the eloquent and passionate man talking on the screen was the same person whose dog had knocked her flying, who she had drunkenly berated on the phone, and who had been both a calm and reassuring presence when she had lost her shit earlier.

He had a face that worked well with the camera, all sharp planes and angles, the high cut of his cheekbones and the smooth line of his jaw, the lens picking up on the light blue of his eyes and the quick flash of lopsided grin that gave a crooked appeal to his almost perfect symmetry. Even the dishevelled mop on his head seemed less... messy; whatever lighting had been used picking out highlights of gold and caramel in his tawny brown hair.

Fascinated, she watched the interview, her ears pricking up when he mentioned the Eileen Wickham project, saying it was the one crime he had always wanted to write about. He didn't expand on why, even though the interviewer did ask, instead leading the conversation in a different direction. Hannah had noticed he was good at doing that and he didn't like to give away much about himself, even if he was in the public eye.

The interviewer then threw her completely by asking if it was true that Liam was planning on donating all royalties from the book to selected children's charities. As he nodded and confirmed it was, guilt stabbed at Hannah.

She had thought the worst of him, assuming that he wanted to profit from their misery and had accused him of doing so.

Why hadn't he corrected her?

The thought played on her mind into the evening. Unsettled, she tried to relax with a soak in the bathtub, but her mind wouldn't switch off.

If she had given Liam the opportunity to tell her everything at the start, would she have had a different view about talking to him?

It was a difficult one, as she was still uncomfortable at the idea of the book, but knowing that while it was about Eileen, it wasn't about validating her, and that the proceeds were going to charity, changed things.

Could it be cathartic? Time to finally put the past to rest, or at least reconcile it and move on?

All of them had received counselling after it had happened, but Rosie was the only one who had kept it up. For Hannah, it was so long ago, she could barely remember what exactly had been said, but she hadn't carried on. Her therapist had shown a severe lack of empathy, instead preferring to tell Hannah how and what she should be feeling. No wonder it had such little benefit.

She wouldn't talk to Liam, not without first discussing it with the others, but equally, she was no longer ruling it out.

She toyed with calling him, needing to know more about the book, but then she had a better idea and found the card he had given her. He had scribbled the address of the Airbnb where he was staying on the back of the card.

Ten minutes later, she was sat on the low wall outside the flats and waiting for a taxi to arrive, pulling on the jumper she had brought with her to ward off the early-evening chill.

It was a reminder of what was to come as September crept closer to October, bringing longer nights and falling temperatures. Hannah loved the beauty of autumn, though she hated the dark and dreary weeks that followed.

Preoccupied, she wasn't aware of the car parked further along the street or the man who was watching her, his fist clenching and unclenching around a stress ball, as he tried to control his rage.

Moments later, her taxi arrived and as she got in, confirming Liam's address, she remained in blissful ignorance as they passed the parked car, unaware when it started to follow.

18

She would be safe here.

That was what Bill had told her when he moved her to the cottage.

Probably because it was in the middle of fucking nowhere, but Eileen had to admit her boy had done well.

She had been unsure when he had first proposed moving, especially when he didn't want her to tell her probation officer where she was going. Bill was convinced that if the authorities knew where she was, the press would soon learn too. It was safer this way.

Besides, his friend had done them a favour, allowing them to stay in his late father's house, and he wouldn't want any attention drawn to him. The place was a bit dated and run-down, but it was better than the cell she had called home for twenty years and at least she didn't have to live in fear that someone might try to break in or set it on fire.

Bill stayed close while she got settled and it was good to know she still had his devotion, that he hung on to her every word.

It had been just the two of them since he was five years old and Eileen knew just how to play him. She had no guilt over that. She had given the boy a good life. He hadn't spent his childhood stuck in the foster system like she had, picked on by the older kids in the home, always overlooked for the youngsters when potential families came to visit. Eileen had learnt her place and it was at the back of the queue. How she despised the kids who stood in front of her. She thought she was lucky when a foster family did eventually take her in, but how wrong she had been.

Even, all these years later, she could remember the creaking of the bedroom door as it opened late at night, the stale breath of her foster dad, Mr Griffiths, as he crawled on top of her.

That was her life. A product of a broken home, having witnessed her father murder her mother when she was eight. No one cared about her, so she had closed her eyes and learnt to survive.

She had been twenty-two when she met Dennis Wickham. She was working in the bar of a village pub and he was a regular. Much older than her and nothing to look at, but he was always nice to her and he quickly made it known he found her attractive.

Eileen wasn't stupid. There had been boys her own age, but none of them had prospects. Dennis was her escape. They were married a year later.

She didn't want kids, but Dennis was desperate for a family of his own. When Bill was conceived five years later, they had all but given up on it happening. Dennis was elated, while Eileen was distraught, hating the idea of having to nurture and raise a snivelling little brat. But as her son grew and she understood how vulnerable he was, how he relied on her for everything, it gave her a sense of power. All of those years being bottom of the pile and finally she was top dog. She could give Bill everything, but she also had the power to take it away. He was hers and he understood his place. He was a good lad and she knew she could count on him.

He had visited her regularly in prison, had put plans in place for her release, and he had been waiting for her at the prison gates. His world still revolved around her and Eileen knew he would likely do just about anything she asked.

She had been goading him about the Hixton girls ever since her release, expressing disappointment that he had never thought to seek revenge on her behalf.

Don't forget they were responsible for you losing your mother.

Those women have never paid for what they did.

They think they are better than us.

You liked that blonde one, didn't you? Hannah. That's her name. Remember the look of disgust on her face when she saw you that day?

I bet you would like to teach her a lesson or two.

She could tell he was getting more and more worked up each time she brought it up.

Good.

Bill would do anything for her. But she wanted him to believe this was all his idea.

19

The sensible thing would have been to ask the taxi to wait.

Stupid, Hannah. Stupid.

Her head had been full of questions and she hadn't been thinking straight, assuming Liam would be at the Airbnb. So no, she hadn't thought it through, which was why she was now standing on the doorstep of his rental, the taxi gone.

What a wasted journey.

And where was Liam? It was a Wednesday night. Was he out working?

Of course she shouldn't have assumed he would be in. Just because her evening plans involved hanging out in her flat, it wasn't the same for everyone else.

She had knocked a couple of times, but knew he wasn't here as she hadn't heard any sign of Tank. Maybe he was out walking the dog, but his car had gone. Why would he have needed to take Tank in his car when there was all this open space?

Resigning herself to the fact she'd had a wasted trip, she debated her options.

She could call another taxi, but she would have to wait

around for it to arrive, or she could walk. It was probably only fifteen minutes back to her flat, though her ankle could be an issue.

Well, that and the fact the house was in the middle of nowhere, so the walk back would take her down country lanes.

She didn't want to be a baby about it, but it was almost dark and just a little bit creepy, and the idea of walking home didn't exactly fill her with confidence.

Damn you, Liam Quinn. Why did you pick somewhere so isolated?

Where the hell was he?

Maybe she should call him. He might be back soon.

As she reached for her phone, the silence was broken by the sound of a car engine, headlights appearing in the distance. Relieved and assuming it was Liam, Hannah watched as the car drew nearer, holding her hand up to shelter her eyes from the headlights. It pulled into the top of the driveway, but then abruptly stopped, the engine still running as a figure got out of the driver's door.

Caught in the beam, she couldn't actually tell who it was and when the figure didn't move, unease crept up her spine.

'Liam? Is that you?'

If it was, he didn't answer, continuing to stand there, and her unease knotted into concern.

'Can I help you?'

Still no reaction, the cool evening air silent except for the purr of the engine.

Hannah wasn't sure what to do. Liam wasn't home and she had no idea who this person was or what they intended.

Knowing it was wrong, but unsure what else to do, she reached her hand behind her, trying the front door. Technically it was breaking in, but she had good reason. Liam would understand, wouldn't he? The door was locked. Of course it was. And that knowledge that there was nowhere for her to go had panic niggling at her gut.

She was overreacting, she told herself. Yet even as she tried to rationalise and steady her breathing, she knew it wasn't true.

'What do you want?'

When the figure failed to answer again, she snapped, unable to bear this game any longer.

'I said, what do you want?'

As she shouted the words, she started limping down the driveway towards the car.

The figure moved quickly. Back in the car. Door slamming, engine revving, then the sound of the car flying backwards, before disappearing at speed back down the country lane.

Hannah's heart was racing, adrenaline rattling through her. She had no idea what the person had wanted, but she suspected it wasn't good.

As the sound of the engine faded, she debated what to do.

After this creepy encounter, there was no way she was going to walk back. She pulled up Liam's number and called it. If he didn't answer, then she would call a taxi. She didn't want to be here if the car returned.

The phone rang before eventually cutting into answerphone and she didn't bother leaving a message. Coming out here without checking he was home first had been stupid. She would live and learn.

She was about to call a cab when she spotted headlights again, her stomach knotting in fear.

It was too late. Whoever it was had decided to come back.

Shit! What was she going to do? There was nowhere for her to go.

Her heart started to thump, and her mouth was dry, as she glanced to the side of the house.

Would there be anywhere to hide round back?

This time, the car didn't pause at the end of the drive, but as it neared, she heard a bark, then saw the silhouette of Tank's big shaggy head poked out of the passenger window, tongue hanging out. He barked again in delight as he spotted Hannah, and her tension eased, relief spilling out.

Tank ran over to her the second he was out of the car and was up on his hind legs, and Hannah wrapped her arms around him, needing a moment to calm herself.

'What are you doing here? Is everything okay?'

She looked up at Liam, aware he seemed more curious than pleased to see her.

Maybe she had misjudged this. 'Yes, I think so. I'm sorry, I shouldn't have come.'

'How did you get here? Did you drive?' As he asked the question, he was looking around for her car.

'No, I got a taxi.' She paused, feeling foolish. 'Look. This was stupid. I shouldn't have assumed you'd be home.'

Liam was thoughtful for a moment, then he nodded. 'Well I am now, so you might as well come in.'

Not quite the welcome she had expected, but then was she really surprised, given how she had treated him so far.

Hannah stepped aside as he unlocked the door, ushering her through. The place was cosy and comfortable. Wooden floors, mismatched sofas, and a large table, an archway leading through to what she could see was a small kitchen. Property was at a premium in North Norfolk and a rental like this wouldn't be cheap. She thought of the car again and the isolated location, still a little jittery with nerves.

'Are you sure everything's okay?' Liam had shut the door now and was studying her more closely. He stepped out of the path of Tank, who barged between them, heading straight for the kitchen, where he started crunching on biscuits. 'You look like you've seen a ghost.'

'Did you just pass another car?'

'No, why?'

'Not on the road leading here?'

'No. What's going on, Hannah?'

'Someone was here.'

'What? Who was here?'

'I don't know. I didn't see whoever it was. The headlights were on. I thought it was you at first. This road is a dead end, so there was no reason for anyone to be down here.' The words were all coming out in a rush and Hannah realised she was shaking, annoyed when she saw Liam had spotted it too.

'Okay, you're not making a lot of sense.' He guided her to one of the sofas, telling her to sit down. As she sank into the plush cushions, he disappeared into the kitchen, returning moments later with a can of Coke. 'Drink this,' he ordered, pulling back the ring cap and pushing it into her hand. 'It will help with the shaking.'

Hannah didn't really want the Coke, was more embarrassed now than annoyed, but she did as told, the cushions dipping as he sat down beside her, aware he was watching her closely. Her face heated, not appreciating the scrutiny.

'I probably overreacted.' She tried to downplay the situation. 'But thank you for the Coke.'

'Maybe.' Liam didn't sound convinced. 'I'd still like to know what happened. Can you talk me through it?'

She nodded, this time taking a calming breath before speaking, determined not to sound like a blabbering idiot. She kept it concise, sticking to the basic facts, relieved when the shaking slowly started to subside, and grateful to Tank who had wandered through, positioning himself on the floor between the two of them, his head resting on Hannah's knee. His warm presence helped steady her further as she stroked the soft fur on his head.

'Are you able to tell me anything about the car?' Liam asked when she finished.

'I couldn't see with the headlights. I think the full beam was on. It was blinding.'

'But did you get a sense of the size of the vehicle? Was it a small car or something bigger like a people carrier or a van?'

She thought about that for a moment and about the SUV that Liam drove. 'It was a similar size to your car. That's why I thought it was you at first.'

'Okay, and was it a man driving?

'I don't know. Maybe.'

'Tall, short, skinny, bulky?'

Again she considered. 'Same sort of build and height as you.'

'Whoever it was didn't speak at all?'

'No. And when I started to go over. That's when they left.'

'You approached the car?'

Hannah couldn't tell if Liam was impressed or incredulous at her stupidity.

'I didn't know what else to do. There was nowhere I could go to get away.'

He seemed to think about that for a moment. 'No, I guess there wasn't,' he agreed, getting up and moving to the window that looked down the drive. He glanced out briefly before closing the blind, then locking the door.

'Whoever it was didn't want to be seen,' Hannah noted.

'So it's possible it could have been a woman?'

Hannah paused. Whoever it was had seemed to be a similar height and build to Liam, but was she really sure? The lights had dazzled her and, honestly, she hadn't seen enough to tell. 'I guess.'

She remembered the flowers, a shiver coming over her. 'You think it was Eileen Wickham?'

'I wasn't here, Hannah. Only you know what you saw.'

It would make sense given that Mrs W had disappeared. Rosie's break-in, the flowers, and the note. It all tied in.

Hannah wasn't quite sure how she felt, knowing the monster from her childhood might have followed her out here and could have been standing just twenty feet away.

What did she want?

She had made warnings when they were kids, telling them terrible things that would happen if they ever revealed to anyone what had gone on, but that had been years ago and they had been empty threats, made purely to buy their silence. She wouldn't actually act on them. Would she?

Ask her that question a few days ago and Hannah would have laughed it off. Now she wasn't so sure.

20

The idea that Eileen Wickham might have spent the last twenty years plotting revenge chilled Hannah. Mrs W was in her sixties now and Hannah could no longer be easily manipulated. However, she knew how cruel and twisted the woman could be, and stupid as it may seem, Mrs W still scared her.

'What is she like... now?'

'Eileen?'

Liam took a moment to consider the question when Hannah nodded. 'I've only met her the one time and I told you she wasn't exactly receptive to my request for an interview.' The corner of his mouth twisted and she was reminded of the YouTube video which had accentuated his charmingly crooked smile. He seemed amused rather than upset by how Mrs W had reacted to his request and Hannah suspected there wasn't much that fazed him. 'She wasn't quite what I was expecting, if I'm honest.'

'She wasn't?'

'I've read a fair bit about her, so I knew she could be persuasive and manipulative, and I guess that's what I was expecting. She didn't appear to be either. She was angry and I sensed she was bitter too. Bitter at what had happened and also that things weren't any better for her on the outside.' Liam took a seat again, but this time on the sofa facing Hannah, his blue eyes on hers. 'Twenty years staring at four walls is going to change you, give you time to think.'

'I guess.' Hannah found herself fidgeting a little under the scrutiny of his gaze as she pulled on the ring of her now empty Coke can. There had been something in his tone that made her feel he was judging her. Of course, she was probably imagining it. She was still a little shaken from her encounter outside and reading signals that weren't there.

Tank picked that moment to whine, getting up and going to the door and scratching at it. He looked at Liam, cocking his head on one side and whining again.

'Seriously, mate? You had enough pees while we were out.'

She watched while Liam let him out, stepping outside with him and pulling the door to. It wasn't enough to stop a cool breeze blowing into the room and Hannah shivered; glad she had brought her jumper. Putting the Coke can down on the coffee table, she shoved her cold hands between her knees.

After a minute or so, Liam whistled to the dog and they both came back inside. This time, Tank didn't go to Hannah, instead settling himself down on the rug.

Liam locked the door again, but remained standing, turning his attention back to her.

'Why are you here, Hannah?'

A very direct question.

She decided to cut straight to the chase. 'Why didn't you tell me the profits from the book are going to charity?'

'You never asked me.'

'I thought you were cashing in on what happened.'

'I know.'

'So why didn't you correct me?'

'Would it have made a difference?'

'Probably not.' Hannah shoved her fingers back through her hair. 'I might have considered it.'

'So you've been looking me up online, I guess?'

The question caught her off guard and heat flushed her cheeks. 'I wasn't snooping. I was just curious.'

'Of course. I mean I get it. I really do. We'd spent most of the day together and you were already missing me.'

What?

Hannah must have looked horrified at his insinuation, because he quickly added, 'I'm teasing you, Hannah.'

There it was again, that appealing lopsided grin. Amusement lighting his eyes.

'I knew that,' she insisted, aware they both knew it was bullshit.

There was silence for a moment, though weirdly it didn't feel uncomfortable. Liam still grinning to himself. Hannah mostly relieved.

'Have you eaten?' he asked eventually.

No, Hannah realised she hadn't. After watching the YouTube video, she hadn't given a whole lot of thought to food and it was only now he mentioned it that she realised she was hungry.

'Not yet.'

'Well, I was going to throw a pizza in the oven. I'm willing to share.'

'I could eat pizza.'

Liam nodded, picking up her empty Coke can before going through to the kitchen, and it occurred to Hannah she was happy to stay and have dinner with him, when just two days ago she couldn't bear to be in the same place as the man. When had that changed? She wondered if she should follow, maybe offer to help. It was pizza though. What was she going to do, take the wrapper off?

Instead, she remained where she was, glancing round the room. There was a small dining table behind the sofa where Liam had been sitting. A laptop open and a pile of notes beside it. That must be where he worked.

As curious as she was to know what he had so far, she wouldn't snoop. Maybe if she spoke to him about what happened, he would offer to show her.

While she waited for him, she pulled out her phone, checked to see if Rosie had been in touch.

She hadn't, and Hannah tried to push down the bubble of worry. She had just one message. It was from her mother reminding her that she needed to know if she was staying over for the party.

Hannah put her phone away, not in the mood for another discussion about this, and she was frowning when Liam came back through holding two glasses of wine.

'I thought you could probably do with this, after earlier.' He caught her expression, eyes narrowing as he handed her one of the glasses. 'Is something wrong?'

'No, nothing.'

'Okay.'

The fact that he didn't push stopped her closing down completely and she stewed over the message for a few moments, wondering if perhaps it would help to talk about it with someone unbiased. Usually, she just vented to Rosie, but, of course, Rosie was of the same mindset as Hannah, so always sided with her, and occasionally Hannah had a niggling feeling of guilt that perhaps she was being unreasonable where her mother was concerned.

'It's my mum's twenty-fifth wedding anniversary next weekend,' she blurted. 'I'll go of course, but she wants me to stay over. I'm just not sure I'm brave enough to do that.'

It might be insignificant to Liam, but admitting to her short-comings, putting it out there that she was scared to go back and stay in the village, was a huge deal to Hannah and she took an anxious sip of wine while she waited for him to react.

'Have you stayed there since you left?' he asked eventually, coming to sit on the sofa beside her.

'Just the once.'

'And what happened?'

He was watching her again, his blue gaze intense, but where before it had made her a little jittery, now it anchored her.

'I couldn't do it. I woke up from a nightmare and found myself in my old bedroom and I panicked.'

Hannah recalled the memory, the shame of it burning inside.

'Did you talk to your mum about it at the time?'

'I tried. She didn't get it though, and kept telling me I just had to move past it.' She gave him a pointed look. 'So am I mad or just pathetic?'

'Actually, I don't think you're either. I do think you should try to face your fears again. But I also get it if it's too tough.'

She noticed he hadn't asked her about her family set-up or questioned that she was nearly thirty-four, yet it was only her mother's twenty-fifth wedding anniversary. That's because he would have done his research, she supposed, so would know that her dad had died when she was six and her relationship with Geoff, her stepfather, had often been turbulent. It was something that had her guards raising again. 'Thanks for listening. I'll figure something out.'

Josh had offered to go with her if she had no choice but to stay. Hannah had mentioned it briefly to him on the way back from Norwich. Taking her ex-husband, though, would likely throw up some awkward questions and she didn't want to give anyone the wrong idea about them.

For now, she pushed the problem to the back of her mind and focused on enjoying the wine and then the pizza as she got to know

Liam Quinn a little bit better, while Tank watched them like a hawk.

He lost interest as soon as the food was gone, clambering up onto the other sofa and sprawling on his back, grunting out gentle snorts, while the pair of them chatted, the conversation easy.

Hannah wasn't sure what she had been expecting. Given the nature of Liam's work, she assumed he would try poking into her past. He didn't though, keeping all talk away from Mrs W and, as Hannah would later realise, drawing her attention away from the car that had scared her earlier, focusing more on the present and, in turn, revealing little snippets of his own life.

Nothing too major, she noted. She learnt he had lived all over, had never married, leading something of a nomadic lifestyle, and that he had taken on responsibility for Tank after his younger sister, Ashley, who had bought Tank as a puppy, decided she couldn't cope and was going to surrender him to a rescue shelter. That thawed Hannah a little bit more. She liked people who were kind to animals. That he had a sister was pretty much all he would let on about his family, though, changing the subject when Hannah mentioned his parents.

In the end, she was the one to bring up the past.

Although she was warming to Liam, was even finding herself a little distracted by the subtle scent of whatever soap or aftershave he was wearing while sat this close to him, she reminded herself this hadn't been a social visit. She had come here to ask questions about his book.

'If I agreed to talk to you, let you interview me, what would it involve?' She asked the question as he topped up their wine glasses, the smooth ruby liquid giving her a pleasant buzz. She was being careful not to drink too much. Relaxed was good, drunk was not.

'It would involve us talking, much as we are now, but I would record it.'

'Record it?' Hannah's eyes widened when he nodded, not sure how she felt about that. 'Do you mean on video?'

'Preferably video, though we could do audio if it makes you feel more comfortable.' He must have picked up on her unease, because he added, 'It's all very informal, Hannah. Just you and me, and we can go at your own pace, stopping whenever you want.'

'What kind of questions?'

'No questions as such. You tell me what happened in your own words, and I will chip in and ask you stuff as you talk.'

It sounded easy enough. Still, she was unsure about being recorded.

'I would need to speak with the others first. Run it by them.'

He nodded. 'That's fair enough.'

Hannah was silent for a moment as she considered. 'Could I talk about it a little now?' At Liam's raised eyebrows, she elaborated. 'I don't mean like properly. Just you and me, no recorder and off the record. I haven't really spoken about it, well, not since when it happened and I'd like to try, to see how comfortable I am with it.'

He took a sip of his wine, studying her over the rim of the glass as he considered her question. The way he was sat, back pressed against the far side cushions and one jeaned leg tucked under him so he was twisted to face her, looked relaxed, but Hannah knew he was alert and could see he was intrigued by her proposition.

'Of course,' he agreed, his tone neutral. 'Whenever you're ready.'

21

2002

After the visit for ice cream, during which Mrs Wickham dressed Tash's knee and Bill fixed her BMX so you could barely tell it had been damaged, the farm became a regular hang-out for Hannah and her friends.

Mrs Wickham, or Mrs W as she came to be known, was so lovely and friendly to them. She had told them they were welcome to stop by any time and could play on the farm, as long as they didn't interfere with any of the equipment.

It was an arable farm, she had told them. Sadly no animals to see, other than the few chickens often poking about at the back of the farmhouse. Mrs W's late husband had been a farmer and she had kept his farm going after he died. It was bigger though and eventually became too much. That was why she had bought this place.

She let them use the land to build dens, play games, or swim in the pond, and quite often she would invite them into the farmhouse, plying them with treats from the freezer or freshly baked pie.

Lauren, Jill, and Miles had been sceptical at first, unsure if the woman was going to be as cool as Hannah, Rosie, and Tash made out, but Mrs W quickly won them over, while they were all flattered that Bill made time for them.

He was slightly older and popular at school, and initially they had been a little shy around him. He didn't hang out with them as such, often busy with chores, but sometimes he would stop to talk to them or join them around the table as they stuffed their bellies.

All had seemed perfect that summer, but as could often be the case, things could sometimes be too good to be true.

The first time Hannah had a sense of foreboding, an under-standing that things weren't quite right, was during her second week visiting the farm. It was one of the hottest days of the summer so far and Mrs W had made lemonade and cookies.

The kitchen had been full of chatter as they had brought their bathing suits and planned to go down to the pond a bit later.

They all loved it when Mrs W invited them inside. Not only did she make them treats, but she was cool too, sitting down with them and showing an interest. Talking to them as if they were adults, not children, and telling them the best scary stories. Like to watch out for the big fish with razor teeth that lived in the pond – they had laughed at that one, knowing it wasn't true, though Hannah knew they had all been a bit apprehensive when first going for a swim. Then there was Mr Bennett, the former owner of the farm who had died after falling down the cellar stairs. They fell silent as she told them how, because he lived alone, no one had realised he was dead. By the time his corpse was found, maggots and rats had been feasting on him. All of them (apart from Jill and Miles) remem-bered Mr Bennett. He had always been crotchety with them if he caught them on his land, threatening and chasing them.

When Lauren told Mrs W this, saying that Mr Bennett hadn't been nice like her, the woman nodded, her expression grave. 'That is why I tell Bill to keep out of the cellar. We can hear Mr Bennett down there sometimes, yelling and banging on the door. He didn't like children and I don't want him hurting my precious boy.' She paused, staring round the table at their wide-eyed faces. 'Of course, rumour has it he only punishes naughty children.'

Hannah glanced at the cellar door. Was he down there now, listening to them? He had hated them all when he was alive. What would he think about them being in his house? She resolved to never go down into the cellar.

When the glass smashed, everyone stopped talking and looked at Bill, who had dropped it while clearing the table.

His eyes went wide as he looked at his mother. 'I'm s-sorry. It was an accident.'

Was Hannah imagining it or was he scared of his mother's reaction?

She looked to Mrs W and for the briefest moment saw something akin to anger pass over her face, but then she was smiling and shrugging the incident off, and Hannah was wondering if she had imagined it.

'What are you like, Butter Fingers Bill,' she laughed. 'How did I manage to have such a klutz of a son.'

While Bill stood rooted to the spot, Hannah got up from the table with the intention of helping to clear up the rest of the table. Mrs W was quick to stop her.

'Don't you worry about that, my lovely. You kids go and enjoy your swim. I will take care of everything here.'

She ushered them outside, still all smiles, and Hannah was thinking to herself how lucky Bill was to have such a cool mum.

It was as they were crossing the field to the pond, Rosie skipping ahead with Miles and Jill and Hannah walking with Tash and Lauren, that she realised that she had forgotten to pack her towel, and her stomach dropped in disappointment, knowing she wouldn't be able to go in the pond.

'Why don't you go ask Mrs W if she will lend you one?' Tash suggested.

'I don't want to put her out.'

'I'm sure she won't mind, Hannah,' Lauren agreed. 'You know how lovely she is, and you want to be able to come in the water with us, don't you?'

She really did and her friends were right.

Leaving them with her bag and telling them she would catch up with them at the pond, she sprinted back to the farmhouse, surprised when she entered the kitchen to find it empty. The leftover cookies and lemonade were still on the table and shards of smashed glass all over the floor.

'Mrs Wickham?'

Hannah wandered further into the house, the coolness of the building a stark contrast to the warm day outside. So far, she had only ever been in the bright sunny kitchen with its yellow painted walls, plus she had used the loo once, that was just off the kitchen. As she made her way across the hall, she couldn't help feel she was trespassing.

'Mrs Wickham?'

There was a sound coming from upstairs and Hannah waited for a moment, not wanting to go up uninvited.

'Mrs Wickham?'

Still nothing.

She wasn't intruding if she was making her presence known, was she?

As she climbed the stairs, nerves jiggled in her stomach, but curiosity pulled her forward. Her hot palm was cooled by the banister and the pine scent of furniture polish lingered in the air. Mrs W had a very tidy house, but it was an old building and upstairs the ceiling was covered in dark wooded beams. Hannah's family lived in a relatively new property and she had never been inside anywhere like this, its low, sloped, stripey ceiling fascinating her.

She was about to call out for Mrs W again when she heard the voices, realising they came from the room opposite the stairs. The door was open a crack and she shyly approached, jumping when she heard the loud slapping sound, followed by a whimper.

Mrs W was talking in a low voice and her tone wasn't the friendly one she used with Hannah and her friends. Peering through the door, she caught her breath.

Bill Wickham was in the room with his mother and she could see his profile as he bent forward, his hands clasping his knees, and he was naked – at least the bottom half of him was, jeans bunched around his ankles, and was that his willy hanging down?

Hannah had never seen a real-life penis before and her eyes widened, her feet rooted to the spot.

Of course, she wasn't quite sure if it was Bill's dangling willy that was shocking her more or the fact Mrs W stood behind her son ferociously smacking his bum with a heavy looking hairbrush. She was barely recognisable, her usually smiling face flushed with rage, calling Bill some of the vilest words Hannah had ever heard. Ones she knew she would never be allowed to repeat.

Instinctively, she knew this was a bad situation, one she was not supposed to see, but her body was refusing to obey her brain's instruction to leave, and she couldn't tear her gaze away from the sight in front of her.

Bill was apologising to Mrs W now, begging for her forgiveness.

'I'm sorry, Mum. I didn't mean to drop the glass. I'm sorry I let you down. I promise I will try to be more careful.'

Another thwack. This one harder.

Hannah winced as Bill cried out, his eyes squeezed shut.

'Take your punishment like a man.' Mrs W snarled the words. 'You snivelling little bastard.'

'I'm sorry. Please forgive me.'

'You're weak and pathetic, just like your father. Do you think I enjoy doing this, having to beat sense into you?'

'No, Mum.'

'Then stop acting like a pathetic little pussy. You're an embarrassment to me.'

It had been an accident. Just a broken tumbler. Why was Mrs W acting like this?

'I promise it won't happen again.'

'No, it won't, because next time I'm throwing you out. You're skating on thin ice, Bill. I'm just about done with you. No sleeping in Mummy's bed tonight.'

'No, please. I'll be good.'

What? Why did Bill sleep in Mrs W's bed?

Hannah's throat was dry, her tongue stuck to the roof of her mouth. She needed to go before they realised she was here.

'I'm doing this for your own good. What woman is going to want a worthless piece of shit like you? Do you think those girls downstairs like you? That they would ever give you a second glance? They know you're a waste of space. I bet they laugh behind your back. What do you think they would say if they knew you liked to suck on Mummy's titties and stick your dick in her mouth? Do you think they—'

The loud creak was followed by deathly silence.

Hannah had finally managed to unstick her legs and make her feet move back, but her exit wasn't as quiet as her approach and she must have stepped on the wrong floorboard.

She froze again, not daring to breathe, fear rattling through her as Mrs W and Bill both looked in her direction.

Bill's face was red and tear-stained as he locked eyes with her, and the horror and humiliation in his expression burned through her. Meanwhile, Mrs W looked shocked.

As the seconds ticked by, no one speaking, fury twisted Mrs W's features. Stepping away from Bill, she crossed the room in quick strides and slammed the door hard in Hannah's face.

Terrified Mrs W might open the door again, she found the use of her legs and they shakily carried her down the stairs and out of the house.

Part of her toyed with going straight home, but her stuff was at the pond.

As she made her way down to join her friends, she wondered whether to tell them what she had just seen.

Would they believe her? Mrs W had always been so nice.

They were all in the water when she arrived, Tash calling out to her.

'Hey, I thought you were going to borrow a towel?'

Hannah hesitated. 'I couldn't find Mrs W.' There it was. The decision had been made. 'I'll just sit on the bank and watch you guys.'

Settling herself on the grass, lying flat on her back, Hannah closed her eyes, the sun on her face and listening to the sound of her friends splashing in the water. Her thoughts remained inside the farmhouse though, as she tried to rationalise what she had seen. What had she just witnessed?

She didn't know how much time had passed, but she must have slightly drifted off. She was woken by voices chatting excitedly close by to where she was laying.

As she opened her eyes, sitting up, she heard Mrs W's voice. 'Oh, there she is, Miss Sleepyhead.'

Hannah immediately remembered what she had seen upstairs, but Mrs W's tone was so friendly again, she actually wondered for a moment if she had dreamt it.

'I brought ice creams,' she told Hannah, handing her a wrapped cone. 'I know all this swimming can be hungry work.'

Hannah accepted the cone with a meek thank you, but she really didn't fancy it. Her friends were all eating theirs, though, and it would be rude not to do the same.

She peeled off the sticky cardboard and licked at the cone, the ice cream cold and heavy as she swallowed.

'How come you're not in the water, Hannah?' Mrs W asked.

'She forgot her towel,' Lauren answered for her. 'We told her to come and see you, that you'd let her borrow one, but she said she couldn't find you.'

Mrs W studied Hannah carefully. 'That's a shame. I guess I must have been upstairs busy with stuff. Of course, I know Hannah would never be rude enough to come upstairs without being invited, would you, love?'

Hannah's mouth was dry, despite the ice cream. 'No, Mrs W.'

'I'm sorry you didn't get to have a swim with your friends.'

'It's okay. I didn't mind.'

She was finding it so hard to reconcile this friendly woman who was here with them right now with the one she had seen upstairs.

Mrs W stayed and chatted with them for a while, but there was no sign of Bill, and Hannah wondered if he was too embarrassed to show his face after what had happened.

As the six of them headed back home, she was still musing it over and talking herself into believing she had overreacted. Her mother had never hit her, but Hannah knew that other families had different rules. It seemed a bit harsh smacking Bill with a hairbrush for accidentally breaking a glass, but maybe it was a normal punishment in their family.

As for the other stuff. Was it normal for some families to share a bed and do the things Mrs W had spoken of? Hannah knew she was quite naïve. She had never had a boyfriend and her mother hadn't ever spoken with her about sex. She should try not to judge.

So she didn't.

Those niggling doubts never left her, though, the next time she returned to the farmhouse – because, yes, she went back again. By this point, her friends were enamoured with Mrs W and they were all going to go anyway. She didn't want to be excluded from the group. But she didn't realise then that things were about to get a whole lot worse.

22

It was the sound of Tank whining and pawing at the front door to go out that woke Liam and he rolled over, grabbing his phone, and swearing when he saw it wasn't yet 6 a.m.

Rubbing a hand over tired eyes, he threw back the duvet and climbed out of bed, tugging on his jeans and heading downstairs.

'Seriously, mate, you couldn't wait another hour?'

Slipping his bare feet into his boots, he unlocked the door and followed Tank outside, wishing he had grabbed a top as the cool air hit him. As he waited for the dog, he looked out across the surrounding fields that led down towards the marshland. It was still dark, though the dawn would soon start to break, and he suspected, if he could be bothered to stay up instead of slipping back into bed, he would get to witness a spectacular sunrise.

He had been lucky getting this place with its pretty location. It was both quiet and isolated, which suited him perfectly, though he could also understand how, in darkness, it had spooked the hell out of Hannah.

She was the reason he had barely slept and he knew revisiting the past had been difficult for her. The conversation had been off the record and he had promised he wouldn't print anything she had spoken about without her permission, though much of it was now stored in his mind. Whether she decided to help him with the book or not, he was keen to talk to her again. Curious to learn more about events through her eyes.

It would be baby steps with Hannah. He understood he couldn't push her. And when she had decided she had relived enough, he had been careful to move the conversation back on to lighter topics. He could tell talking about Eileen had drained her, which was why he had persuaded her to stay the night.

As Tank finished his business and they both went back inside, he thought of her now in the spare bedroom. The door was still closed as he climbed the stairs, and he wondered if she had slept better than him, not replaying everything they had talked about like he had. Of course, knowing she was in the room next door hadn't helped. He would be a liar if he said he wasn't attracted to Hannah Cole.

It was important that he keep any relationship between them professional, however. Hannah was simply business and he needed to stay focused.

Keeping his movements quiet, he slipped into the bathroom, figuring he would have a shower and maybe check out that sunrise after all.

* * *

When she wandered downstairs a couple of hours later, he had already drunk two cups of coffee, the first watching the sunrise, which had been worth staying up for, the sky a spectacular blaze of orange hues and moody purples, the second after returning from a walk with Tank and while typing up some notes for the book.

'Hey, you sleep okay?'

She nodded, yawning, blonde hair tousled and still wearing the T-shirt he had lent her to sleep in, though she had put her jeans on with it. It was too big for her and he thought made her look a little vulnerable. He ignored the kick inside his chest as his heart hitched a little.

'How's your ankle?'

She hadn't appeared to be struggling with it, but that didn't mean she wasn't still in pain.

'It's okay. Still a little sore, but getting better.'

'Sit down. I'll get you a coffee,' he told her, getting up and heading into the kitchen as Tank went over to her for a fuss.

'Thank you for letting me stay last night.'

'No problem. Are you hungry?'

'No, I'm fine. But thank you. I'll call a taxi and get out of your hair.'

'I'll give you a lift home.'

'You're busy. I've already put you out enough.'

'You've not. Have your coffee and then I'll take you.'

Milk and two sugars. That was how she took it, he remembered, dumping both into the cup.

She was sat on the sofa when he brought the drink through, though didn't seem comfortable. Her back was rigid and her hands folded in her lap. She looked more like she was waiting for a job interview than coffee.

'Thank you,' she said for the third time, not meeting his eyes as he handed it to her, and it occurred to him that the way she was acting, all overly polite and a little self-conscious, was how she might have done if they had slept together then woken to regret it.

Given that they definitely hadn't done that, he suspected it was instead the shadow of the past and that she had started to open up to him last night about Eileen. Although she had been calm, almost detached, as she had talked, Liam knew it couldn't have been easy for her

He would let her work through things at her own pace, but it wouldn't stop him being direct with her when he felt it was necessary.

He sat down beside her, perhaps a little closer than was necessary, jolting her from her thoughts. 'You're acting weird.'

'What? No I'm not.' Her eyes widened as they met his, then she quickly looked away again.

'Yes, you are. You've thanked me three times in the space of five minutes and now you're worrying about putting me out and—'

'That's called being considerate.'

'Usually you're telling me to piss off.'

'That's a little hard for me to do when I'm in your house.' She gave him a quick smile, her eyes flashing with humour, and he saw a spark of the Hannah he knew and preferred.

'Ouch!' he told her, playing along.

She plucked at a loose thread on the T-shirt with her mug-free hand. 'Besides, you're gradually becoming less irritating.'

'I am?'

'You are. Don't push it though,' she warned.

That was something, he guessed.

He decided to cut to the chase. 'So how are you feeling about what you talked about last night?'

Hannah was silent as she considered the question and he mentally kicked himself for pushing, scared she was going to shut down again.

'It was weird talking about it after all this time and because I did, I couldn't stop thinking about it afterwards, about her and where she is. I didn't get much sleep,' she admitted.

'You said you slept okay?'

'I was being polite.'

'See. I told you! You were acting weird.'

She glared at him. 'You know that less irritating thing? It's wearing off!' She tried for annoyed, but failed, and he caught the smile on her face as she looked away.

'So you think Eileen is behind last night then?' he asked, wanting to know how convinced she was. Would she involve the police? He thought not, as she hadn't wanted to call them last night. Probably because she knew there was nothing they could do. Someone standing outside a car at the end of a driveway was hardly a crime.

'I don't like that she has disappeared.' Hannah looked right at him then, her clear green gaze steady. 'Why would she do that unless she was up to something?'

He answered as honestly as he could. 'I don't know.'

Her phone buzzed, distracting her momentarily, and she frowned as she stared at the screen, putting her coffee down before hurriedly typing back.

Liam waited until she had finished, aware she was still distracted. 'Everything okay?'

'Yeah.' She let that one word hang there for a moment and he thought it was all he was getting, but then she huffed a little, before picking up her cup again and taking a sip. 'It's Rosie. She ran off Tuesday night and I haven't been able to get hold of her.'

'But she's okay?'

'So it would seem. Apparently she's coming over later, so I'll find out.' Hannah was silent for a moment. 'There is something else that happened, that I haven't told you about.'

Liam kept his tone neutral. 'There is?'

He listened as she told him about Rosie, the break-in at her flat and her subsequent disappearance.

'This isn't new for her. She's... sensitive and freaks easily. When she does, she often disappears, gets wasted, and tries to forget her problems.'

'And doesn't let you know she's okay.' He tried hard to keep the judgemental tone from his voice.

'She panicked. Someone broke into her home, the one place she feels safe. And she's convinced it was Eileen Wickham.'

'Do you think it was Eileen who broke in?'

Hannah shrugged. 'I don't know. The call had to have been from her. Who else would know about the music box? And I guess it would be a coincidence someone breaking in on the same day. That woman really won't let it drop, will she?'

He couldn't answer that or give her the reassurance he suspected she needed, so he didn't. 'Have you spoken to the others who were there that summer? If Eileen is really behind what's been happening to you and Rosie, surely she will have been tormenting them too.'

Hannah nodded. 'I WhatsApped Tash, Lauren, and Jill after the break-in and the flowers. Rosie doesn't know about the flowers yet. I was worried I might spook her further. Nothing has happened with any of them. They don't know about last night with the car. Or that Mrs W is missing. I should update them.'

'You should.'

How would they react to the news that Eileen had vanished? The dynamics of the group intrigued him. The five of them had stuck together as kids, their evidence a crucial part of Eileen's trial. Did they still have that closeness, that special bond?

He was curious to find out.

23

Hearing footsteps out on the landing, Rosie threw open the door, expecting it to be Hannah, rolling her eyes in frustration when she saw instead it was everyone's favourite ex-husband, Josh, standing on the threshold.

'What the hell are you doing here?'

'You finally decided to show up then,' he smirked.

'What's that supposed to mean?' She would have slammed the door in his smug face, but he already had a foot inside Hannah's flat, irritating Rosie as he stepped inside, shutting the door.

She wanted to remind him that he didn't live here, but given that she didn't either and had used Hannah's spare key to let herself in, she didn't really have the higher moral ground on that one.

Hannah knew she was coming over. Rosie had just made it earlier than agreed. She would rather be here than in her flat, which was still tainted by the break-in. She had stopped at that little bakery Hannah liked and picked up pastries. It was her way of apologising for disappearing again. She didn't want Hannah to be mad at her. Her world felt like it was unravelling and she needed her best friend.

'You know Hannah's been worried about you.' Josh stared down at her, his tone patronising. 'You really need to stop pulling this shit and stressing her out.'

How fucking dare he?

She adopted her best haughty tone. 'I already messaged her. She knows I'm fine. Anyway, my friendship with Hannah is none of your business, so stop sticking your beak in.'

'I beg to differ.'

'No one cares, Josh. Ex means ex for a reason. You're no longer a part of Hannah's life and you don't get to speak on her behalf. You should go.'

Rosie had never been a Josh fan, their personalities clashing from the offset.

'I think Hannah gets to decide that. Where is she?'

'She's out, but she'll be home soon. I'll be sure to tell her you stopped by.'

'No need. I'm not in a rush, so I'll wait.'

As if to infuriate her, Josh slipped out of his jacket and took a seat on Hannah's sofa, making himself comfortable.

Damn him. She should have known he would dig his heels in.

Ignoring him, Rosie went through to Hannah's bedroom, slamming the door. She didn't need his attitude and already had enough on her plate to deal with, the Mrs W stuff scaring the shit out of her, and her head was about to explode. She just wanted Josh to go so she could chill with Hannah.

Where the hell was Hannah, anyway?

Rosie had messaged to say she was back and would come over later and all she'd had back from Hannah was a brief reply saying she was out, but would be home soon.

Out where? She had hurt her ankle, so it wouldn't be walking the dogs, and her bed was made, so she must have been up early.

Maybe the pain in her ankle had worsened and she had gone to see the doctor.

Or something more sinister had happened.

No! Don't go there.

But Rosie's overactive imagination couldn't help it and over the next ten minutes she conjured up all kinds of scenarios. She was already in a skittish mood and had managed to work herself into a panic that Mrs W had done something to Hannah and that she was the one who had sent the message from Hannah's phone, when she heard the front door open.

She rushed through from the bedroom, relieved to see Hannah step through the door, a look of surprise on her face when she saw she had visitors.

'Rosie, I didn't think you were coming over till later. Josh? What are you doing here?'

'Those theatre tickets for your mum's anniversary arrived,' Josh told her, getting to his feet and sounding a little distracted as he looked past Hannah. 'I'm on my way to see a client and had a bit of time to kill, so I thought I'd swing by and...' He trailed off, seeming more interested in the man who had followed Hannah into the flat.

Liam Quinn.

Rosie wanted to scream. What the hell was he doing here?

'Hi, I don't believe we've met.' Josh offered his hand to Quinn as Hannah made the introductions.

'This is Liam Quinn, Josh. Liam, my ex-husband, Josh Cole.'

No elaboration of who Quinn was or that he was writing a book about Eileen Wickham. Rosie was sure Josh would have something to say about that when he knew the truth.

Quinn's eyes had widened slightly at the ex-husband mention, though given his profession, he would surely know all about Hannah's life and that Cole hadn't been her maiden name. Maybe it was surprise at Josh being in her flat.

'Good to meet you,' he told Josh, giving nothing away.

'Likewise.'

Well, wasn't this all very civil?

'Why is he here, Hannah?' Rosie was aware she sounded petulant, but honestly she didn't care. Who the hell did Liam Quinn think he was interfering in their lives, and worse still, why was Hannah letting him?

'Liam gave me a lift.'

'Have you been talking to him about us, about what happened?'

Rosie could see that Josh's curiosity was piqued by her question, but Hannah ignored it, instead firing back at her.

'Where have you been, Rosie?'

'I had to get away. You know how it is.'

'I've been worried sick about you. You call me telling me that someone has broken into your flat, then you disappear.'

'I couldn't stay there.'

'I get that. But you could have answered your damn phone and let me know you were okay.'

Seriously? Hannah was twisting this back on her?

She could see Josh nodding in agreement, that superior smirk back on his face, while Quinn didn't seem surprised by anything Hannah was saying, so she'd clearly told him everything that had happened. How dare she do that? She had no right.

'I'm sorry, okay, but me disappearing for a few days is not as bad as you talking to him.' Rosie poked her finger in Quinn's direction. 'Have you gone crazy, Hannah?'

'Anyone care to tell me what's going on?'

Josh wouldn't be her first choice of ally, but given that Hannah appeared to have lost her mind, Rosie had little choice. 'Liam is writing a book about Eileen Wickham. He's been pestering us to talk to him about what happened. Hannah promised me she wouldn't agree to it.'

'Rosie!' Hannah's tone was angry.

Josh was viewing Quinn through different eyes now, though he kept his tone diplomatic. 'It pains me to agree with her, but Rosie's right. Is this really a good idea, Han?'

Quinn said nothing to defend himself, Rosie noted, though he didn't appear in the least bit bothered that he was being talked about, instead seeming intrigued by the dynamics between the three of them

When Hannah spoke, her irritation was clear. 'With all due respect, Josh. It's not really any of your business who I decide to speak to. Not any more.'

Those last words were a low blow and Rosie saw Josh's expression darken as they sunk in. 'I guess not,' he said tightly. 'I think I should go. Tickets are on the counter. Transfer the money when you get a second.'

Quinn stepped to one side to let him out. 'Do you want me to leave too?' he asked Hannah, his tone low.

She shook her head, glaring at Rosie as she answered. 'No, I want you to stay.'

The words hurt Rosie like a slap. What the fuck was going on with Hannah? She was taking Quinn's side now? Honestly, this was getting too much.

Furious with the whole situation, she stormed from the room, slamming the door of Hannah's bedroom and throwing herself on the pretty blue duvet.

She expected Hannah to follow, to try to put things right, her rage growing when she didn't and fresh tears falling. Hannah never took sides against her. It was all Quinn's fault. Somehow he had wormed his way in and was making her act irrationally.

The man was dangerous and Hannah couldn't see it.

Hannah had always been the protector, the one who looked

after Rosie, but now the roles were reversing, and Rosie knew what she had to do.

Pulling Josh's number up on her phone, she hit call and waited for him to answer.

'Rosie?' He sounded both wary and intrigued. 'What do you want?'

She swiped at her wet eyes, determination setting in. 'I need your help. I want you to look into Liam Quinn.'

24

Lauren was the first to react to the news that Eileen Wickham had disappeared, her reply coming shortly after Liam had left.

Were the police aware? What were they doing about it?

Tash had been next, just a few minutes later. She was less focused on Mrs W, instead telling the group that her girlfriend, Sam, had heard someone in their driveway a few nights ago. It might be nothing, but she wanted them to be aware.

Jill was the only one who didn't reply and Hannah could see she hadn't read the latest messages. Throughout all of this, Rosie had remained in Hannah's bedroom, oblivious to what was going on.

Before he left, Hannah had apologised to Liam for Rosie's behaviour. He had seemed unfazed, but still it had been an uncomfortable situation to walk into. She would need to say sorry to Josh too at some point. Yes, she was annoyed at him for overstepping, but she knew his concern came from a good place. He was just trying to look out for her.

Hannah was not in the mood to deal with that now or a sulking Rosie. She was tired, after a sleepless night, though not so much from talking about the past, as she had told Liam. That had actually been therapeutic, like unloading the heavy box she had been carrying around for a long time. No, her lack of sleep had come from knowing a man she was finding herself increasingly attracted to, much to her annoyance, was sleeping just across the landing.

There had been the odd date since her divorce from Josh, but nothing memorable, and finding herself awake and thinking about sex for the first time in God knows how long had been both a surprise and a bit of a shock.

Nothing could happen, she knew. This whole situation with Mrs W and the fact Liam was writing the book just muddied the waters. She didn't want to complicate things.

She had agreed to meet with him in the morning, to talk some more about what had happened, again off the record.

Right now though, she needed to put Rosie in the picture about what had been going on.

* * *

Forty-five minutes later, they had cleared the air and Rosie was up to speed. There had been panic over Eileen and plenty of tears, but finally she had calmed down.

They had also reached a tenuous compromise. Rosie had grudgingly admitted she was in the wrong for fleeing again and cutting off contact, while Hannah apologised for backtracking on talking to Liam. She was going to continue doing so, but she promised not to drag Rosie into it..

She knew her friend was unsettled by everything that had been happening and after deciding it was safer that she stay the night, Hannah contacted the police to update them on Rosie, knowing they were keen to speak with her about the break-in.

The PC who came out to take their statement didn't give much away, though she did show concern that Hannah and Rosie believed Eileen Wickham was responsible for the things that had happened.

Hannah didn't mention that she had gone to see Mrs W, planning to confront her. She didn't think that would go down well with the police.

After the PC left, Hannah excused herself to her bedroom and phoned Josh, thanking him for the tickets, knowing he had called in a favour with a client to get her the best seats in the house for her mother's anniversary present, and she apologised for how they had left things earlier.

She had just ended the call when Rosie started screaming.

25

The body of Jill Peters (nee Goldberg) was found by her husband, Adrian, when he returned home from a business trip on Thursday morning. After the police were called and Adrian had answered their questions as his wife of eight years was zipped up in a body bag and taken away, his best friend, Baz, had made coffee. While Adrian waited, still in a state of shock, he had messaged some of Jill's closest friends, trying to figure out what the hell had happened.

An accident or maybe not. Jill had been found at the foot of the stairs. Had she simply tripped or had someone pushed her? It would be easy to assume it was an accident, but her phone was missing.

One of the friends Adrian messaged was Lauren Bell.

Lauren was the only one of the Hixton gang who regularly saw Jill, but she hadn't seen her in a couple of weeks. She broke the news to the other four women in the Hixton Five by WhatsApp. Perhaps she should have phoned them all instead, but she was busy getting ready for a meeting that couldn't be avoided, plus the news had shaken her. WhatsApp was easiest.

* * *

That was where Rosie saw it, and she was still screaming when Hannah rushed through to the living room, convinced her friend was being attacked.

'Rosie? What the hell?'

Unable to speak, her screams now turning to sobs, Rosie handed over her phone and Hannah read Lauren's message, her skin chilling.

Jill was dead. Bright, vivacious and confident Jill Goldberg, who had always been up for adventure, had the brightest smile, and had been so full of life.

It had to be an accident. And it had to be a coincidence.

That was what she kept telling herself as she comforted Rosie, replying to Lauren and then Tash when she commented. None of them mentioned whether they thought Jill's death was connected to Rosie's break-in or the incidents that had happened to Hannah, but she knew they were all thinking it.

Numb with shock, Hannah sat with Rosie for a bit, then WhatsApped Josh to let him know.

She decided to tell Liam too, and ask if they could postpone meeting up tomorrow. She wasn't sure she would be in the mood for talking about the past given what had just happened. He would understand. They could talk again in a few days.

She dialled his number, but it went straight to voicemail, so she asked if he could ring her back.

He didn't call and, when she eventually heard from him, it was via WhatsApp, his tone striking her as both terse and vague.

Something's come up and I'll be away for a few days. Need to reschedule tomorrow. I'll be in touch.

Okay, so he had cancelled on her.

Hannah sent a brief message back.

No worries. Hope all okay.

She tried to take the message for what it was and not read too much into it, knowing that tiredness and stress was probably leading to paranoia.

By the time she crawled under her duvet, she was exhausted.

The beep of a text came just as Hannah's head hit the pillow and she reached for the phone, the screen illuminating in the darkness as she opened the message.

Bad girls need to be punished.

She sat up in bed and reached for the light, blinking as she read the message again and trying to ignore the build-up of nausea in her gut.

She didn't recognise the number and debated for a moment whether to reply or ignore it.

The terminology was pure Mrs W and Hannah could remember exactly when the woman had spoken those words to her, and the horror that had followed.

She tried to force the images from her mind. There was nothing she could do about the message tonight and dwelling on the past was going to send her crazy. She didn't want to tell Rosie and risk panicking her further. The two of them were safe together inside her flat, and she had deadbolted the door. Tomorrow she would speak to the police again.

She tried to settle herself back down, this time leaving the light on, hoping it would chase the shadows away, but when she did

eventually find sleep, the dark memories of Hixton pushed back to
the surface.

26

2002

'What are you doing in here?'

Hannah's eyes widened as Bill blocked the doorway to the garage.

She had been after one of the old towels Mrs W kept in here, needing something to wipe the wet seat of the swing that hung from the old oak tree down by the pond. After three weeks of dry heat, the heavens had finally opened last night and everything was now soaked.

She had been trying to avoid Bill since the incident she had witnessed in the farmhouse bedroom, unable to forget the look of humiliation on his face. It wasn't always easy though.

Hannah had a feeling that what she had seen wasn't quite right, but what was she supposed to do about it? Mrs W was an adult, Hannah still just a child, just thirteen years old. If she told anyone what had happened, would Mrs W really admit to what she had done? Worse yet, if she was confronted, she would know Hannah had told on her.

She had been lovely to Hannah and her friends, allowing them to hang out on the farm, feeding them treats and always there with a friendly word. But that day in the bedroom, it was as if a mask had slipped and Hannah couldn't help worry that there was perhaps a not-so-nice side to her.

The following day she had tried to persuade her friends to go somewhere different. There was the woods and the old bridge. It was unfair to keep imposing on Mrs W, she'd argued.

Her suggestion hadn't gone down well, the others lured by whatever goodies would be on offer at the farm, and she had been overruled.

Since then, she had hung in the background, trying to appear invisible to both Mrs W and Bill, terrified that one of them would say something about what she had seen or tell her off for snooping.

Neither of them had, but cautious now, Hannah was starting to question everything. The dead mouse that had ended up in Lauren's shoe. Had it really been an accident like Mrs W claimed? Lauren had just before spoken about her phobia and Mrs W was the only one in the house where the shoes were at the time. Lauren had freaked out, screaming and crying. And Hannah had noticed Mrs W had seemed more amused than concerned.

Then there was the day they were all sick. Their parents had put it down to a bug, but Hannah remembered the lemonade Mrs W had given them hadn't tasted quite right. She always made her own, but it seemed stronger than normal with a weird aftertaste, and she had been so insistent they all finish their glasses. Had she done something to it?

Mrs W was back to being all smiles, which had Hannah wondering if she was overreacting. As for Bill, on the odd occasion their paths crossed, she had caught him watching her. It made her uneasy. Yes, he was popular at school and he was good-looking too. Under different circumstances she would have been flattered. Ridiculously embarrassed too, because she hadn't yet come close to having a boyfriend. He wasn't looking at her in that way though. It was more like they shared a secret and he was trying to figure out how he felt about that.

She suspected, as he stared at her now, he was thinking about what she had witnessed.

'You shouldn't be in here. What do you want?' he demanded; his voice gruff.

'I... I was just looking for something to wipe down the swing.'

He seemed to consider that.

'Is that why you really came in here?' he asked eventually.

Hannah's heart was thumping, her voice sounding so small when she answered him. 'What do you mean?'

'We both know what I mean.' When she didn't react to that, he frowned. 'Come here.'

Hannah didn't move. Her feet seeming as if they were glued to the floor.

'I said come here.'

His tone was rough and demanding, and her legs were lead heavy and shaking a little as she did as he asked.

At least they were standing by the doorway of the garage, so she didn't have to try to get past him.

Breathe, Hannah.

It was all okay. She was just panicking because of what she had seen.

She dared glance at him now, not liking the mean look on his face.

'You're a snoop.' He said the words cruelly, glaring at her.

'I'm not. Honestly, I just wanted a towel, but it's okay, I can go without.' The words were tripping over themselves in their haste to get out.

'You're a snoop and a liar. You were spying that day in the house.'

'What? No, I promise I wasn't.' Hannah's cheeks flamed. She was mortified. 'I didn't mean to see anything.'

Bill's face was red too, but she wasn't sure if it was with embarrassment or anger.

'If you ever tell anyone what you saw, I'll—'

'I won't and I haven't, I promise.'

'How do I know? You could just be saying that. I bet you've told your friends.'

'I haven't told them. I haven't told anybody. You can trust me. I swear on my life.'

'*I swear on my life!*' he mimicked, making her sound pathetic.

'I won't tell. I promise.'

'I don't believe you.'

'Honestly, I won't say anything.'

Her bottom lip was trembling and she hated that she thought she might cry. Why was he being so nasty to her?

'I guess there is one thing you can do to make me believe you.'

'What? Tell me. I'll do anything.'

'You saw me. I want to see you.'

Hannah's eyes widened. 'W-what?'

He leant in close, his sickly-sweet breath warm against her cheek. 'You saw my willy, so I want to see your pussy. That way, I know I can trust you not to tell.' In that moment, he looked older than fifteen, which only intimidated her further.

'I can't do that.'

'Why not? It's fair.'

'I'll do anything else you want, but not that.' She was making promises she knew she couldn't keep, but didn't care. She just needed him to back off so she could get away.

'But why? Are you a little scaredy-cat?'

'No, it's wrong.' Her voice faltered on the last word, exposing her, proving that she wasn't as brave as she was trying to make out.

Bill huffed. 'I thought you were cool. I might have known you wouldn't dare do it.'

'It's not that.'

'Well, what is it?'

'I'm not supposed to.'

'Says who? Your mummy? Do you always do what Mummy tells you? You're such a baby, Hannah.'

'No I'm not.'

She wasn't being a baby, was she? What he was asking her to do was wrong.

Her humiliation was complete when the tears started to spill. He looked at her with such disgust, she wanted the ground to swallow her up.

'Forget it,' he told her sulkily. 'I didn't realise you were such a loser. Wait until I tell everyone at school what a saddo you are. Crybaby Hannah, the goody two shoes.'

He wouldn't, would he? Panic overrode everything else. 'No, please.' She grabbed for his arm when he started to walk away and he shook her off.

'Get lost, you big baby.'

'Wait. Okay, I'll show you.'

He paused, turning around, not quite failing to hide his smile. 'You will?'

Hannah's heart was thumping. If her mother found out, she would be so angry. But if he told everyone at school…

Knowing she didn't have a choice, she nodded.

It would just be quick. She would show him and it would be over.

'Go on then.'

Her fingers fumbled with the buttons on her jeans, her skin burning hot as she pulled them down her legs.

'Lower,' Bill demanded when she paused.

Hannah did as he asked, yanking them further down until they were around her knees.

'Now your knickers.'

For a moment, she froze and didn't think she could do it.

'Pull them down.' His voice was stern, but he also sounded a little excited.

One quick flash and it would be over.

She didn't dare look at him as she hooked her thumbs over the elastic waistband, slowly lowering the briefs until she was fully exposed.

She squeezed her eyes shut, hating that he was looking at her private parts.

'Nice,' she heard him mutter, followed moments later by. 'Oh shit.'

The last words sounded panicked and Hannah opened her eyes, blinking at the furious face of Mrs W.

'What the hell is going on here?'

Bill's eyes were wide. 'She asked me if I wanted to see. I told her no, Mum.'

Mrs W whirled on Hannah. 'Pull your knickers up now! Is this true?'

Hannah didn't need to be asked twice, cheeks flaming as she yanked both her underwear and jeans up together.

'No, no! It's not true,' she protested, finding her voice. Although she was scared, she was also angry. How dare Bill blame her. 'He's lying. He made me do it.'

'You know I wouldn't do that. Mum, you have to believe me. She's always following me around the farm. She's just a stupid little kid. I told her I wasn't interested, but she won't leave me alone.'

'It's not true. Stop lying!'

The smack when it came caught her around the head, knocking

her off her feet. Hannah didn't fall because Mrs W caught hold of her by a handful of her hair.

'I think you and I need to have a talk, young lady.'

Hannah was still stunned as the woman dragged her out of the garage towards the farmhouse and she stumbled over her feet, before finding her voice.

'Please, Mrs Wickham. I swear he's lying. He made me do it because I saw him.' She tried to free her hair from the woman's grip, certain it was going to rip right out of her scalp.

It wasn't until they were inside the farmhouse and Hannah had been pushed down into one of the kitchen chairs that Mrs W spoke again.

'You saw what?' she demanded.

Hannah's heart was thumping as she rubbed at her sore head. 'That day in your bedroom,' she squeaked, afraid of what reaction she was going to get.

There was a long pause. 'I have no idea what you're talking about.'

'You were with Bill and telling him off.'

'I think you're confused. You didn't see anything, so—'

'But I—'

'Don't interrupt me when I am talking to you.' Mrs W's face was stone.

'Sorry, Mrs Wickham.' The tears were falling again now and she couldn't stop them.

'Stop crying, girl. Your tears don't wash with me. You clearly have a problem with the truth. Lying about me and about my son.'

'I'm not. I promise.'

'There you go again. Do you have any idea how disgusting that is? Dropping your knickers for a boy? They have names for girls like you. Dirty little sluts. I wonder what your mother and stepfather will say when I tell them what you did.'

'Please, no. Please don't tell them.' Her mum was going to be so disappointed.

'She needs to know what a dirty little girl she has.'

'Please, I'm begging you, Mrs Wickham.'

'You need to be taught a lesson, young lady. My Bill is a good boy. I won't have you trying to seduce him and turn his head with your filth.'

'It... wasn't... like... that...' Hannah was struggling to speak now between sobs.

'Stop it with your lies! I'll give you something to cry about.'

When Mrs W went over to the cellar door, unlocking it, Hannah froze. If she hadn't been sitting down, her legs would have probably collapsed beneath her. What was the woman going to do?

'Get inside. Let's see what Mr Bennett thinks about liars and sluts.'

'No! Please, no.'

'Get inside, Hannah, now. Bad girls need to be punished.'

Hannah glanced at the back door, wanting to make a run for it, but she was too scared. Every part of her was wobbling like a jelly. 'I don't want to go down there. Please don't make me.'

She could barely see through her tears now and they turned to screams as Mrs W dragged her off the chair, pushing her inside the cellar and down the stairs. Had the woman not had hold of her, she would have stumbled and fallen.

The air was damp and musty, the temperature cool, and even through her tears, Hannah could see there was barely any light.

Mrs W pushed her over to another door, pulling up the bolt and swinging it open to reveal a tiny room. A cupboard of sorts, though it was mostly empty. And then she was shoving Hannah inside, hard enough that she fell back against the wall, and although Hannah tried to fight back, to get out of the cupboard, she wasn't strong enough, the door slamming shut and almost catching her fingers.

She was in complete darkness now, banging frantically on the door and begging to be let out.

Mrs W didn't speak again and Hannah heard the bolt click into place, then Mrs W's footsteps growing more distant before the slam of another door.

That was when Hannah realised she was all alone.

27

Liam finally made contact on Sunday afternoon, about four hours after Hannah had reached the conclusion she would never hear from him again.

When her phone rang, she was out for a test walk, making sure her ankle would hold up if she resumed her dog-walking duties in the morning. Confident it would, she stopped by to see her dog charges and their humans to let them know she was back in business.

It was as she was walking back to her flat that Liam called, and she blinked at the screen in surprise, hesitating for a moment before answering. He had cut her off with no contact, simply saying something had come up and he had to go away. She had no right to be upset about that. He owed her nothing. She wasn't a part of his life. They had simply connected over an interview for his book.

'Hello?' She kept her tone casual.

'Hannah, it's Liam. Sorry I've been off the grid. Something came up.'

There it was, that vague 'something' again.

She kept her tone breezy. 'It's not a problem. Is everything okay?'

'Yeah, just family stuff.'

She knew nothing about his family, except there was the sister who had given him Tank, but that, of course, was because they had only ever talked about Hannah and her life. She didn't push it, knowing he would only change the subject.

'Look, sorry I had to cancel on you. I wondered if we could catch up this evening. If you don't have any plans, of course.'

She was certain he had only added that last sentence out of politeness. They both knew she was unlikely to have plans. Still, her heart hitched a little at the thought of seeing him, which in turn annoyed her, because it wasn't supposed to be about that.

'I can do this evening.'

God, Hannah. Stop sounding so eager.

'Great. Are you okay to come here again? I'll feed you.'

'Sure, and thanks.' Now her ankle wasn't hurting so much, she could take her car.

'Shall we say about seven? I should be back by then.'

'Seven is fine.'

* * *

His car was there when she arrived and the front light on, much to Hannah's relief. Still, as she parked in the driveway and headed up the steps on to the porch, she couldn't help but think back to the last time she visited, remembering how defenceless she had been when the car had pulled up, and the memory sent an icy shiver down her spine.

The door opened before she could knock, and she stepped inside to an enthusiastic greeting from Tank.

'I brought this,' she said, making a fuss of the dog before

handing Liam the bottle of wine that she had stopped to buy. She had debated whether to bring it or not. They were meeting to talk about Mrs W, it wasn't a date. Still, he was making her dinner and good manners told her she should bring something.

The briefest of hesitations as he accepted the bottle had her questioning herself again. Was she making this into something more than it was?

'Thanks.'

As he took the bottle through to the kitchen, Hannah followed after him, Tank practically attached behind her, and she spotted the large paper bag on the worktop and could smell the Chinese food.

Okay, so he wasn't actually cooking then.

'I only just got back,' he apologised. 'Traffic was a bitch, so I had to compromise. Are you okay if I nip upstairs for a quick shower?'

'Yes, of course.'

'Great. Give me ten minutes.'

Left alone, Hannah found plates and cutlery, put on the oven to keep the food warm, then wandered back through to the front door, where Tank was pawing and whining, wanting to go out.

She opened the door for him and while she waited, she glanced at the table where Liam's MacBook sat. Unlike last time she had been here, it wasn't open, probably because he had just dumped it there after coming indoors. The pages of notes she had seen before were piled on top of it and curiosity had her itching to go and have a look.

She couldn't. It would be an invasion of his privacy, even if the subject matter he was writing about did involve her.

Of course, if she was setting the table and happened to glance at the top page...

No, she shouldn't.

Tank came bounding back in at that moment and she was grateful for the distraction. She wasn't a snoop, knew only too well from her past that prying into other people's business never ended well. Instead she indulged the fluffy hound with an ear rub, before following him through to the kitchen, noting his bowl was empty. Clean too, which suggested Liam hadn't yet had time to feed him.

As if to emphasise that point, Tank plonked himself down next to the bowl and looked at her expectantly, his big pink tongue hanging.

'You're going to get me in trouble,' she mock grumbled to him, picking up the bowl and hunting for his food. She found a half-used tin of dog meat in the fridge and a bag of dry food in the cupboard under the sink, guesstimating what she thought Liam would feed him.

Tank whined as she put the bowl down, tucking in straightaway.

'I see he's got you wrapped around his paw,' Liam commented from behind her, his voice making her jump.

'He was hungry. I hope you don't mind me feeding him.'

'Not at all. You've saved me a job, so thanks.'

He brushed past her as he went to the oven and she caught his fresh citrusy scent, ignoring the little kick in her groin. He had changed into a navy T-shirt that hung on broad shoulders and swapped his jeans for a pair of grey joggers, and his usually unruly hair was still damp and a shade darker than normal. She watched as he bent down to open the oven door, appreciating the curve of the joggers as they tightened over his bum, then immediately berated herself. What the hell was wrong with her? She was acting like a horny teenager.

'Do you want me to take anything through?' she offered, needing a distraction. It was getting too hot in this tiny kitchen. 'Have you got place mats?'

'I think there's some in the cupboard behind you.'

Hannah found them, taking them through and glancing at the notes on the table again.

She set the place mats down, could just about read the first few words of scribble, immediately recognising the name Jill Goldberg, then Liam was beside her, picking up the MacBook and notes and moving them out of the way.

'Sorry. I haven't been using the table to eat at. It's a bit of a mess. Do you want a glass of wine or a soft drink?'

'Um, a Coke please if you have one.'

He didn't seem too stressed that she might have seen the page, but was that an act? He had been quick to come through and remove them. Was that because he didn't want Hannah to see them?

And why was Jill's name on top? Hannah hadn't yet spoken to him about Jill's death and Liam had told her he was yet to talk to any of her old friends.

Why did he have her name written down?

That question stayed with her as they sat down to eat, both keeping the conversation light and off topic to start with, while Tank sat between them, his own dinner finished and now hopeful that he might share theirs.

'Where did you have to travel back from?' Hannah eventually asked, deciding to try to find out a little bit more about this man sitting opposite her. She took a sip of her Coke, scooping up another forkful of noodles as she waited for him to answer.

'Down south.'

Another vague, frustrating answer. And then he did that thing she was learning he was so good at doing. He flipped the subject.

'How were things after I left the other day?'

'What do you mean?'

'Well, we already know Rosie's thoughts, but your ex-husband didn't seem too thrilled to see me either. I hope they haven't given you a hard time.'

'Rosie will come around.' That was actually more a hope than a belief. 'She's fragile and finds it difficult to trust.'

'And what about the ex? What's the story there?'

'Josh? As we're divorced, it's not really any of his business.' That was unfair. Josh cared and he was good to her. Her tone softened. 'He worries about me, which is nice. It's good to know he's in my corner.'

'You guys sound close. How come you split up?'

Hannah shrugged. 'I guess we were both young and rushed into it, not really considering the commitment needed to make a marriage work. It didn't last long. I was divorced when I was still in my twenties.'

'And now you're both older, hopefully wiser, you don't fancy giving it another go?'

'No.' She shook her head. 'It's not like that for us. I guess what we have figured out along the way is that we work far better as friends.' It was the truth and Hannah forked up more of her noodles, aware that Liam was studying her. Why did he want to know about Josh and her relationship with him? Was his interest personal, or was that just wishful thinking on her part? 'You've never come close to marrying, then?' she asked, throwing the question back.

'I was engaged once, but it didn't work out.'

'How so?'

'We were incompatible, I guess.' He looked thoughtful for a moment, glancing at the food on the table. 'Do you want any more of the orange chicken?'

'No, I'm good.' Hannah handed him the dish, watching as he scooped the rest onto his plate.

Considering his job involved asking questions, he really didn't like answering them himself.

'So, has anything else happened over the last few days?'

The abrupt change of subject threw her, not giving Hannah an opportunity to consider how she should answer. So far, she had kept quiet about Jill's death. She had planned on updating Liam while they ate, but seeing Jill's name on the top page of his notes had thrown her.

'Not really,' she lied.

Liam actually paused eating to study her, his eyes slightly narrowed. 'And what about the others? How did they react to Eileen vanishing?'

Did he know she had lied to him? Come to think of it, why was she lying to him?

'They were a little freaked out.'

'But nothing has happened to them?'

'No.'

Hannah was pretty certain her guilt was written all over her face. She never had been any good at deceiving people. If he knew, he didn't call her out on it, instead returning his attention back to his food.

Hannah wrestled with her conscience, the weight of the lie growing inside her, hating that they had fallen into a silence. 'Jill's dead,' she blurted, needing to break it.

Liam paused again, his eyes meeting hers. He didn't look surprised or shocked, but he also didn't admit that he already knew.

'Jill Goldberg?' he asked eventually, and the fact he had wanted clarification suggested perhaps he didn't know.

'Yes.'

He nodded curtly, perhaps annoyed that she had planned to not say anything, though he didn't question why. 'Tell me what you know.'

She did, which actually was very little.

'Do you believe it was an accident?' he pressed when she had finished.

'I honestly don't know.' Hannah put down her cutlery and scrubbed her hands over her face. 'She fell down the stairs. It could easily have been an accident, but the timing? It's all a bit coincidental, don't you think?' She paused in frustration. 'Honestly, I really have no idea. What were the circumstances? Had she been drinking? Was there anything she could have tripped over? Had anything happened to her in the days before she died?'

'Maybe it really was just coincidence.'

'Is that what you think, after everything that's happened?'

'Well, I agree the flowers had to have come from Eileen Wickham, but perhaps there is a more innocent explanation for the car that was here. Think about it. You were here alone. If the driver had really meant you harm, they had the perfect opportunity to attack you. Then there's Rosie's break-in. I know she told you she heard the music box, but you've admitted yourself, Rosie gets confused sometimes. If someone had broken into her flat, she would have been upset and not thinking clearly. Is it possible she imagined hearing the music?'

It was true; Rosie often had a distorted view and version of things, very likely a way of coping with her past trauma. The break-in would have scared the hell out of her and it was very likely her brain would struggle to cope. Was it possible she had mistaken hearing the music box?

'Together these things create a pattern, especially when you throw in Eileen going AWOL, but we're talking about three incidents, plus a quite likely accidental death.'

'It's not just three things though. Tash had someone snooping around outside her house. Then there was the message I received.'

'What message?'

Shit.

Liam's sharp blue gaze told Hannah she had been caught out.

She sighed, annoyed with herself for lying in the first place. 'I received a text a couple of nights ago.' It was still on her phone and she reached for it now. Showing him was easier than saying the words aloud. She watched him read the message, saw the flicker of irritation, then he smoothed it over.

'Did you call the number?'

'No. I did report everything to the police though.'

She didn't have to tell him that while they logged everything, there was little they could do. He would already know that.

'Can I?' He was holding up her phone and she saw he had the call button up.

She shrugged, watched him put the phone on loudspeaker. It went straight to voicemail. No surprise there. He handed her the phone back.

'Why didn't you tell me any of this, Hannah?'

He sounded more frustrated than annoyed, which didn't help her bubble of guilt.

Why hadn't she told him? Lack of trust over Jill. She couldn't shake the feeling that he had already know. Her name was written at the top of his notes and he hadn't seemed surprised at the news she was dead.

He didn't know. When you told him, he wanted to know what had happened.

She recalled his words: *Tell me what you know.*

Actually, that wasn't the same thing at all. He hadn't asked her to tell him what had happened. He had simply wanted to know what Hannah knew.

Everything inside her went cold. 'Did you already know Jill was dead?'

He had a good poker face because he didn't flinch. 'Why would you think that?'

'Answer the question, Liam.'

For a moment, they stared at each other.

'No,' he said eventually. 'I didn't.'

'Your notes. Why do you have her name written down on the top page?'

She could see the disappointment on his face before he spoke and guilt stabbed at her.

'You were going through my research?'

'No! I wasn't. I would never snoop. But it was sitting on the table when I set it. It was impossible not to see.'

Liam didn't say anything. Instead he got up, retrieving the notes from the bookshelf where he had put them. He slammed them down on the table in front of her.

'You want to see what I'm working on, Hannah? Then go ahead and look. You know what I am writing a book about and, like it or not, you, Jill, Rosie and the rest of your friends are a part of it. Yes, Jill's name is there. You're all mentioned. So is Scott Copeland,' he told her, mentioning the name of Eileen Wickham's first victim. The boy from before. 'If not on the first page, then certainly later on. Knock yourself out. It's all there.'

He was angry with her and both annoyance and embarrassment heated her face. She could now see that Rosie's name was also mentioned. Miles's too.

'I don't want to look at your notes.' She shoved them towards him, pushing back her chair and getting to her feet. The food she had been enjoying now sitting uncomfortably in her stomach. 'Thank you for dinner, but I think I should go.'

He looked exasperated, though didn't say anything as she got up, picking her bag up from the sofa. She expected him to stop her as she opened the door, letting herself out, but he didn't.

It wasn't until she had reached her car that she heard his footsteps.

'Hannah! Wait.'

Ignoring him, she started to open the door. He caught up to her quickly, and she flinched as he touched her elbow.

'Don't go.'

No, it would be a mistake staying and she turned to tell him that, finding he was standing much closer to her than she realised. She backed up a step, her bum pushing the door shut. He was still too close, but the tremor in her belly wasn't from fear.

She looked up at him, certain from his expression that he could feel it too.

For a moment, neither of them spoke, then Liam broke the silence.

'I'm sorry I accused you of snooping. I've had a shitty few days and I'm tired and a little irritable. That's no excuse. I shouldn't have taken it out on you.'

He looked so apologetic, the fight went out of Hannah.

'I'm sorry too. I shouldn't have jumped to conclusions about Jill.'

'I don't want to keep secrets from you. If it makes you feel more comfortable seeing exactly what I'm writing about, what notes I am making, I will go through it with you.'

'No, you don't have to do that. I don't need to see.'

'I want you to learn to trust me, Hannah.' He reached up and caught a strand of her hair between his fingers, giving it a gentle tug. The move could be read as friendly or more, and she wasn't quite sure how to interpret it.

When her eyes widened, he let go, backing away a step.

'Will you come back inside? Please? I'd like you to.'

It was a simple request, but Hannah still took a moment to consider. Something had shifted between them and she would be a liar if she said she wasn't attracted to this man. But did she trust him?

She nodded. 'Okay.'

She guessed she was about to find out.

28

'Have you found anything yet?'

'Rosie. Hello to you too.' Josh's dry tone irritated like nails on a blackboard and she clenched her free hand into a fist, wishing that she'd had another choice of ally. Hannah kept her circle tight and Rosie and Josh were the two who were closest to her. Which was another reason why Quinn was annoying Rosie so much.

Why was Hannah lowering her defences around him so easily? Rosie didn't trust him one iota. There was something fishy about the man and with everything going on at the moment, the timing of it all was rather coincidental.

Hannah wouldn't like her prying, but Rosie was only looking out for her.

'Hello, Josh,' she snapped back, her tone impatient. 'Well, have you? Found anything?'

'I haven't really had much of chance to look yet. He's a writer and I've glanced over his website and publisher. It all seems legit. He's had several successful books too.'

Rosie snatched up her wine glass and took a drink. 'I'm not interested in his writing career. I've already looked at his website.'

'Then what is it that you want me to do?'

She could hear the weary note of impatience in Josh's tone, and she clenched her teeth in frustration. The man really didn't get it.

'What I want you to do is use your contacts and find out what the real deal is with him. I know he's hiding something.'

By Josh's contacts, she meant at the solicitors firm where he worked. Surely he knew people and could find a way to cut through red tape to help them get some answers?

'I'm not a private investigator, Rosie.'

'I know that, but you must be able to do something.'

'You know it's quite possible there is no dirt to find and you're just jealous because he's spending time with Hannah.'

'I am not jealous!' This was typical Josh. Pushing her buttons and twisting things around to try to make her look a bad person. Besides, he could talk. She had seen his face when Hannah had shown up with Quinn, and he wasn't happy. 'I don't like how he has her hooked. You know what Hannah is like. She doesn't trust easily, but for some reason, he has managed to worm his way beneath her defences so he can dig into the past. What if he is trouble?'

Josh sighed, loud and exaggerated, as if to make a point, but Rosie knew she had his interest. He was far too overprotective of Hannah and while that normally annoyed her, in this instance she could use it to her advantage.

'Okay, okay. Leave it with me. I will make a few phone calls and see what I can find out about him.'

That was better.

'Let me know as soon as you find anything.'

Rosie was convinced there would be something she could use, but she had to act quickly. The deeper Hannah became involved with Quinn, the more difficult it would be to make her see sense.

It was unlike her friend to get duped. Normally she was the one with her head screwed on and Rosie was able to rely on her. There had been countless times that Hannah had helped her out of trouble. Now it was time to return the favour.

Quinn showing up at the same time Mrs W started terrorising them was too much of a coincidence to ignore. Were they somehow connected? Mrs W wanted revenge and Rosie knew she wasn't going to rest until she had taken it. Was Quinn going to help her get it? Mrs W had been forced to give up twenty years of her life and she blamed the five of them for it. Now she wanted their lives in return.

Rosie closed her eyes and for a moment she was back in the darkness, the scent of the earth and that awful cool moist air. There had been two of them that last awful night and although there had been tears and moments of panic, knowing they were together made it easier to cope.

At least it had until eventually there had just been one voice and Rosie had realised she was there all alone.

She knew what evil Mrs W was capable of. The cruelty she had shown them as children had been hidden behind a smiling mask, as she lured them in with ice cream and cookies. She was the witch in Hansel and Gretel, the wolf in Little Red Riding Hood, the faceless monster who they had all been warned never to get in the car with.

She had warned Hannah there would be consequences if they ever betrayed her, if they ever told anyone what she had done, but they hadn't listened. They had told and Mrs W had gone to prison where she had no doubt planned her revenge.

As a child, Rosie had gone from adoring Mrs W to being terrified of her in the course of one night, but as an adult, recalling what truly awful things Mrs W was capable of was even more frightening.

There had been six of them as children, but Miles had died. Now his sister, Jill, was dead and as awful as it was, part of Rosie actually envied her. Jill had nothing to fear. It was those who were left, Hannah, Lauren, Tash and Rosie, who needed to be on their guard.

Eileen Wickham was coming for them and they needed to find out what she was planning. So far, she had just been playing games with them, but soon she would strike and their nightmare would begin again, and Rosie didn't know if she could survive this time.

29

'Have you considered Bill Wickham might be involved or helping Eileen?'

They were back at the table, the dishes mostly empty, though Tank was still keeping a close eye for scraps, and the bottle of wine that Hannah had brought was now open. Liam had persuaded her to have a small glass and she had been nursing it, looking like she wished she could have a top-up.

He was tempted to tell her to stay the night again, but it probably wasn't the wisest idea.

The earlier argument might have been smoothed over, but there was now a tension of a different kind between them and he knew they were both trying their best to ignore it.

If she stayed, he wasn't sure it would be in the spare room, so it was better if she remained sober enough to drive. Perhaps wise for him to keep a clear head too and stay focused on the Wickhams.

He watched her reaction to his question carefully, aware of the history between her and Bill.

To her credit, she didn't give much away, her expression carefully blank, though he noticed her hand shook a little as she picked up her glass, taking a bigger sip.

'I have, but why would he wait this long to take revenge?'

'His mother is finally out of prison. Maybe she has asked him to help her, or it could be it has triggered something. You said the message on the card with the flowers is a phrase she used several times, so it would have been one Bill was familiar with too.'

He could tell she didn't like the idea, which wasn't a surprise, given that Hannah had feared Bill Wickham as much as she had his mother.

'Has he ever tried to get in touch with you over the years?'

She shook her head. 'No, fortunately. Do you know much about what happened to him?'

'From what I've been able to find out, he managed to get on an apprenticeship on a building site after he was released from the young offenders' institution. He moved up to Yorkshire to be closer to his mother, never settled, never married, then a couple of months before Eileen's release, he moved back to Suffolk and rented the house in Sudbury, the one we went to.'

'He was living there with Eileen?'

'Technically yes. His name is on the paperwork, but he works away during the week. She was mostly there alone.'

'And what about now? He must know where she is.'

'He claims not. Of course he's lying.'

'She was horrible to him too. Why did he always take her side?'

'Blood ties run deep. She's still his mother, his responsibility.'

'Do you think it could have been Bill who followed me here the other night?'

Yes, but Liam didn't say that, going for the more diplomatic, 'Possibly.'

He was scaring her a little and wondered if she found the idea of Bill coming after her even more frightening than Eileen. Bill had just been a kid at the time he had terrorised her. A fifteen-year-old boy. But then, Liam supposed, to a thirteen-year-old girl that age gap had probably seemed much bigger. 'You were his favourite target.'

It wasn't a question, but she nodded anyway. 'I don't think he ever got past the humiliation that I saw him that day. He wanted to redress the balance. Have me feel that same shame.'

They had talked at length about the beating Hannah had witnessed, Liam pointing out the impact it would have likely had on Bill. How the humiliation could easily morph into something darker.

'Are you comfortable telling me what happened after that day you saw Eileen hitting him? When you next went back to the farm?'

Hannah hesitated for so long that he thought that was going to be a no. 'Still off the record?'

'Still off the record.'

She reached for the wine bottle, looking resigned. 'I can try, but I'm going to need more of this.'

Liam didn't say anything, watching as she filled her glass and took a generous sip.

She wouldn't be driving home then. He tried very hard to ignore the kick of lust that burned through him.

He waited until she was ready to talk, then listened as she recounted the incident in the garage, unable to make eye contact with him, her cheeks flushed as she told him how Eileen had caught her in a compromising position. As she talked about the cupboard in the cellar, she closed her eyes and he knew from her words that she was back there.

He could only imagine how frightening it must have been for her as a young girl.

Without thinking, he reached across the table and took hold of her hand, only conscious he had done it when her cold fingers tightened around his, clinging on. Eventually, she fell silent and he gave her a moment to gather herself before speaking.

'How long were you in the cupboard?'

'About an hour, I guess. It felt much longer.'

'And what happened after?'

'She let me out. I was numb by that point, and maybe a little in shock. The others had already gone home, so it was just me there. She was nice to me after. I had peed myself and she took my damp underwear and jeans and said she would get them washed for me, then she let me clean up in the bathroom and borrow a pair of Bill's jeans. Afterwards, she gave me a ride home.'

'But you didn't tell anyone?'

'She was acting like nothing had happened for most of the ride home, but as we got closer, she threatened me. She said that if I told, my mother wouldn't believe me, because it would be my word against hers and everyone knows to believe adults over children. She also warned me that if I said anything, she would have to come after me. That she would lock me in the cupboard again and next time she wouldn't let me out.'

'Did your mother question why Eileen had driven you home?'

'She had her story all figured out, telling my mum that I had gone into the cellar of my own accord and the door had shut behind me. She had hidden my bike and told the other kids I must have gone home, which is why they left without me. And she said it wasn't until later when she went down into the cellar to get something that she realised I was down there. She was very convincing and my mum even thanked her for lending me the jeans, apologising that I had peed on her floor. I didn't dare tell anyone what had really happened and I was terrified each time I left the house that she might grab me and force me to go back.' Hannah finally looked up at Liam. 'When you're just a kid, threats like that seem like such a big deal.' Her gaze dropped to study their linked hands, but she didn't let go. After a moment, she reached for her glass with her free hand, gulping down the rest of her wine.

'Thirsty?' Liam asked, amused.

'Dutch courage.' When he arched a questioning brow, her words tumbled out. 'I don't want to be alone tonight.'

Shit.

He pulled his hand free and got up, starting to clear the table, knowing if he looked at her, it would be game over. It was talking about the past, he guessed. She was vulnerable right now and as attracted as he was to her, he couldn't take advantage of that. 'You don't have to be alone. You can stay in the spare room again.' He kept his tone light, knowing he had to nip this in the bud.

'I don't want to sleep in the spare room.'

'Hannah, this isn't a good idea.'

'I don't care.' She was also on her feet now, her hand on his arm. 'Liam—'

He turned to tell her no, but she caught him off guard, her mouth crushing against his, and he tried to resist her advances for all of about two seconds before lust took over common sense, his dick telling his brain to shut up.

She was intoxicating, both the taste and the feel of her as she pressed against him, and heat exploded in his belly as his hands moulded over her arse, pulling her closer as he drank her up.

He wasn't supposed to sleep with her, this was never part of the plan, but he couldn't think rationally while her hands were working their way under the back of his T-shirt and her breasts were mashed up against his chest.

As her mouth left his to graze down his jawline, he made one last half-hearted attempt to stop her. 'Are you sure you want to do this?'

She paused briefly, pulling her head back to look in his eyes, her own heavy with lust.

'I'm sure.' Her kiss-swollen mouth curved up on one side, both in humour and in challenge, and that was it. He was undone.

This might be a huge mistake, but he was in too deep now and he would worry about it tomorrow.

30

Had it not been for Tank sticking his face in Hannah's and trying to poke his big slobbery tongue up her nose, she likely wouldn't have woken in time to remember she was back on dog-walking duty.

Pushing him away, she rolled back against the hard warm body beside her and started to drift back to sleep again, then awoke with a start as she realised she was going to be late.

There was no time for any morning-after shyness as she threw back the duvet, earning herself an annoyed grunt from Liam, and she dashed from the bed, hunting around the room for her clothes.

'All of your stuff is downstairs,' he told her, and she shot him a look, saw he was now propped up on one elbow, watching her with lazy interest.

Her cheeks heated as she recalled the frantic fumbling of the night before, both of them hurriedly undressing each other. They had been worse than a pair of horny teenagers.

For all of his initial reluctance, once Liam was on board with the whole 'let's have sex' thing, he hadn't held back, and Hannah was glad she had made the first move. It had been the most enjoyable night she had experienced in a while.

'Oh wait.' He frowned, reaching beneath the duvet and pulling out her knickers. He held them out to her with a devilish grin. 'Not quite all of it.'

Hannah snatched them from him, then, with as much dignity as she could muster for someone who was completely naked, she walked out of the bedroom, heading for the stairs. Tank hot on her heels, clearly hoping she was heading for the kitchen.

She had her jeans on and was fiddling with her bra when Liam came down the stairs a couple of minutes later, fastening his own jeans.

'So, do you always cut and run after a one-night stand?'

So that's what he thought this was? 'Actually, I don't do one-night stands.' When Liam arched his brow, she admitted, 'You're the first.'

If he was surprised by that, he didn't show it, nodding as he headed through into the kitchen.

'Do you want coffee?'

'I don't have time.' Hannah found her jumper down the back of the sofa, slipping it on. 'I'm supposed to pick the dogs up in twenty-five minutes.'

'Are you free later?'

'Um...' She considered the question, trying to decide how to interpret it. Was he asking because he wanted to resume talking about Mrs W or did he want to have sex again?

She wasn't opposed to either, but he had just referred to her as a one-night stand and she wasn't quite sure how she felt about that.

When she didn't answer, he poked his head round the door, eyebrows raised. 'Is that a yes or a no?'

Hannah ran a self-conscious hand through her hair. They had both just rolled out of bed, but he was looking surprisingly fresh and sexy in a slightly scruffy, dishevelled way, while she was pretty certain she looked like she had slept in a hedge. 'I guess so. Maybe.'

'Hannah, is this going to be weird now between us?' he asked, coming towards her, a faintly amused look on his face.

'No of course not.'

'Good, because it was just sex. It doesn't have to complicate anything.'

Just sex? Okay, well that told her. Maybe she was a little out of practice, but she'd never had any complaints.

'It doesn't,' she agreed a little huffily. 'Anyway, I need to go.' She found her bag and pulled out her keys, waving them at him. 'Dogs are waiting.'

'So I'll see you later?'

'Sure. Whatever.'

Bloody *just sex*. For a writer, he certainly had a way with words.

She stewed a little on the ride home, struggling to lift her black cloud.

And even later, when she was on the beach, the dogs frolicking in the waves, she couldn't shake it.

It was her own fault, she supposed. She had pushed for last night, even when Liam had tried to stop her. And of course it was just sex. Yes, there was an attraction there, but he had never intimated that he wanted more. He didn't even live around here and would be gone in a few days. Hannah had known exactly what she was getting into last night. She only had herself to blame.

It didn't stop her brooding and when her phone rang and she saw it was her mother, her heart sank further.

She didn't need to answer to know why her mum was calling. It was going to be about the anniversary party again. When they had last spoken, her mother was trying to pin her down for an answer. Hannah had promised she would let her know within the next couple of days.

Guilt swamped her as she stared at the phone, not in the right frame of mind to answer. If she said no, they would get into a fight.

Hannah would be reminded how important this party was for her mother and that she was a selfish and inconsiderate daughter, her mother having no concept of how difficult it was for her to return home in the first place.

Jane Lawrence had been as shocked and horrified as the other parents when they had learnt about Mrs W, but as the years rolled by, she had never been able to understand why Hannah couldn't simply put everything behind her. It was over. Mrs W had gone to prison. It was time to start living her life again.

And, to an extent, Hannah agreed. But that life couldn't be in Hixton, and even though she was trying her best to enjoy the new one she had built for herself, she had no control over the nightmares or the panic attacks that occasionally happened when she did return home.

Moments after the call ended, a WhatsApp came through. Hannah left it unread for now, knowing her mum would see if she read it. She would reply, but later.

She slipped her phone back into her pocket and whistled to the dogs, attaching leashes before rewarding all three with a treat. As they walked towards the woods, she considered the rest of her week and the other pets she had scheduled. She only had her regulars lined up, and she was feeding Tango and Cash, a couple of senior cats, while their owner was away on a work trip. She needed to start trying to pull in some new business. Maybe it was time to do another leaflet drop.

She was considering that as she walked deeper into the wood when her ringtone started playing, the harsh sound cutting through the silence and startling her.

She pulled her phone from her pocket, surprised to see Lauren Bell's name appear on her screen. Although they had spoken on WhatsApp, she hadn't had a physical conversation with Lauren in a couple of years. Was there an update on Jill?

'They don't think she was alone,' Lauren was quick to tell Hannah, not bothering to return her hello. It was as if they had already been mid-conversation, not speaking for the first time in forever.

That was Lauren all over, Hannah remembered. The pair of them had been friends since they were six years old and Lauren had never been one for pleasantries, always cutting straight to the point.

'Who wasn't? Jill?' Hannah asked. She was perhaps stating the obvious, but Lauren hadn't said, so she wasn't certain.

'Yes,' Lauren told her impatiently. 'I went to see Adrian on Saturday, offer my condolences. Jill's stepmother and stepbrother were there too. I've never met him before. Anyway, we were all talking and Adrian told us the police are saying it's possible she was pushed.'

That wasn't good. 'Do they have any suspects?'

Thoughts of Mrs W and Bill raced through Hannah's mind. Would they have travelled down to Croydon to get to Jill? And if they had, why hadn't they targeted Lauren too? Sevenoaks was less than an hour away.

'No, not yet.'

'But they don't think it was anyone she knew?'

'The door was unlocked and there were a couple of windows open, so it could have been anyone. Adrian is kicking himself because they had cameras, but they weren't working. He had been promising Jill he would get them fixed.'

And he was going to feel guilty about that for a long time, Hannah thought, though didn't say it out loud. Poor bloke.

'I reminded him about Mrs W's release and also told him about what's been happening recently. He's going to mention it to the police.'

'You think it's connected, don't you?'

'Honestly, I don't know, Hannah. Maybe. The timing is a little too coincidental for my liking. I have a private investigator who is doing some digging for me. I'm going to see if I can track Mrs W down.'

'We don't know if she's dangerous, so be careful.'

'I can take care of myself.'

Hannah didn't doubt she could. Lauren had always been independent and not afraid to go after what she wanted in life. She had been one of the luckier members of the Hixton Five, and aside from the mouse, she had never experienced what Mrs W was really capable of.

They left the conversation with Lauren promising to keep Hannah updated if she found anything out, while Hannah agreed she would update Rosie, and Lauren would call Tash.

Should she have told Lauren about Liam? So far, Rosie was the only one who knew about him and Hannah felt a little guilty about that. She decided she would tell Lauren and Tash, but she wanted to wait a bit, unsure how they would react if they knew she was both talking to and sleeping with the man writing a book about them.

It didn't look good.

31

Hannah tried calling Rosie while she was walking to Lexi Hartman's house, on her way to see Lexi's cats, Tango and Cash. The property was about a twenty-minute walk, but it was a pleasant afternoon and Hannah fancied the exercise. When the call went to Rosie's voicemail, she left a message asking Rosie to give her a quick call back. Rosie had returned to her flat after her landlord had fixed the broken lock, and Hannah had been checking in with her regularly, wanting to make sure she was okay.

Hannah was in Lexi's kitchen, filling up a bowl with fresh water, when Rosie's name flashed up on her phone screen, and the tension dropped out of her shoulders.

'Hey, how's it going?' she asked, purposely keeping her tone light.

'You remember that audition I had for that new police show?'

'I do.'

'I've had a call-back. They want to see me again.'

'That's brilliant news. When is it?'

'The day after tomorrow. I really want this, Hannah.'

This was the most enthusiastic Hannah had heard Rosie in

days. She had been subdued and not her usual perky self since the break-in and had admitted she hadn't been sleeping well. Getting the call-back was a boost she needed and Hannah was thrilled for her.

She toyed with not telling Rosie the latest developments with Jill, not wanting to burst her bubble, but if Rosie found out from Lauren or Tash and realised she had been left out of the loop, that would be worse. As the conversation turned to other topics, Hannah decided to bite the bullet and Rosie fell quiet as she learnt Jill's death might not have been an accident.

'So the police think that Mrs W killed her?' she asked eventually, her voice no more than a whisper.

'They don't know what happened. They're just investigating every possibility.'

'But they said it was an accident.'

'And it might still be,' Hannah said, trying to placate her, even though she didn't really believe it herself. 'Lauren has hired a private investigator.'

'What? Why?'

'She's going to try to find Mrs W. If she did kill Jill, we need to know.'

'That's a really bad idea. Is she going to approach Mrs W if she finds her? That could be dangerous for us all.'

Hannah could hear the panic in Rosie's tone and tried her best to defuse it. 'She didn't say, but this is Lauren. She's the most sensible one of us. She's not going to do anything stupid.'

'If Mrs W finds out we're looking for her...'

'She's not going to find out.'

'I don't like any of this. I should go and talk to Lauren. I'm going to be in London for my audition. She's still in Sevenoaks, right? It's not that far.'

'Just leave it, Rosie, please. I need you to keep out of this, to stay safe. Lauren's already hired someone. Let her see what she can find out and you focus on your audition. She isn't going to put us in danger.'

Rosie fell silent.

'Promise me you'll stay away.'

'Okay, but I'm telling you, I don't like this.'

Hannah was wishing she'd gone with her first instinct and kept Rosie in the dark. She had known the news about Jill would upset her, but she hadn't expected her to overreact about Lauren hiring a private investigator. Lauren had always been the least tolerant of Rosie. If Rosie showed up on her doorstep, Hannah would likely get it in the neck.

'You don't have to like it, but I agree with Lauren. Trying to get the upper hand with Mrs W can only be a good thing.'

'It's that bloody Liam Quinn. Don't think I haven't noticed all of this has started happening since he showed up. You need to tell him to get lost.'

'You can't blame Liam for this. He hasn't done anything wrong.'

'Of course he has. He's dredging up our past and is making everything worse. And you keep defending him. How do we know he's not in cahoots with Mrs W? Don't you think it all seems rather odd that he shows up saying he is writing a book about her and now all these things are happening?'

'I promise you, he's not—'

Hannah froze. The noise sounded like a stone hitting one of the back windows.

'Hannah? What's wrong?'

'Nothing. I just heard something outside.'

'Where are you? Are you at home?'

'No, I'm at a client's house.'

'Are you there alone?'

'Yes.'

'So what made a noise?'

'I'm sure it's nothing. Just you making me paranoid.'

Not quite the truth, but Rosie didn't need to know that. It was probably just one of the cats had knocked something. Still, Hannah crept out into the hall and peeked into each of the rooms.

'Look, I need to sort Tango and Cash. I'll give you a call a bit later.'

'You're sure everything is okay?'

Hannah was in the living room now, looking over the back garden. She couldn't see anyone outside. Maybe a bird had flown into the window. 'Everything is fine.'

She ended the call, taking another look outside. Then, convinced she had overreacted, she sorted food and water for Tango and Cash before going in search of them, wanting to give them both some affection and a few treats. In her instructions, Lexi had explained they might be upstairs under one of the beds, and after finding downstairs empty, that's where Hannah headed.

Tango was sprawled across the landing at the top of the stairs, rolling over to expose his big ginger belly as Hannah approached, while sleek black Cash with his wide worried eyes watched her cautiously from under the bed in the spare room.

She spent some time making a fuss of Tango, while working on Cash, trying to lure him out with a combination of sweet talk and treat temptation. It was likely the latter that won, but he at least let her coax him while he enjoyed the biscuits.

Another loud bang had Cash running back to his hideout and even Tango flinched.

Rolling onto her knees, Hannah crawled across to the window and tried to discreetly peer out.

Her heart caught when she spotted the flicker of movement down below.

She barely saw him before he moved out of sight, certainly not enough to identify him, but she knew it had been a man. Who the hell was he and what on earth was he doing? Her client's gorgeous house was in a remote location with no close neighbours, a mile and a half from town.

Had she locked the front door? She was certain she had, but now she was doubting herself.

Climbing to her feet, annoyed her legs were shaking, she left the bedroom, heading across the landing. Her stomach felt like it was going to drop as she crept downstairs, and she hated how unnerved she was.

She had worked so hard over the years to build up her confidence and a tough exterior, hating the idea of anything that made her weak, and all it had taken was a handful of unsettling incidents to reduce her to a quivering wreck.

As she reached the bottom step, she saw a flash of black through the living-room window and nearly tripped over as she ran to the front door, tugging on the handle to make sure it didn't open. She heaved out a breath when she realised it was definitely locked. Someone was out there and she had no idea who they were or what they were doing there.

Yes, it could be completely innocent, but she couldn't be sure, and she wasn't about to stick her head out of the window and ask.

Retreating back to the stairs, she concentrated on her breathing, angrily telling herself to get a grip. She was still sitting there minutes later, trying to figure out a plan of action, knowing that if she called the police over something that could easily be a misjudgement on her part, she would be made to look a fool, when her phone rang. She glanced at the screen, expecting it to either be Rosie or her mother, surprised when she saw Liam's name flash up, and she hesitated briefly before answering. 'Hello?'

'Hey, you still up for meeting later?'

He hadn't made it clear why he wanted to meet. Was it personal or because he wanted to talk more about her past? Hannah wanted to kick herself for blurring those lines, but truthfully, as uncomfortable as it had made things, she couldn't regret what had happened last night. Besides, right now she was grateful he had called. 'Are you still at the cottage?'

She kept her tone low. If the man was still outside the house, she didn't want to advertise the fact she was indoors. Maybe he thought the property was empty and had come to burgle it...

'Yeah, I'm working. Why?'

'I'm at a client's house. Someone is... was outside.'

'What?' His tone was sharp, alert now. 'Hannah, where are you?'

'I might be overreacting. It could be—'

'Tell me where you are.'

She rattled off the address, a little embarrassed, but mostly relieved when he told her to sit tight and keep the doors locked, that he was on his way.

'Do you want me to stay on the phone with you?'

'No, I'll be okay. I'll see you in a bit.'

She ended the call, wondering if this could be chalked down to her paranoia. Although she wanted to believe that, her gut told her she wasn't overreacting.

A noise at the front door had her looking up, and she watched the handle moving up and down as whoever was on the other side tried to gain entry.

Okay, it was locked, but how tough would it be to break down if someone wanted in badly enough?

Not waiting to find out, Hannah ran back up the stairs and locked herself in the bathroom. She pulled her phone out and with trembling fingers called 999.

32

After speaking with Hannah, Lauren called Tash, explaining the situation with Jill and her plan of action. Tash took the news in her usual matter of fact way and Lauren was pleased she had left Rosie the basket case for Hannah to talk to.

She liked her other friends fine, but couldn't deal with Rosie and her meltdowns, so these days tended to avoid her. She had successfully managed to do so now for the past four years. Yes, Rosie had suffered worse than the rest of them, but she could be so melodramatic. Lauren would never say it out loud to the others, but she sometimes felt her old friend needed a good slap.

Nipping outside for a cigarette, she messaged her private investigator, asking if there was any update, aware she had only hired him a couple of days ago and not wanting to seem too pushy, but conscious that she needed answers fast.

Noah Keen had come highly recommended by Lauren's boss and she understood why, impressed when he called her back fifteen minutes after she chased him.

'I've been following up on Bill Wickham,' he told her. 'He's told the police he doesn't know where his mother is, but I don't buy that.

Everything suggests he dotes on Eileen. He had been visiting her regularly in prison and was there to pick her up when she was released. His name is also on the tenancy agreement of the house she was living in.'

'Do you know where he is?'

'He works away. Not easy to track down, as he flits between jobs, but I've spoken with his most recent employer, who happens to be up on the North Norfolk coast. Bill was staying in a caravan during the week.'

'You think he is responsible for harassing my friends?'

'Honestly? I don't know, but the close location suggests so. I have the address of the site, but he hasn't been in work in over a week and apparently his things are gone from the caravan. I do have his phone number, email, etc. Do you want me to try and talk to him?'

Lauren wasn't afraid of contacting Bill directly. She told Noah that and said she would be in touch, then she looked at the information he had given her.

The site address, a phone number, and an email address.

Deciding to cut straight to the chase, she dialled the number, unsurprised but still disappointed when it went to voicemail. She didn't leave a message, wanting to catch the man off guard.

Was he involved in Jill's death and the other things that had been happening to her friends?

He didn't call her back, but given that he wouldn't recognise her number, Lauren hadn't expected him to. She decided she would leave it an hour and then try him again.

33

Liam arrived at the house just a few minutes after the police had shown up.

Hannah hadn't left the bathroom until she saw the police car from the window and she was in the kitchen talking to the female PC when her colleague escorted Liam through. Tank was hot on his heels and Hannah hoped both the cats were still upstairs.

She gave the officers a statement, though her description of the man wasn't really going to help them, as she hadn't seen him properly.

'Do you think he followed you?' Liam asked, earning himself an annoyed look from the PC taking her statement, for interrupting.

'I honestly don't know. I didn't see or hear anyone.'

She had been on foot, so surely she would have noticed if she was being followed. But then again, why would the man show up at the empty house at the same time as her, unless it was to frighten her?

Mrs W's name was mentioned again, as was Bill's, and the PC made a note, assuring her that Eileen Wickham's disappearance was being taken very seriously.

She was in Liam's car, getting a lift back to her flat when Lexi called.

'Are you okay? The police contacted me.'

'I'm fine and so are Tango and Cash. It was just a bit of a shock.'

'I'm not surprised. I'm sorry you were there alone. I have no idea what that man was doing there.'

Hannah did. She didn't say that to Lexi though. If the woman knew the incident was likely personal, she might not want her to cat-sit for her in the future.

'Is there anything I can do to help?' she offered instead.

'Thank you, but there's no need. I'm heading home early, so I'll be back later this afternoon.'

While it was a pain financially, Hannah was also relieved, knowing she would be nervous about returning to the house alone. At least Lexi left the conversation saying that she would use Hannah's services again.

Slipping her phone back into her bag, Hannah shoved her hands through her hair and gave a frustrated sigh, earning herself a side glance from Liam.

'You okay?'

'No. I'm not.' She didn't like how scared she had been in the house, how vulnerable she had felt waiting in the bathroom for the police to arrive, terrified that whoever was outside might find a way into the house. But worse than that was the worry that whoever was harassing her, be it Mrs W, Bill or someone else, was now affecting her business and her clients. That just pissed her off. She explained it now to Liam. 'I just want it to stop.'

He nodded, though didn't say anything. Instead, he reached across and gave her hand a comforting squeeze. It struck Hannah as an intimate gesture, taking her a little by surprise, but she didn't comment.

They drove the rest of the way back to her flat in silence, the only sound coming from the low rumble of the engine and Tank panting on the back seat. Hannah was brooding, mostly about Mrs W, but also about the man beside her, still trying to figure out what he wanted, though unsure what she wanted for herself, while Liam seemed caught up in his own thoughts.

She didn't invite them in, but wasn't offended when both man and dog followed her inside anyway. It felt natural and it crossed her mind that perhaps it shouldn't, given they had only known each other a week.

'I need a shower,' she muttered, throwing her keys and phone down and heading to the bathroom, leaving him to his own devices.

When she emerged twenty minutes later, she was feeling fresher and a little perkier, standing under the warm spray, having soothed the edges of her bad mood.

Liam was on the sofa, feet up and his phone to his ear, Tank snoozing at his feet, though seeing her coming through, he quickly ended his call, getting up.

'Is everything okay?' she asked.

'Yeah.' He put his phone away before changing the subject. 'I made you a coffee.'

Hannah glanced at the mug on her counter, then at the drink he had made for himself. He certainly had no qualms about making himself at home. 'Thanks. Did you want to stay for dinner?'

'Sure. Thanks. Your phone keeps beeping. Someone's trying to get hold of you,' he told her.

'It's probably Rosie.' Hannah glanced at her WhatsApp, her heart sinking when she saw she had two more messages from her mother, plus another missed call.

She couldn't keep putting off getting back to her.

She read the messages, her mum pushing for an answer. They were only five days away from the party and Hannah really needed to let her know what she was doing.

She swore, understanding she really didn't have a choice.

'It's my mother,' she told Liam when he gave her a questioning look. 'That anniversary party I told you about is on Saturday and she's pushing again for me to stay.'

'Are you going to?'

'I want to. I just honestly don't know if I can do it.'

'So tell her no.'

'Suggested by someone who has never met my mother.'

'I haven't. But I could if you want me to.' He held her gaze, eyebrows raised in suggestion.

'What?'

'I'll come with you.'

Hannah was taken aback. 'You'd go to my mother's twenty-fifth wedding anniversary party with me?'

He shrugged like it was no big deal. 'Sure, why not? You're worried about going alone. I don't have plans.'

'But we'd have to stay over.'

'I know.' He grinned. 'That's the idea of me going, right? So you don't have to stay there by yourself.'

He made it sound so simple when it really wasn't. How was she supposed to introduce him to her mother? As a friend, as her one-night stand, as the man she had only met last week, who was digging into the past? And what about sleeping arrangements? The house only had two bedrooms, the third having been converted into her mother's sewing room.

'I don't see how that would work,' she told him.

'Why not? I stay with you and hopefully you don't freak out. How would that not work?'

'Well, my mother is going to wonder who you are for starters.'

'Tell her we're friends.'

'There's only the one free bedroom.' As she said it, heat crept up her neck.

'Oh.' His grin widened. 'You know I've already seen you naked, right?'

'That's not what I mean,' Hannah was annoyed he was making her spell it out for him. She couldn't decide if he was genuinely baffled or purposely winding her up. 'How is my mother going to react if I rock up and introduce you as my friend, then we sleep in the same bed?'

'I see.'

I see? What was all he had to say?

'Is your mother prudish about couples who sleep together out of wedlock then?' he teased.

'She will be if she knows they've only recently met.'

'Okay, so we don't tell her that. I'll pretend to be your boyfriend for the weekend.'

When Hannah simply stared at him like he was mad, he raised his brows.

'Would that work?'

'She's going to wonder why I've never mentioned you.' And rightly so. It was a little unsettling, the idea of Liam posing as her boyfriend.

'I'm sure we can come up with a reason for that. I'm good at making up stories.'

He winked at her and Hannah shook her head in exasperation. He was enjoying this.

'Look, it'll be fine. Message your mum back and tell her we're coming. We have a few days to figure out what to tell her.'

Maybe he was right and she was overthinking this. It was her mother's twenty-fifth anniversary party and she couldn't miss it. Having Liam there would anchor her.

She sent the message, getting the read tick almost immediately. She hadn't even had a chance to put her phone back down on the counter when it started ringing.

Hannah stared at in alarm, glancing to Liam for help. 'It's her.'

'Well, you'd better answer it.'

Yeah, he was going to be no use whatsoever. She put the call on loudspeaker.

'Hi, Mum.'

'Why didn't you tell me you're dating someone?'

'Umm, we decided to keep it quiet and see how things went.'

'I'm your mother though.'

'I know, Mum. Sorry.'

'How long?'

Hannah looked to Liam in panic, who was listening in amusement. He helpfully shrugged and shook his head. 'No idea,' he mouthed.

'Umm, it's been about six months.'

'Six months? It's serious then. I can't believe you never mentioned it when we came up to visit last.'

'It was still early days.'

'So it would seem. It's about time you started dating again, Hannah. You've already let one good man slip through your fingers.'

'Josh didn't slip through my fingers. The marriage wasn't working.'

'Perhaps you didn't try hard enough. He was solid and dependable, and had a good job.'

Hannah rolled her eyes. Her mother bloody loved Josh.

'Can we not talk about my failed marriage please?'

'So who is this new one? I want to know all about him.'

No. She wasn't doing this now. Not only did she not have the inclination; she didn't have the time either. Plus this wasn't the most comfortable conversation to be having in front of Liam.

'You'll meet him on Saturday.' Hannah gave Liam a sly smile. 'You can fully interrogate him then.'

Ha, that got him back.

'Well at least tell me his name.'

'Liam.'

'Liam,' her mother repeated, as if testing it out. 'And what does Liam do? Has he got a good job?'

'You'll meet him at the weekend, Mum. I have to go now. I'm late for an appointment. Love you.'

Hannah ended the call before her mother could ask any more questions and shot Liam a challenging look.

'Sure you still want to come?'

'I can't wait,' he told her dryly.

As he spoke, his own phone started ringing and he frowned at the screen, before rejecting the call.

'You're popular today,' Hannah commented. It was the second time in the space of an hour he had ignored whoever was trying to get hold of him. She watched as he fired off a brief text. 'No one you want to speak to?'

'Actually, I do, but it can wait.'

He glanced at his phone again as a text pinged through, frowning as he read it.

'Is everything okay, Liam?'

'Sorry? Yeah, it's fine.' He set his phone down and smiled at her, but it looked a little forced. 'So, what do I need to know about your mother?'

Another convenient subject change, but Hannah played along. She noticed he seemed distracted though.

A short while after he had finished his coffee, he got up to leave.

'I thought you were going to stay for dinner?' she asked, surprised.

'I actually forgot I have an appointment.'

Really? Where had that suddenly come from? Was he blowing her off?

Hannah slipped her cool, couldn't care less, mask into place, as she watched him attach Tank's leash and both of them left, thinking only after the door had closed that no arrangements had been made for the weekend.

Given how he had just reacted, would he even be going?

She wouldn't lower herself to ask. She was certain she wasn't being paranoid.

Whatever it was, she wouldn't chase. If he wanted anything else from her, she was sure he would soon be in touch.

34

Callers who don't leave messages make me nervous.

I have two different phones. One for work and one for playing games, and I am careful who I give my number to. Anyone who needs to get hold of me is already on my contact list.

I was busy when the first call came in and wariness had me declining the second one.

It seems someone wants to speak to me urgently, so why have they not left me a voicemail?

After the second missed call, curiosity got the better of me and I sent the unknown number a text. Three simple words.

Who is this?

The reply hadn't taken long to come.

Is this Bill Wickham?

Who wants to know? I am desperate to find out, but I don't reply immediately, instead making sure I am alone before I reply.

Who are you and what do you want?

It feels like forever, staring at my phone, waiting for a response. My skin is crawling with paranoia.

Eventually it comes.

It's Lauren Bell. I'm sure you remember me from Hixton. I need to talk to you. It's important.

What the fuck? How has that stuck-up little bitch managed to get my number?

My reply is blunt and instant.

Fuck off.

No pleasantries. We're not friends, and Lauren played a role in sending Mum to prison. She has a bloody nerve contacting me.

I am about to block her number when another message comes through.

I need to talk to you and it's urgent. This involves your mother, so please call me. I would hate for her to get in trouble again.

Seriously? The bitch is threatening me?

I remember her smug face. She was the hoity-toity one of the group. Always looking down on us, thinking she was something special. She was demanding and precious, the one who always had the newest and the best of everything and how she loved to brag and let everyone know about it.

This involves your mother, so please call me back.

Why the fuck does she want to talk to me about Mum? Does she not realise she's already caused enough trouble and misery?

I would hate for her to get into trouble again.

Is that supposed to be some kind of warning? After everything that has happened, she actually has the audacity to threaten me? It's that last line of her text that really sticks in my throat. Who does she think she is?

Tormenting Hannah and Rosie has been fun, but now Lauren commands my attention. I've enjoyed messing with those two bitches, and I'm not done yet, especially with Hannah. I have special plans for her.

Even now, all these years later, it makes me sick inside whenever I remember what she saw.

Mum was always calling me a butter fingers and warning me to be more careful, and I had known I was going to be punished the moment the glass smashed.

She was good that she never yelled at me in front of the other kids, believing that punishments should always be dealt with in private.

It was my own fault that she had to do this, I understood that. I had been clumsy and had to be taught a lesson. And it hurt her more than it did me, she told me, as the pain brought tears to my eyes. I resolved that I would be a better son. I would try harder and I would make her proud of me, so she didn't have to go through this again.

I have never managed to block out the look on Hannah's face as she had peered through the door, her eyes widening in shock. She saw it all and my face heats up as I remember how everything had shrivelled up inside of me.

After that day, she looked at me differently. She barely made eye contact and on the occasions she did I could see her disgust.

For years I have fantasised about evening the score with her, but those plans would have stayed in my head if she hadn't started poking around. She was the one who started this, but I will end it.

As for Lauren Bell. She needs to keep that stuck-up nose of hers out of my business. It doesn't involve her. She's snooping in my private life and that's unacceptable.

If she has my phone number, then what else does she know?

I haven't targeted her. Partly because she lives the furthest away, but also because she was the least involved. Yes, she might have told tales to the police with her friends, but she was never directly involved in the games we liked to play.

Because that's all they were. Stupid little games. And okay, sometimes games end with accidents. Miles Goldberg got unlucky, just as Scott Copeland did years before.

I suppose Scott was the closest thing I had to a best friend growing up, but he started turning into a bossy little shit, always trying to tell me what to do, and I didn't like it.

That's why I dared him to get on the swing that went across the pond. He couldn't swim, but I kept calling him a chicken shit and he didn't like that. I could see he was getting more and more anxious as Mum pushed him higher. He wanted to get off, but Mum ignored him and I encouraged her to keep going, enjoying the fear on his face as he struggled to hold on.

Eventually he slipped and I remember watching as he fell through the air, the look of horror on his face as he fell, his body creating a huge splash as it broke through the water.

I looked at Mum, expecting her to panic, but she was impassive, watching him thrash about in the water.

'Shouldn't we help him?' I whispered the words, knowing it was the right thing to say, but a perverse part of me didn't want to break the moment. I was enjoying Scott's struggle.

She never answered me and we stood side by side at the edge of the pond, watching until the water finally stilled.

When Mum was arrested, the police started looking at Scott's death again. It was ruled as an accident at the time. Scott was playing on the tyre swing alone and Mum had found him face down in the pond. That was what we told the police when they first came looking for him. Mum said as long as we stuck to the same story we would be okay, and she was right.

That was the first time I really felt how proud she was of me. I had done well and she rewarded me with my favourite ice cream after the police left.

And, okay, it was a shame Scott had died, but there would be other friends, and there had been, until they had ruined everything.

I barely think of him these days, but Hannah is often on my mind. For now I have just been toying with her, but soon I will take my revenge.

First I need to nip this thing with Lauren in the bud.

The woman is a pain in the arse and an inconvenience I really don't want to have to deal with.

I type Lauren's name into Google and the various social media platforms where I have fake accounts. Her name is fairly common, so it takes a little while to locate her, but I'm pleased to see she is active on Facebook and Instagram. People give too much away online and it makes it so much easier to track them down.

By the time I have finished with Lauren, she will regret ever trying to contact me.

35

Bill had instructed her to stay in the cottage, but Eileen was growing bored. There was only so much housework she could do and TV shows she could watch.

He had given her a phone and she tried to keep up to date with what was going on with her disappearance. She had seen the reports that she was missing and knew the police were looking for her, but if they had any leads they weren't saying.

With the worldwide web at her fingertips, she had not been able to resist looking up the bitches who had ruined her life, positively bursting with glee when she read about the death of Jill Peters. Would they be burying her near the body of her snivelling little brother, Miles?

Eileen had despised that kid and enjoyed feeding on his fear.

Just a shame the brat had pegged it. If he hadn't be so weak and pathetic, she wouldn't have lived in hell for twenty years.

It had taken having a kid of her own to realise quite how much enjoyment she got from tormenting children. They were little brats, all of them, but she learnt how to paint on a friendly face and lure them in with smiles and treats, passing off her cruel pranks as funny games, and she understood how to manipulate them into not telling. They looked up to her and they trusted her and she fed on that. There was nothing more satisfying than finding an excuse to punish them, then seeing their frightened faces the moment she let her mask slip.

And she had moulded Bill to be her little helper. All she had to do was knock down his confidence, keep him in line with occasional punishments and reward him with treats when he did her bidding. And as he got older, she could see a little of herself in him, understanding that he had the same cruel streak.

She had seen that with the death of Scott Copeland.

Of course she hadn't planned to watch Scott die that day, but she had been enjoying his fear so much as she kept pushing him out across the pond and she had got carried away. And it wasn't as if she had killed him; she just hadn't helped him, fascinated as she watched his struggle to survive, then intrigued when she saw Bill's reaction.

By the time they moved to Hixton, Bill was a willing participant in her games, even suggesting and building their special box. Eileen had been grooming those kids for weeks and had way more planned for them. It was a shame their fun had ended so abruptly.

Now Jill was dead, but Lauren, Tash, Rosie, and Hannah were still breathing, and that bothered her. She looked at the pictures of Rosie whoring herself all over social media, then at Hannah's pet website. Hannah had been her favourite target, Eileen furious with her when the girl had snuck upstairs and caught her in the bedroom with Bill.

They had set her up in the barn, Bill persuading Hannah to remove her underwear, while Eileen waited to pounce, ready to dish out one of her punishments. It had been perfect.

Reliving the good old days was making her restless. If she could just get out for a little while, away from these four walls. She had already snuck out for a few short walks, hiding her hair under a cap and donning sunglasses, but it wasn't enough.

The old bloke who had lived here had a car in the garage. Eileen had checked it and it worked. Was it worth the risk of taking it out?

As she toyed with the idea, the washing machine beeped and she went to empty it, loading her basket.

Bill had told her to stay put, but he wasn't here. She could take the car out and be back before he returned. He would never know.

As she took the washing into the garden and started hanging clothes on the line, continuing to mull the idea over, the sound of footsteps crunching against gravel had her looking up and her mouth dropped open.

'What the hell are you doing here?'

36

Lauren couldn't remember getting into bed, but then the truth was that right now she didn't remember much about anything.

It was Wednesday and she had been at work. Of that she was fairly certain. She vaguely recalled arriving home. Had she eaten?

Perhaps that would explain the feeling of nausea and why she felt so out of it. She must have food poisoning.

Seriously, she couldn't remember the last time she had felt as ill as this. Her vision was swimming, her limbs so heavy. She tried to sit up, but it was too much effort. Instead she focused on the air vent at the top of the wall, tried to count the metal strips to anchor herself.

Something was glowing through them.

Eyes.

Was she being watched?

No, it was impossible. There was nothing in the vent. It wasn't big enough. And what had green glowing eyes anyway?

As she told herself she was being stupid, the bars started to throb, almost like something was trying to get through them.

Lauren watched in horror. This wasn't possible.

She squeezed her eyes shut, opened them again, relieved to see whatever was there had gone.

This wasn't good. If she was hallucinating, perhaps she needed medical care. She should call for help.

She managed to roll over so she was on her side with one half of her face mashed into the pillow, but still she was too weak to raise her head. Instead, she blinked, trying to gain her focus.

Her phone should be on the bedside table. Where was it?

She must have drifted for a moment because when she gained consciousness again, she was no longer alone. Someone, something, had dipped the mattress behind her, the warmth of a body pressing against her back, one arm holding her in place as the other stroked her hair.

Lauren tried to turn again, but didn't have the energy.

'Help me.'

She wasn't sure if she had said the words aloud or if they were just in her head.

'Shh.'

Who was in bed with her?

And then she remembered.

The doorbell ringing and how she had opened it without checking the peephole. Oh, how she wished she had checked the peephole.

She had purposely picked a door with one because of the village location of her house, but time had made her lax with security. If she had checked the peephole, she perhaps wouldn't have opened the door.

Instead her eyes had opened wide as she had stared at the face from her past.

'You did this to me,' she managed as she was rolled over so she was lying flat on her back. It was the drink. It had to be. She recalled it had a slightly odd taste.

A finger pressed against her lips, then that creepy 'shh' again.

Lauren started to cry, her vision swimming with tears as she tried to focus on the face looking down at her. She was being straddled now, could feel the weight pushing her down into the mattress. For the briefest of moments, the blur cleared and she could see the determination, the intent, as their eyes met. And she understood.

This was more than a warning. She was really in trouble.

And if she was in trouble, then so were the rest of her friends.

'Please.'

She felt the mattress shift slightly, and for a moment wondered if she was actually getting through as her hair was smoothed back from her face, the cool hand caressing her cheek in what seemed to be a gesture of affection.

But then the mouth was pressed against her ear. 'It's time to go to sleep, Lauren.'

She barely had time to react to the words, to comprehend what was about to happen, before the pillow covered her face.

37

Lauren is sprawled on her back across the queen-sized bed and rage is heating up inside of me. She actually looks peaceful, like she is simply asleep.

I don't want her that way. I need her to be afraid, remorseful, to understand just how much pain she has caused.

This whole scenario was supposed to play out different to this. Yes, she is no longer a problem, but I didn't get to punish her. She has deprived me.

I want to scream in frustration, but instead I sink to the floor and rake frustrated hands through my hair as my tears flow freely. Tears of anger and bitterness for a stolen childhood, for the injustice of everything that has happened, and for being denied the chance to punish someone who really deserved to suffer.

Caught up in my self-pity party, I lose track of time, and when I eventually look up, I am shocked to see it's already light outside.

Fool. Fool. Fool.

Darkness gives safety. People will now be waking up. Lauren's house is on the outskirts of a village with no close neighbours, but I still risk being seen as I leave. Unlike Hannah and Rosie, I haven't been following

Lauren and I came here for the first time last night. I have no idea of her routine.

I know she lives alone, but what if she is expecting visitors?

Quickly I gather my things, glance down at the ice queen on her bed, struggling to swallow the ball of irritation stuck in my throat. I know it will remain there until I have a release for my anger.

After carefully wiping down surfaces and door handles, I let myself out, hoisting my bag onto my shoulder. At least I had the foresight to park a distance away, leaving my car down a dirt track about a mile from the house.

I am welcoming the one wise decision I have made when the silence is broken by the sound of an engine drawing closer. The front door is already closed, the lock having clicked into place and I glance around the small front garden frantically looking for somewhere to hide.

It's too late. The red postal van is already close enough for the driver to see me and I freeze, my mouth dry and adrenaline pumping through my veins as the van stops and the postie climbs out.

I realise I have two choices. I either try to act normal, like I am supposed to be here, or I try to take the man down. If I do that though, I will have another body on my hands and things will spiral out of control.

'Morning.'

The guy doesn't seem suspicious. Maybe early fifties with a greying moustache and shorts. And he is slight in build. If I attack, I am certain I could overpower him. It is too risky though.

Instead I take the letters and the parcel the man hands over, thank him, aware my voice sounds reedy and more high-pitched than normal, then watch him head back to the van.

I wait until the van has disappeared from sight, then I throw the mail in the wheelie bin.

Despite the coolness of the morning, sweat pools in my armpits and on my upper lip, and I think I might throw up.

I made a huge mistake and when Lauren Bell's body is found, this man is going to be a prime witness.

The police are going to know I have been here and as I quickly make my way down the lane and back to my car, I feel trapped, aware the net is closing in on me.

These games I have been playing have been a huge waste of time. Yes, I have enjoyed a perverse thrill tormenting the little bitches, but it isn't supposed to end this way.

Keep calm and carry on. That is what those stupid gimmicky signs say. Right now I need to follow their advice. Hopefully the body won't be found for a bit and I will have time to get my affairs in order, then I can get the hell out of here and find somewhere to lie low for a while.

Jill Goldberg is dead, so is Lauren Bell.

Tash Hogan, Rosie Emerson, and Hannah Freemont need to watch their backs.

38

Liam didn't make contact until Friday and although that bothered Hannah more than she cared to admit, there was no way she was reaching out first, not after the way he had abruptly left her flat on Monday.

That decision came with its complications, namely in the shape of her mother. Now Jane Lawrence knew he existed, she was badgering Hannah with messages, all disguised as questions she needed answers to in order for the party to run smoothly, though Hannah knew exactly what her game was.

She had debated saying that Liam couldn't make it now, but that would bring with it a fresh headache. Besides, she had committed to staying and she couldn't really drop out now. Somehow she was going to have to face this weekend alone.

Again, like when he had disappeared for his family crisis or whatever it had been, it occurred to her she might not hear from him again. Last time it had been mildly annoying, but given how he had just walked out on with no explanation, plus the fact they had now slept together, it cut a little deeper.

By Friday, she was certain he had moved on and she had given herself a stern telling off that she would not mope after a man she had met only a short while ago, and a pep talk that this would be the weekend where she started to conquer her fears about returning home, so when he rang her on Friday afternoon, her spine bristled with irritation and she let it go to voicemail. She wasn't in the mood. Although the week had passed quietly, apart from her mother's nagging, frustration was kicking in. The police had no updates for her and there had been no word from Lauren.

Liam left her a message, which she refused to listen to, then he became as persistent as her bloody mother, calling another half a dozen times, before taking it a step further and showing up on her doorstep with Tank in tow.

'I've been calling you,' he told her, catching her off guard. She hadn't been expecting him, assuming the knocker to be either Rosie or Josh. Both of them had been quiet the last couple of days.

'I'm aware.'

'So why didn't you answer?'

She would have shut the door on him, but noticed he had one of his big feet conveniently over the threshold, so instead she turned to walk back into her flat, could hear footsteps as both Liam and Tank followed.

'Hannah?'

He sounded exasperated, which had her hackles raising. This was his doing. He had no right to be annoyed with her.

'Stop right there.' She put her hand up. 'You do not get to walk in here acting like everything is okay after ignoring me all week.'

'I haven't ignored you. I wasn't aware you'd tried to contact me.'

'I didn't!'

She said those two words with such annoyance, Liam's blue eyes widened and even Tank looked at her in concern. 'So what's the problem then?'

Seriously?

She wanted to rage at him, but he seemed genuinely baffled, and a tiny part of her couldn't help wondering if this was who he really was. He led such a nomadic lifestyle, perhaps he simply wasn't used to having to consider someone else.

No, stop making excuses for him.

'You can't just waltz in and out of my life like you're doing,' she told him, trying to keep her tone even-tempered. 'You're either full on one hundred miles an hour or nothing at all. You were here on Monday and we talked about you coming back to Hixton with me this weekend, but then you vanished and I've had no idea what your plans are. Whether you are still coming with me or not. If you were even planning on getting in touch again.'

'If you'd have bothered to listen to the message I left you, then you'd have known that was why I was getting in touch.' He sounded a little testy, like he still didn't understand what the issue was.

'It's Friday!' Hannah fumed. 'We're supposed to go tomorrow. I've had a million messages from my mother and I've had no idea what to tell her, if I should pretend this fake relationship of ours is already over. We've had no time to figure a cover story so we don't trip each other up when she starts with the questions.'

'Okay, I'm sorry.' He really didn't sound it and when Hannah glared at him, he shrugged. 'Look, I got caught up writing and when I do, I get pretty intense. I tend to lose track of things. I'm used to having just myself and a dog to take care of. It's why I work better alone.'

'You still could have called sooner. Just so I knew you hadn't dropped off the face of the planet.'

'You know this phone thing works both ways, right?'

He was right, but that wasn't the point. Why should she have chased after him when he had been the one to leave here so suddenly?

'Josh offered to go with me,' she grumbled, ignoring that Josh's offer had been over a week ago and she had already turned him down.

Liam's nostrils flared and Hannah enjoyed the flicker of satisfaction at his reaction to the mention of her ex-husband.

'So are you saying you don't want me to go with you now?'

'Yes! I don't know. Maybe.'

While Liam looked exasperated, Tank let out a whine and sank to the floor, as if resigning himself to the fact this argument was set to roll on.

It would be easier to kick Liam out, tell him she didn't want to see him again, but that meant she really would be going by herself. And as humiliating as it was, the idea of that terrified her.

'Look, I'm sorry I've upset you.' He moved towards her and Hannah took a step back, annoyed when she found herself pressed up against the counter. Yes, he was sounding a little more contrite now, but she wasn't ready to forgive him.

Why though? If she thought about it rationally, he hadn't really done anything wrong as such. Okay, so he could have called sooner, but she had no claim over him.

She was still a little too het up to be logical, and as he stepped into her personal space, reaching to touch her arm, she flinched.

It was the tension that had built knowing she had to return home that was causing her to behave like this. Deep down, she knew that. Although she had tried her best to ignore it, as the date neared, her nerves had grown. Then the unfortunate timing of Liam going quiet on her and that added fear that she would have to face going alone had manifested itself into panic.

The episodes didn't happen often. She liked to think she was a well-adjusted woman who looked forward and tried not to dwell on the past too much, but recent events hadn't helped.

It had been a cause of conflict with Josh. Sometimes she had behaved irrationally in their short-lived marriage and even though he understood everything that had happened, he would grow frustrated with her, taking it personally.

Liam was watching her closely and she expected him to turn and head for the door at any moment. Why the hell would he want to put up with this level of drama? Therefore it shocked her when he stayed where he was.

'Tell me how I can fix this.'

When she opened and closed her mouth, unsure quite how to respond, he stepped closer, not touching, though she was aware of the heat from his body. What did he mean, 'fix this'? Was he talking about how he hadn't contacted her or her overreaction to it? She honestly wasn't sure.

This time when he touched her arm, she didn't flinch. His other hand went to her face, tilting her chin with his thumb. 'Hannah, look at me.'

She didn't want to, was almost afraid in case she saw pity, but the way he had positioned himself had her trapped and she couldn't really manoeuvre herself away without causing a scene. Slowly she raised her eyes, found herself locked into a gaze of crystal blue, but rather than cause distress, it centred her. There was no pity. What she saw was understanding. That and something else. Something deeper.

'Let me go with you tomorrow. We'll deal with it together, okay?'

He made it sound like they were a team and she found herself conveniently forgetting about her anger with him and how he had gone AWOL on her. A team meant she didn't have to face going home alone. A team meant he would be there to help her get through it.

Needing that support, she nodded. 'Okay.'

His mouth was close to hers and as his gaze dipped slightly, she wondered if he was going to kiss her, but then his lips curved and he leant forward, grazed them in a gentle kiss against her forehead before wrapping her in his arms.

The heat from his body radiated into hers, energising her, awakening her belief that she was strong enough to face her fears, and she relaxed into him, snaking her arms around his waist and hugging him right back.

Tomorrow she would head home to Hixton. She would spend the night in her old family home, sleeping in her childhood bedroom for the first time in years.

She wouldn't bolt and she was determined she wouldn't have a panic attack. Instead she would face her fears head on.

She could do this.

39

They arrived in Hixton a little after noon on the Saturday, plenty of time before the party, which was due to start at seven.

Hannah had insisted on driving and Liam guessed it was a distraction for her. As they approached the village where she had grown up, she had fallen silent, the colour draining from her face as she turned into the close where her mother and stepfather still lived.

The driveway she parked on belonged to a modest semi-detached house. Nondescript, but well cared for, the picket fence freshly painted and the hanging baskets either side of the front door filled with colourful flowers. Here he hoped to learn more about the real Hannah. The one behind the barriers he was struggling to fully break down.

'You okay?' he asked as she turned off the ignition. She actually looked like she might throw up. When he had left her flat on Monday, it had been touch and go if he would make this weekend. Unlike Hannah, he was glad he was here.

When she nodded, he took her clammy hand, giving it a

squeeze of encouragement. 'It's just one day. This time tomorrow we'll be on our way back to Norfolk.'

She smiled weakly. 'I'm already looking forward to it.'

Tank picked that moment to poke his head between the seats, probably more out of curiosity as to why they had stopped but were still sat in the car. Seeming to pick up on Hannah's nerves, he stuck up his front paw, prodding at her shoulder, and when she turned to acknowledge him, licked at her face.

Liam had been relieved Hannah's mum had been okay with the dog coming, unsure what he would have done with him if she had refused. It had also been good for Hannah to have him along for the weekend. Tank was a distraction and would also serve as the perfect time-out if things got a little too much for her.

The front door opened and he recognised the woman who was stood on the front step beaming at them as Jane Lawrence, Hannah's mother.

'At last, here they are.'

She watched them get out, the smile slipping slightly when she saw Tank. Liam wasn't sure what sort of dog she was expecting. Probably something smaller and daintier from the look on her face.

Oblivious to the slight and simply excited by new places, smells and people, Tank's tail was thumping hard. He would soon win her over.

Naturally inquisitive and generally at ease with meeting people for the first time, Liam had to remind himself to hold back instead of going straight over to introduce himself. This was Hannah's mother, her weekend. He was just here for support and it was important to let her take the lead. Instead, he busied himself clipping on Tank's leash waiting until Hannah was ready, then followed her to the door.

'Hi, Mum.'

'Hannah.'

Jane looked her over, almost as if wanting to check this was her daughter and not an imposter, before pulling Hannah into a stiff hug. Before she had even let go, Liam could see her curious eyes glancing up at him.

'You must be the new boyfriend,' she gushed.

'This is Liam.' Hannah made the introductions awkwardly. 'Liam, my mum, Jane.'

'It's good to meet you.' Liam held out his hand, taken aback when Jane threw herself at him instead. As she embraced him – far more warmly than she had her own daughter – Tank started barking in delight.

Jane released him pretty quickly, eyeing the dog warily, and Liam glanced at Hannah, who had an amused expression on her face.

'Come on in, come on in.' Jane was beckoning them inside, linking her arm through Liam's. He shrugged in apology at Hannah, who was left to trail behind with Tank.

'Geoff, is the kettle on? Liam, it's so nice to finally meet you. It's about time Hannah started dating again. I kept telling her she was going to be left on the shelf.'

Liam cringed on behalf of Hannah, beginning to suspect it wasn't just memories of Eileen that kept her away from Hixton.

Geoff and the boiling kettle were in the kitchen waiting. He was a man of few words, Liam soon learnt, giving them both a cursory nod as Jane made the introductions.

As he made cups of tea for them all, Liam considered what he knew about Hannah's stepfather, which was actually very little. Geoffrey Lawrence had come into Jane and Hannah Freemont's life just a year after Hannah's dad had died, marrying Jane when Hannah was eight. Hannah had never taken her stepfather's name and, according to people Liam had spoken to, her relationship with him was cordial at best.

Aware he was currently hogging too much of the attention, and wanting Hannah to have a few private moments alone with her mother and stepfather, he excused himself to go and fetch the overnight bags and let Tank have a pee.

He used the time alone to run over the cover story he had agreed with Hannah on the drive down. They had decided to keep it as simple and as close to the truth as possible, saying they had met on the beach in Wells after Tank knocked Hannah over, just changing a few small details. Firstly they would make out that the incident had happened months earlier and also they planned not to mention that Liam was writing a book about Eileen Wickham. It was safer, they decided, if they stuck to saying that he was simply a writer.

Jane loved the idea of having a celebrated author in the house, Liam discovered a short while later while being interrogated over the tea that Geoff had made, and he suspected she would be dining out on it for ages, telling all of her friends that Hannah was dating someone famous.

Not that he would ever consider himself well known. A few of his books had been big hits, but people tended to know the titles and the stories, not the man who had written them, and that was exactly how he liked it. Privacy was important to him.

Over the years, he had become a pro at diverting questions and avoiding any prying into his personal life, learning how easy it was to distract people if you gave them the opportunity to talk about themselves, and this wasn't going to be an issue with Jane. Although she had bombarded him with questions, clearing dying to know everything about her daughter's mysterious boyfriend, he had brushed her off, smoothly giving enough of an answer to pacify her curiosity before twisting the conversation back onto her. And Jane, he quickly established, loved talking about herself.

Eventually they were able to escape, Tank in tow, and the look of relief was clear on Hannah's face as she led him up to the stairs to her old bedroom. The room had been redecorated since she had left, she told him, closing the door to give them a little privacy, and her mother was now using it as a second guest room.

He glanced at the double bed, knowing they would be sharing it, though he had no intention of having sex with her while they were under her mother's roof.

Actually, scrub that. He should never have slept with her in the first place. It just complicated everything. What Hannah needed this weekend was a friend, so he would try his best to be supportive. He wasn't going to lie though. He was expecting a long and frustrating night.

The plus side for him being here (not that he would ever tell her) was that he was also getting to see the dynamics of the family at play. It was all good background research for his book.

Liam had seen pictures and some video footage of Jane Lawrence sitting in the courtroom, but as she had welcomed them into her home, he soon realised he had her all wrong. She had always seemed to be protective of Hannah, wanting to shield her from the glare of the press, and of the parents, she had been the most indignant, the one who shouted the loudest for justice, while Rosie's parents simply fell to pieces. For those reasons alone, he had expected her to be nurturing and perhaps overprotective. In his head, he had imagined Hannah perhaps found her to be a little overbearing.

While he would never dispute Jane's love for her daughter, it had quickly become apparent that nothing was about Hannah. This was the Jane Lawrence show and the woman clearly loved the limelight and being centre of attention.

'Are you okay?' he asked, dumping his bag on the chair in the corner of the room and unrolling Tank's bed for him in front of the radiator.

'Yeah. It's just one night, right?'

She didn't sound very convincing and there was little Liam could say that would make the next twenty-four hours pass quickly, so he didn't, instead straightening up and glancing out of the window at the long narrow garden. Like the rest of the property, it was well cared for, filled with mature shrubs and pretty flower beds.

'I take it your mum and stepdad like living here. They've never thought about moving?'

'They love the house and the village, and all of their friends are local. I think Mum might have considered it, but Geoff is never going to leave.'

She didn't sound bitter, though it must have been difficult for her living here in the aftermath of the trial, where everyone knew what had happened, and having to pass the farmhouse on a frequent basis. Of the families involved, only the Lawrences and the Emersons had stayed in Hixton, though Roland and Denise Emerson had been planning to move four years later, shortly before they were both killed in a car accident.

After Rosie left to live with her aunt, it had just been Hannah who remained. No wonder she escaped the village as soon as she was able.

As he turned away from the view of the garden, he found she was watching him, the frown on her face creasing two little lines between her eyebrows.

'Why Eileen Wickham, Liam? Surely there are a dozen or so more interesting crimes to write about.'

She had asked him that question once before. Had she forgotten or was she trying to trip him up?

'I already told you, it's one that stayed with me. I was a kid too when it happened and I remember reading about it. It resonated and stayed with me. A neighbour, someone you should be able to trust, and a village where most people knew each other. It could have been any of us.'

He held her gaze, her green eyes studying him intently, seeming to reach inside of him, stabbing in his gut. It was partly with denied lust, though mostly he knew it was because he was lying to her. Why was that starting to sit so uncomfortably with him?

She seemed to buy what he was saying, nodding as she sat on the edge of the bed, fussing at Tank when he rested his head on her leg. 'I guess we all feared monsters when we were kids. Finding out they were real was a shock. It stays with you.'

She was right. It did stay with you, though not quite in the way she thought.

Liam couldn't tell her that. He was committed to this path, and the less she knew the better. If she found out the truth it could change everything, and he couldn't take the risk of that happening.

Another week and he would have all he needed, then he would force himself to move on. It was easier that way.

40

It wasn't just coming back to the village that Hannah found difficult. The worst bit was having to catch up with all of the neighbours she hadn't seen since she was a kid. It was a tight-knit community and aside from a handful of people, most of the residents had lived there for years. She remembered when they had first learnt the truth about Mrs W and how shocked they had been. Most people had been kind, but there had also been gossip and staring, some crossing the road to avoid her, unsure how to treat her. She had felt like a freakshow.

She mostly kept her visits home brief and low-key. If she could get away with never returning to Hixton she would, but her mother would never stand for that, so instead there were three or four yearly trips down from Norfolk, where Hannah would have one eye on the front door, ready to escape as soon as she thought it was politely acceptable. On occasion, she would run into Joan and Fred, who lived next door, but mostly she saw no one else outside of the house.

This whole party scenario was one of her worst nightmares, with everyone gathered in the village hall and so many familiar, albeit older, faces, many of whom she could see were eyeing her with curiosity, some even being so blatant as to rudely whisper.

She knew they would be talking about Eileen Wickham and she hated that all these years later it was something she was still so closely associated with. At least locally.

'Do you want a drink?'

Liam removed his hand from where it had been reassuringly placed at the small of her back and Hannah immediately missed his touch. She had questioned again how wise she was bringing him while on the ride down to Suffolk, but it had been a good call. Having someone with her who understood how difficult this was for her was helping to combat the nerves.

Yes, she wished she wasn't here, but at least that awful sense of claustrophobia as she battled to hold herself together was for the moment kept at bay.

'Please. Can you get me a white wine?'

It was tempting to ask for a bottle, but maybe that wasn't a wise idea. Besides, her mother would frown on her if Hannah drank too much.

She glanced at Jane now, noting she was lapping up attention as she received congratulations from her friends and neighbours, the present table that had been set up at the back of the room – a trestle table covered in a white sheet and decorated with a banner – filling up with gifts and cards.

Hannah had given her mother and Geoff her own gift back at the house before they left for the party and they had seemed delighted with the theatre tickets.

To give her mother her dues, she looked good for her age. Her hair now expertly blonded by her hairdresser and styled in a severely short cut that most women couldn't pull off. On Jane Lawrence, with her even features, wide eyes and high cheekbones, it looked striking.

As her mother hugged a woman with red hair, she caught Hannah's eye and beckoned her across. 'There she is.'

Hannah reluctantly made her way over and Jane immediately linked arms with her, so she was conveniently trapped.

'Darling, you remember Gail Andrews, don't you?'

Hannah did and she fixed a pleasant smile on her face. Gail was an old friend of her mother's and had been a permanent fixture at the village hall for as long as Hannah could remember, running various groups over the years, from flower arranging to yoga. Apart from the hair, which had originally been a mid-brown, and the added lines to her face, she hadn't changed much, her eyes, which Hannah always remembered as being beady, looking her up and down.

'Hannah Freemont. Look at you, all grown up.'

It sounded like something you would say to a teenager rather than a woman in her mid-thirties. Still, Hannah forced her smile up a notch.

'It's actually Cole now. And it's nice to see you, Gail. How are you?'

'Can't complain. Can't complain. Your mother said you'd married.'

'She's divorced now,' Jane helpfully pointed out. 'It didn't last long, did it, Hannah. That's the problem with young people these days. They're not prepared to work at a marriage.'

Hannah ignored the dig. It was something she had come to blows with her mother over many times across the years, but tonight wasn't the time or the place. Instead she made awkward small talk, wishing the minutes away.

'So are you in touch with any of the other girls?' Gail eventually asked, her tone conspiratorial. She didn't have to say who she meant. It was obvious she had been dying to ask. And she wouldn't be the only one. Most of those here probably wanted to pick at the old wound to see what would happen.

'She still sees a lot of Rosie, don't you, darling,' her mother answered for her.

It was twice Jane had used the endearment since arriving at the village hall. Hannah remembered she liked to make use of it in front of company.

'Is she well?' Gail pried.

'She is,' Hannah lied. There was no way she was sharing anything of Rosie's life with a gossip like Gail. 'She's carving quite a name for herself.'

'She's an actress,' Jane pointed out. 'Been on the soaps.'

Hollyoaks and only fleetingly, but Hannah didn't correct her.

Gail seemed impressed. 'I'm so pleased. Such a sweet girl.' She shook her head pitiably. 'Poor thing didn't deserve what happened that summer. She was just a baby.'

Hannah knew where this conversation was going and suddenly she was too hot, wishing she could loosen the high collar of the dress she had chosen. This was why she had been nervous about coming to the party. It was one of her worst nightmares playing out. Gail was still talking, but the words weren't registering now. Sweat pooled in Hannah's armpits, her brain fogging up and shutting out the conversation.

But then it stopped, Gail looking towards Hannah, but past her, her mouth slightly open, and Hannah realised Liam was by her side.

'I got you a large,' he told her, the smile on his face telling her he knew she needed it.

He handed her the wine, then, with a hand free, placed it once again in the small of her back.

It was comforting and a reminder that she didn't have to do tonight alone.

Gail was still gawping at him and Hannah's mother was quick to make the introductions, eagerly telling her friend all about Liam's books. She must have googled him, as she suddenly seemed to know an awful lot about them, and Hannah hid her smirk as Liam actually blushed.

She took a big sip of her drink, grateful the conversation had shifted, Gail now fascinated by the 'celebrity', as she referred to him, in the room. Hannah knew he valued his privacy, so was grateful when he took the heat off of her, engaging both women with a few author tales, even promising both of them signed copies of his books. She watched him as he spoke, realising he could actually be quite charming when he wanted to. His conversation was smooth, and the stories he told interesting.

He might have his faults, but he had stuck to his word and come with her this weekend, and she was glad he was here with her now. Although they had slept together, there was no relationship between them, no commitment, and in a few days he would be leaving Norfolk, so she would likely never see him again. The idea of that coiled something deep inside her. Was it disappointment?

* * *

'Thank you,' Hannah told him later when they were able to take a brief interlude. The evening wasn't over yet, but at least she had survived so far.

Liam had guided her into the main entrance hallway, where the loos and the reception were, but instead of stopping, he led the way outside.

Hannah breathed in the cool night air, appreciating the cloak of darkness. The only light coming from the front windows of the village hall, the music from the disco muffled by the walls.

'How are you coping?' he asked, sipping at his pint.

The beauty of the venue's location was the walking distance to Hannah's old home, meaning they could at least both have a drink. Although she hadn't drank too much, and neither had Liam, a few glasses had been required to get through the evening.

'I'm okay. You really rescued me tonight.'

'That's why I'm here.'

He studied her for a moment, his face partially in shadows, and although his expression was unreadable, the heat in his blue eyes was clear.

Hannah's arms goose pimpled when his gaze dropped to her mouth, and it had nothing to do with the cold.

This man had secrets, of that she was sure, but it didn't stop her growing attraction to him.

Perhaps her mother was right when she said Hannah had never been the best judge of character when it came to men. Aside from Josh, who really should have stayed in the friend zone, she had never picked well. Of course, her mother was biased where Liam was concerned, her delight at his author status overriding any shadows of doubt, and she had been showing him off to friends, family, and neighbours all night, allowing Hannah to mostly remain in the shadows. Jane Lawrence was going to be devastated when she found out their 'relationship' was over.

'Hannah Freemont? Is that you?'

Hearing her former name called, Hannah tensed, and as she turned to see who had called her, the moment with Liam was broken.

She spotted the woman crossing the car park, but didn't recognise her. As she grew closer, there was a spark of remembrance.

'Nicola?'

'I wasn't sure if you would remember me.'

'You look so different.'

'In a good way, I hope.'

'Yeah, in a good way. You look great.'

It wasn't a lie. Nicola Finch had been a couple of years ahead of Hannah at school and their mothers were good friends. Her long brown hair was now worn in a stylish blonde bob and both her braces and her NHS glasses had gone, while the dress she wore accentuated a figure that she clearly looked after.

'Thank you. You do too.'

Hannah glanced down at the understated black dress she was wearing. It wasn't anything special and Nicola was just being kind. Hannah had picked it hoping to fade into the background. Still she thanked her and they spent a little time catching up, as she learnt that Nicola still lived in the village and was now a teacher at the local primary school.

She had introduced her to Liam, who had made small talk for a few moments before disappearing inside to get them both a drink and, as he returned, Nicola was studying him carefully.

'You know, there's something really familiar about you,' she told him, thanking him as he handed over her glass of gin and tonic.

'Liam's an author,' Hannah told her. It was quite possible Nicola had seen him on social media or perhaps read one of his books.

'No, that's not it.' She cocked her head on one side. 'I'm sure I know you from the past. You've been here before, haven't you? When you were younger.'

Had he? Hannah stared at Liam. His poker face gave nothing away.

'You must be getting me confused with someone else. It's my first time here.' Although his tone was amiable, there was the slightest edge to his words.

Was he telling the truth?

Hannah could tell Nicola wasn't convinced either, but she didn't push it, telling Hannah it was lovely to catch up and thanking Liam for the drink again before excusing herself.

Although the moment was over, it stayed with Hannah throughout the rest of the evening and was still on her mind when they returned home at the end of the night.

'It's weird how Nicola thought she recognised you earlier.'

'Is it?'

She'd had her back to him as she undressed, slipping into an oversized T-shirt, more than a little self-conscious about being naked around him, which was laughable considering he had already seen everything the night they had slept together. Now she turned, wanting to see his reaction. He wasn't looking at her though as he knelt on the floor beside Tank's bed, making a fuss of him as he settled the dog down.

'She just seemed so certain she had known you.'

'I guess I must just have one those faces.' He shrugged, getting up. 'What time do you want to head back tomorrow?'

There it was again, the subject change. Always when he wanted to divert attention away from himself. It was getting irritating and only made her more suspicious.

'You always do that.'

'Do what?'

'Change topic when you want to avoid talking about yourself.'

Liam laughed, but she could see the annoyance in his eyes. 'I've no idea what you're talking about. I asked a simple question.'

She could push it, but suspected it would result in an argument she didn't have the energy for. 'After breakfast,' she said snappily. 'No point in hanging around.'

Ignoring the confused look he gave her, she pulled back the duvet.

It was weird getting into a bed with him just to sleep, their one night together now almost a distant memory. She hadn't given this scenario a whole lot of thought when she had agreed to the whole fake boyfriend thing, but now it was all she could concentrate on and she hated the awkwardness.

At least it was keeping her distracted from being back in Hixton.

Stiff British politeness had her rolling over to face the wall when he started to undress and she tensed as the mattress dipped and he climbed in beside her.

They lay in silence for a few moments and Hannah was aware of everything. The heat from his body, his light masculine scent. Every movement, every tiny noise, from the ticking of the alarm clock to her shallow breathing and the thump of her heart.

She couldn't spend the whole night like this. It was painful.

'Hannah—'

'What are we doing?'

They both spoke at once, rolling over at the same time and bashing elbows and heads.

Rather than make things more uncomfortable, it broke the moment. Hannah getting the giggles, which in turn brought a burst of laughter from Liam.

'We didn't think through how awkward this bit might be,' she spoke eventually, candidly, studying his face in the shadowy darkness.

He didn't speak for a moment, rolling onto his back again and staring up at the ceiling, huffing out a heavy sigh. 'Awkward and difficult,' he agreed eventually. 'You know this is killing me, right?'

Hannah's throat constricted. Her mouth was dry. 'It is?'

Shifting again, Liam propped himself up on his elbow, looking down at her. 'What happened before was a mistake.'

Ouch. She tried to ignore the sting. 'Maybe for you.'

'For us both. I should have never slept with you.'

As her ego crumbled, Hannah tried for humour. 'Keep going. You're doing a lot for my confidence here.'

Liam grimaced. 'I'm not explaining myself properly.'

'Says the writer.'

'Look, it's complicated, okay. Complicated because I'm here on work and you're part of that work. And you're making it really difficult because—'

'It's okay. I get it. Can we drop the subject now please?' She wished to hell she had kept her mouth shut and pretended she was asleep. How humiliating. And they still had the rest of the night to get through, as well as the drive home together tomorrow.

'Would you let me finish? I was going to say it's really difficult because you're driving me crazy.'

What? She stared at him, wondering if she had heard right.

'I didn't expect this... you. And if things were different. If we had met under different circumstances...' He trailed off, looking frustrated. 'In a few days, I have to leave.'

Hannah didn't buy that. He was a writer. Surely he could work from anywhere. Besides, if he liked her as much as he was saying, he would be looking for solutions, not obstacles. She didn't tell him that. He had just dropped his guard with her. That was enough for now.

'Define crazy,' she said instead, her tone playful.

She liked him. He liked her. They were both adults and there was nothing wrong with a bit of fun if they were both up for it.

Liam's mouth curved into a sly grin. 'Let's just say I won't be sleeping on my front tonight.'

His comment had Hannah laughing again, her earlier unease now gone. 'I can help with that if you'll let me.'

When her hand slipped beneath the covers, he caught it, entwining his fingers with hers.

'We're not having sex with your mother in the next room,' he told her, his tone firm.

'You're such a prude,' Hannah groaned, before giving it one

more shot. 'I was hoping you could distract me from having to spend my first night in this house in fifteen years.'

Liam pulled her hand back up from under the covers, kissing her knuckles. 'I can do that without sex.' He looked at the bracelet she wore round her wrist, a cheap piece of string that meant more to her than any other piece of jewellery she owned. 'What's this?' he asked, running his finger along the band.

'It's a friendship bracelet. We all have one. Me, Rosie, Lauren, Tash, Jill. Miles had one too.' Tash had made them the summer Miles had died, and Hannah had never taken hers off since.

'Tell me what it was like growing up here and about your friends.'

'You want to talk about that now?

'I don't mean about Eileen. I want to know how it was before. The happy stuff. Tell me about your friends. What they were like?'

41

2002

It had always been the four of them – Hannah, Tash, Lauren and Rosie.

They had grown up in the village together, their parents all friends, attended the same schools, birthday parties, and other events.

Lauren and Tash were the most assertive. Bossy Lauren usually trying to self-appoint herself as leader of their little gang, while tomboy Tash tended to challenge and bicker with her. Hannah was happy to take a back seat. Taller than the others, then the first to start developing breasts, she was more self-conscious of her appearance and tried to blend into the background, happy to let the others lead, while Rosie was the baby of the group. Nearly a year younger, tiny and fragile, but stunningly pretty, even from a young age, Tash and Hannah tended to mother and protect her, especially when she got on Lauren's nerves, which was often.

They hung out together most days, walking to school together, sitting at the same table in the canteen at lunch, and spending their weekends bike riding, exploring, and building dens when the weather was good or watching movies and playing board games when it wasn't.

Lauren was the most fashion-conscious and as they moved to high school, her interest grew in the latest trends in hair, clothes, and make-up. The group became more interested in boys – even Tash pretending to show an interest at that young age – and with secrets shared about crushes, the little group became even more tightly knit.

That was why Lauren had formed such strong opinions about Jill and Miles Goldberg.

Like the others, she was curious about the newcomers, but, while she was intrigued enough by Jill to welcome her into their circle, she didn't want to start hanging out with Jill's younger brother.

Jill was in their year at school and cool, confident and pretty, but Miles was two years younger and shy. His small frame and huge glasses that swamped his face, and the inhaler he was always puffing on, quickly made him a target for bullies.

But the pair of them came as package, which caused Lauren a problem.

Miles was a boy, she had pointed out, and they had a rule. No boys in the group.

'You just made that up,' Tash laughed, calling her out.

'No I didn't. We agreed.'

'We've never agreed no boys.'

'But it wouldn't be right having him hanging out with us. Not with the stuff we talk about. Besides, he's too young.'

'I like Miles,' Rosie sniffed. 'And he's nearly twelve.'

'He needs to find his own friends.'

'But why can't I be his friend?'

'Have you not been listening, Rosie?' Lauren sounded exasperated. 'He's a boy, so he needs to play with boys.'

'No he doesn't.' Tash, who sometimes hung out with her older brother and his friends, protested. 'Girls can be friends with boys. Boys have a lot more fun than we do,' she added slyly.

Lauren bristled. 'They cause a lot more trouble.'

'Says who.'

'My mother.'

Lauren's mother had a lot of opinions, some of them really quite strange, and Lauren was always quoting her.

As usual, Hannah and Rosie exchanged a smirk, while Tash rolled her eyes.

'Hannah. You're very quiet. What do you think? Do you have a problem with Miles hanging out with us?'

'I don't mind.' Hannah had only seen Miles a couple of times and he seemed very quiet and shy. She had heard that some of the other kids his age had been mean to him and that sat uncomfortably with her. Maybe having a group of slightly older friends would help to bolster his confidence.

'So that's three against one,' Tash smiled smugly at Lauren, whose face crumpled.

'This is so unfair. You can't just all go against me.'

'It's not unfair at all. We have all had a say instead of you deciding for us.'

Lauren had stormed off in a tantrum that day, telling Tash, Hannah and Rosie that she no longer wanted to hang out with them.

Of course, she calmed down when she realised she had overreacted, and after a day of sulking and pretending to avoid them, she had gone creeping back, and the hand of friendship had been extended to Jill and her younger brother.

Those first couple of days, even Hannah would admit it was a bit weird. It had been the four of them for so long, it was strange having to build a friendship with new people. Especially ones with different accents, who had come from so far away. Jill and Miles had lived in a place called Kissimmee in Florida, which was close to Disney World. That had the four of them all green with envy, certain through their young eyes that living next to one of the best theme parks must be a dream come true.

Jill and Miles had been in the UK now for about three years, relocating with their father when he transferred jobs. Their mother had passed away when they were both still young, and they were adjusting to a new home and now life with a stepmother.

Neither sibling was keen on their stepmother, Veronica; Jill had clashed with her on several occasions, while Miles was scared half to death of her.

Veronica's insertion into their life had been sudden. She had been married before, they told their new friends, and she was quite set in her ways about parenting and how things should be done. That certainly didn't wash with Jill, who had grown up looking after Miles herself. She was already a teenager and did not need some stranger telling her what to do, especially one who had walked out on her family to begin an affair with her dad. Veronica had married him just two months after her divorce had been finalised.

Hannah thought Veronica Goldberg sounded like hard work. Possibly more difficult to deal with than her own mother, and she felt sorry for Jill and Miles having to put up with her.

She liked them both and was glad they had invited them to hang out. Jill was cool, capable, and easy to talk to, while Miles came out of his shell the more time he spent with his new friends. He bonded in particular with Rosie, the two of them often engaged in little chats, though Hannah grew close to him too. She had always been drawn to the underdogs and, like she had done with Rosie, she took him under her wing, wanting to protect him and look after him, especially as things weren't great for him at school or home.

As the school term ended and the summer holidays began, the six of them became inseparable and were a familiar sight around the village. Lauren always neat and presentable with her red pigtails, Tash generally a scruffy mess from whatever mischief she had been up to, tall and lanky Hannah, stylish Jill, then the tiny twosome, Rosie and Miles, usually bringing up the rear, too engaged in conversation to keep up with their friends.

Some speculated that the six of them had been targeted from the start and that Rosie and Miles had been the ones Mrs W coveted most, because they were the most vulnerable. Others, though they were few and far between, thought it was a tragic accident. A terrible prank gone wrong.

Now when she looked back, Hannah realised there had been so many signs she should have spotted. It wasn't just the mouse or the sickness after drinking Mrs W's special lemonade. There were so many other little things. Incidents that blurred on the edge of her memory, unsettling murmurs of events that maybe she had buried. At the time, Hannah wasn't sure if she was on to something or if she was being paranoid and, because of that, Mrs W's cruelty had escalated.

Just a few weeks later, any innocence the group had was gone.

Now when Hannah tried to remember looking back at Rosie and Miles, wanting to make sure they were keeping up pace and hadn't stopped to chatter again, Rosie walked alone.

42

Hannah woke early on Sunday morning, momentarily forgetting where she was.

It took a second or two to come flooding back, the once lemon walls of her bedroom now painted in a rich teal and the furniture different, but then she remembered. How she had survived the party, Liam telling her he was crazy about her, then lying in bed next to him talking about the past, but not the terrible bits. He had pushed her towards happier memories of her friends, ones that she remembered fondly, asking her questions and seeming genuinely interested, and it was only now that she realised he had probably been keeping her purposely distracted so she didn't dwell on the negatives of being back in Hixton. She had eventually drifted off, the monsters of her past at bay, and had slept fitfully all night.

He was still here in bed beside her, and over the course of the night, she had rolled into his space. She was aware of the heat of his body against her back, of his arm sprawled across her, and his warm shallow breath close to her neck, and certain he was still asleep, she was loath to move, too comfortable and wanting to savour the moment of closeness, aware she was falling for a complicated man. One she couldn't have.

They would head back to Norfolk after breakfast and she suspected whatever was between them would move back into a professional capacity. At least the ordeal of having to revisit her childhood home would be over – well, until the next time. The relief Hannah felt on that front was immeasurable. She had done it. She had faced her demons and the encounter hadn't broken her. Knowing that gave her strength and had her considering the farmhouse again.

She had tried to go back the last time they were in Suffolk, but it had been a step too far. Was it worth trying again today before they headed home?

She proposed the idea to Liam as she reversed out of her parents' driveway, waving goodbye to her mother and Geoff. It was a bright sunny morning and it felt like a wasted opportunity if she didn't at least try again.

Part of her wondered if he would protest, see it as a waste of time after what had happened before, but he surprised her, agreeing it was a good idea.

As they headed out towards the farm, her confidence started to wane, the urge to ease her foot off the accelerator and turn the car around overwhelming. Anger built inside her.

She was determined to do this.

Liam must have picked up on her vibes, or perhaps had noticed she was clenching the steering wheel a little too tightly, her knuckles white with the pressure. 'We don't have to go there if you don't want to.'

'I do want to go there,' Hannah insisted, trying to convince herself as well as him.

As she turned into the road that led to the farm, nausea swam in her stomach and she thought she might throw up.

Fight it, Hannah. It's just a fucking house.

She would not let the bitch defeat her again.

'Can you pull over?'

Liam's request took her by surprise, but she did as asked, grateful for the distraction, pulling off the lane and stopping in a clearing by the woods.

'Is everything okay?'

He didn't answer her, instead getting out of the car. He opened the back door, clipping on Tank's leash before letting the dog jump down, then he wandered round to the front of the car, opening the driver's door. He leaned in, catching her off guard, when he turned off the engine and snatched the keys out of the ignition.

'What are you doing?'

'Tank could do with a walk. I only let him out to pee this morning. I thought we could leave the car here and walk down to the farm.'

Was that really why he has asked her to stop or was it part of a crafty plan because he had picked up on her nerves and thought it would be easier approaching on foot?

Either way, she was grateful, getting out of the car as asked.

Liam clicked the locks then pocketed her keys, before offering her his hand.

Hannah took it, comforted that she wasn't doing this alone. This was a route she had walked many times that summer. Although her legs wobbled and her stomach churned, she pushed herself forward, appreciating that he was in a chatty mood, distracting her with conversation about the party and the people they had met.

As the lane curved and the woods to the side of the road became denser, she spotted the farmhouse in the distance. It was all so familiar and she half expected to hear the chatter of her childhood friends, as they walked beside her. When she slowed her pace, Liam tugged on her hand.

'Come on, Hannah. You can do this.'

'Yeah, I can. Just give me a moment, okay?'

They stopped walking, much to Tank's frustration. He had been pulling ahead, wanting to sniff at and pee on everything, and realising they were going nowhere, he plonked his sizeable bum down and gave Hannah the evil eye, sensing this was her doing.

She stared ahead at the farm, so many memories resurfacing. No one had lived there for a long time and the signs of neglect were evident, even from this distance.

'How are you feeling?'

'I'm okay. It's weird being back here. It's like being thirteen again. I keep expecting to see her step out of the house with a basket of laundry.'

Liam dropped her hand and moved to stand behind her, slipping his arm around her waist and positioning her so they were directly facing the farm. 'I know the memories are bad, but the evil is no longer there. It's just bricks and mortar.'

His mouth was close to her ear, the warmth of his breath caressing her neck as he spoke.

'I know that. And they're not all terrible. There are ones from before too. I can hear the others. Their laughter as they're cycling past us. Is that odd?'

'Not at all. You're back in a place that's evoking a strong reaction.'

'I'm going to conquer this.' Hannah spoke with more conviction than she felt. 'I won't let that witch define me.'

For too long, she had given into the fear of returning here. Just the thought making her heart start racing and breathing difficult. Although the nerves still churned, there was a newer steely determination behind them.

'I have been bitter about what happened for so long. It's time to let it go.'

Liam was silent as he considered her words, but he didn't move his arm, and Hannah sank back into him, drawing extra strength from the steadiness of his heartbeat and his rhythmic breathing. On the ground in front of them, Tank yawned and whined a little, letting them know of his dissatisfaction at the hold-up.

'I know how easy it is to hold on to bitter memories,' Liam said eventually.

'You do?'

'I don't have the easiest relationship with my mother. She's been absent for a lot of my life.'

'She has?'

Was he actually opening up and revealing something personal to her? Hannah held her breath, waiting for him to continue.

'When you're young, you look up to your parents and you think they will always be there to protect you.' Liam gave a harsh laugh. 'After my mum went away, I realised it was all a lie. I struggled with that for a while. But then I realised that if I didn't want it to destroy my life, I had to find a way past it.'

Hannah took a moment to process that. He seemed so confident, so self-assured, and it was hard to imagine him as this hurt and unloved little boy.

'And did you?' she asked quietly. 'Did you find a way past it?'

'She's back in my life now. We're never going to have a typical mother-son relationship, I will never forget what she did, but she's my flesh and blood. The tables have turned and she needs me now more than I need her. I've tried to be a better son to her than she was a mother to me.'

'And is that working?'

'Some of the time.' Liam released her, caught hold of her hand again and pulled her round to face him. 'So I have tried to conquer my demons. How about we now go and try to conquer yours?'

Hannah looked into his steadying gaze and nodded. It was time to cut Mrs W out of her life.

'Okay, let's do this.'

43

There was something fishy about Liam Quinn, and Josh Cole was certain it had nothing to do with the bristle of jealousy he had experienced when Quinn had shown up with Hannah at her flat.

By jealousy, he didn't mean he was still in love with Hannah; that boat had sailed a long while ago. He had been in love with her once, desperately so, and when she had finally given in to his pleading for a date, he had felt like the luckiest man in the world. But then they had married and, while he still adored her, they had jointly realised they weren't compatible in that way. He liked to think it was credit to both of them that they had managed to part amicably and salvage what was a great friendship.

To Josh, Hannah was still as important as family, which is why he looked out for her.

He hadn't taken Rosie's concerns seriously at first. Rosie liked having Hannah to herself, so she was always going to put obstacles in the way. She was overreacting and simply looking for a way to cause trouble.

But the book bothered him. Quinn was poking into Hannah's past and Josh couldn't believe she was okay with that. Was she really that smitten with the guy? She had always been so private about everything that happened and now here was Liam Quinn wanting to tell the whole world what had happened to her. Was he cosying up to Hannah purely to get her story?

Not that Josh was suggesting Hannah was unattractive. She was gorgeous. Of course, he was biased, but he was certain he wasn't alone in that opinion. And it wasn't just a physical thing. She was kind, compassionate, and stronger than most people he knew. But she was also vulnerable, even if at times she didn't realise it. If Quinn was taking advantage of her, he would have Josh to answer to.

Hannah would kill him if she realised he was interfering, but on this occasion Josh felt he was justified. He was just looking out for her and in order to do that he needed to know more about Liam Quinn.

The guy had experienced plenty of success with his books, but it seemed he liked to keep his life as private as possible. Quite the irony since he was now making a career of poking about in other people's business, and it had Josh all the more curious. Guarded people tended to have secrets.

Frustratingly, the man was squeaky clean from what he'd discovered so far and Josh tapped his pen in frustration against the jotter pad where he had been making notes.

Born in Devon to James and Jennifer Quinn thirty-five years ago, with one younger sister, Ashley. He had gone to university in Nottingham, held down a number of jobs, mostly in television production, before getting his first book published when he was twenty-eight. He had never married and had lived all over the country, never seeming to stick in one place for too long.

What was he hiding?

It was a random search on Sunday morning that led Josh down a rabbit hole and eventually to Liam Quinn's secret.

What he found out was unexpected, shocking even, and had him questioning Quinn's motives all over again. This had nothing to do with wanting Hannah's story, of that he was certain, and he didn't believe for one second that she knew the truth. Quinn's motives were personal and Josh needed to fill her in as soon as possible.

He knew it was the weekend of Jane and Geoff's party, so Hannah would be away. He had offered to go with her, but she had turned him down. While he knew she had been uncomfortable with going back to Hixton, at least she was safe there and away from Quinn.

Still, he picked up his phone and dialled her number, wanting to put her in the picture.

Frustratingly, it cut to voicemail, but he left a message, urging her to call him as soon as possible.

'Han, it's me, Josh. I need you to call me urgently. It's about Liam Quinn. Don't shoot me, but I did some digging. You need to stay away from him. He's not who he says he is.'

44

Tash was outside cleaning her car when Rosie's sporty little KA pulled into the close, and her brows raised as her old friend pulled to a halt, climbing out of the driver's seat.

'Hello, this is an unexpected visit.'

'I had to come. Hannah's away and I didn't know where else to go.'

Rosie's face crumpled, tears filling her big blue eyes, and Tash tensed in alarm. Had something else happened? She dropped her sponge in the bucket, wiping her hands dry on her jeans and went to Rosie.

'Why are you crying? What's wrong?'

'Everything.'

'Everything?'

'I'm in such a bad place, Tash. All of this stuff with Mrs W. I'm trying to be brave, but it's so hard.' Rosie's tears fell harder, smearing mascara down her cheeks.

'Look, why don't you come inside. I'll make some tea and... have you eaten? I can cook you some eggs on toast?'

'Is Sam home?'

'She's at work. Come on, come inside and let's get some food into you.'

Rosie sniffed and nodded. 'I'd like that.'

She took Tash's hand like she was a child and let her lead the way into the house.

'You sit down,' Tash told her, moving the Sunday paper and magazines out of the way and plumping the cushions before urging her to take a seat. 'And I'll go put the kettle on.'

She glanced back at Rosie before leaving the room, a frown creasing her brow. She hadn't seen her in this kind of state in a long while, and given they didn't see each other that often these days, her visit was really out of the blue.

Rosie was glassy-eyed, anxious, and so frail; Tash feared she could be taking drugs again. They had always been her downfall. Mrs W's release, the break-in at her flat, then Jill's death. It was a lot to deal with and she had never been able to cope well. No wonder she was the first to crack.

Hannah tended to shoulder a lot of the responsibility where Rosie was concerned, but she was away and it wasn't fair to ruin her weekend. Tash knew Hannah had been under enough stress of her own and she would not add to that. Instead she took Rosie her tea, sat with her, and tried to calm her down.

'Can I stay here with you for a while?' Rosie's eyes were wide and anxious. 'We could watch movies like we used to.'

Tash nodded. If Rosie wanted movies, they would watch movies.

If she could keep her occupied and get some food inside her, maybe persuade her to rest for a while, it would do her the world of good.

She made more tea and some scrambled eggs on toast, coaxing Rosie to eat. Then, noticing she was shivering, she wrapped her in a fleecy blanket and switched on the TV, clicking on to Netflix.

'What do you fancy watching?'

'Something happy.'

They settled on *Bridesmaids*, though Rosie seemed mostly distracted and kept glancing at her phone. When the film had finished, Tash persuaded her to try to rest, while she cleared up in the kitchen. She put the radio on, hoping the music might serve as a more soothing backdrop than silence.

She had just finished loading the dishwasher when Rosie appeared in the doorway. She seemed perkier, though her eyes were still red from all the earlier crying.

'How are you feeling? Did you manage to get any sleep?'

'A little.'

'Are you going to stay? You can have dinner with us when Sam gets home.'

'That would be nice. Can I have another cup of tea?'

'Of course you can. I'll put the kettle on.'

'I can do it. I'll make you a cup too.'

This was good. She seemed to be returning to normal Rosie. Tash eased out a sigh of relief, turning her attention to the vegetables they would need later for dinner.

As she started peeling potatoes, the purr of an engine had her looking out of the kitchen window.

It was Sam's car. What was she doing home so early?

As her girlfriend joined them, explaining she had left work early as she felt unwell, Rosie fell quiet, an almost petulant look on her face.

Luckily, Sam didn't pick up on the vibes and she excused herself to go lie down.

'What's got into you?' Tash demanded in a hushed whisper after Sam had left the room.

Rosie shrugged, the canister of tea bags still in her hand. 'I was just enjoying it being the two of us. It's been like old times, don't you think?'

'It has.' Tash's tone softened. 'But Sam is happy to have you here too, and she's gone upstairs, so technically it is still the two of us.'

Rosie nodded, her expression turning vacant. 'I guess.'

'Are you okay?'

'I should go. I'm going to head to Hannah's. She might be back now.'

'I thought you were going to stay for dinner?'

'I'm feeling much better now.' Rosie threw her arms around Tash, hugging her tightly. 'Thank you for letting me stay'.

'You're welcome, but what about dinner?'

Rosie wasn't listening. She had gone through to the living room to fetch her phone and bag, then was in the hallway slipping on her boots and jacket.

Tash watched her leave, her mouth open. Sam and Rosie had always been on good terms. Why was Rosie acting like this? She stood in the kitchen and watched as her old friend climbed into her car and sped off up the road. She had to be taking drugs again. She would message Hannah and warn her.

As she reached for the phone, the newscaster on the radio spoke and she froze.

'The body of a woman who was found on Friday has been identified as Lauren Bell.'

Tash reached for the counter, needing something to hold on to, a pulse beating between her ears and growing louder. Reeling in shock, she didn't focus on the full report, but picked out a few key words. 'Suspicious', 'police want to speak to a man', 'eyewitness'.

Lauren Bell wasn't an uncommon name. It wasn't their Lauren. It had to be someone else.

But Tash knew she was kidding herself.

* * *

They had been having such a nice time. Why did Sam have to come home and spoil it?

Never mind. Rosie would drive to Wells and go and see Hannah. She would surely be back from her weekend in Hixton by now.

As the radio station she was tuned to cut to the news, she slammed her foot on the brake. That was the last thing she wanted to be listening to. She needed happy, happy.

Behind her, a car hooted, making her jump, the driver waving his fist and swearing out of his open window as he overtook her. Rosie ignored him, fiddling with her Bluetooth.

She connected her phone to the speakers, her favourite playlist blasting out.

That was better. No news. She didn't want any of that doom and gloom, thank you.

Instead she cranked the volume even higher, the sound of Green Day already lifting her spirits, and told herself that everything was going to work out okay.

45

She was done being scared.

Eileen Wickham had been in control for so long and it was all Hannah's fault because she had let her. It was ridiculous. She hadn't even seen the woman in years and shouldn't have allowed her to have this headspace. It was time to take that control back.

Although the nerves still knotted in her stomach as they passed through the entrance to the farm, anger was now building and pushing them aside. She considered herself to be a rational woman, so why had she allowed this to happen?

For so long, she had been afraid to come back here, but Liam was right. This was just the shell of a building, and okay, bad things – very bad things – had happened here once, but that was in the past.

'Are you okay?'

It was the second time he had asked and now when she answered, it was with more confidence.

'Yes, I really am.'

As though to prove that point, she strode ahead to where the front door of the farmhouse was hanging off its hinges, Tank scrambling to keep up with her, not liking that he was no longer in front.

Pushing it open, she stepped through into the kitchen where they had once sat, the room filled with excited chatter as Mrs W served up cakes and cookies and the other treats she had used to lure them in.

The table was still there, the wood faded and dusty, and two of the legs broken so it stood like a slide and the curtains that hung at the window were dirty and torn, now little more than rags. The glass was smeared with filth and cracked, probably from where a stone had been hurled at it, and rubbish was everywhere, while cobwebs and graffiti adorned the once bright yellow walls.

Bitch
Murderer
Burn in hell

They were all messages for Mrs W, but she would likely never see them.

Hannah glanced at the cellar door, remembering the day Mrs W had revealed her true colours, locking her down there with Mr Bennett. Although she was older, wiser, didn't even believe in ghosts, recalling how she had felt that day, trapped in the dark cupboard, sent an involuntary shiver skittering down her spine.

'I've often wondered why they don't tear the place down,' she commented, as Liam joined her. 'No one wants to live here.'

'There's been talk over the years. A couple of developers have been interested, but nothing's ever come to fruition. The only people interested in coming in now are the ghoul hunters or kids daring each other to explore.'

'And us.'

Liam's mouth twisted into a crooked smile. 'And us,' he agreed.

As they stared at each other, Hannah's phone picked that moment to ring, vibrating loudly in her pocket. She pulled it out, saw Josh's name on the screen, and swiped to send the call to voicemail.

This moment was too important. Josh would have to wait.

'Everything okay?'

She nodded. 'Just Josh. He can wait. How safe is it upstairs? Are we okay to go up?'

He nodded. 'Yeah, it's okay structurally. Just be careful. There are a few loose floorboards.'

Hannah went through to the hallway, could hear Liam telling Tank to stay as she started to make her way up the stairs, to the place where she had first seen Mrs W's mask slip.

'No, Tank! Sit! Dammit, Tank!'

Of course the dog wasn't paying any attention and moments later they were both following after her.

'He really would benefit from obedience classes,' she said as Tank charged past her.

Liam muttered something non-committal about how he might look into it, though they both knew full well that he wouldn't. Honestly, though, Tank was a welcome distraction.

As Hannah approached the landing, saw the low ceiling with its dark beams, the ones that often haunted her nightmares, her chest tightened.

Although her legs were heavy with reluctance, she pushed on, determined to prove to herself once and for all that nothing in this house could hurt her.

The door to Mrs W's bedroom was wide open. The once ornate bed still dominated the room, though it was missing the mattress and the base was broken in two. The wallpaper was mostly torn from the walls and there was a gaping hole in the ceiling. Hannah had seen inside this room just the once and found it difficult to wipe the image of what she had long ago witnessed.

'This was where I first knew something wasn't quite right,' she told Liam, finding it easier if she spoke about what she was remembering.

He didn't say anything, but she saw she had his attention.

'It's where I saw her with Bill. He was bent over, his jeans and pants down, and she was hitting him. I've never been able to shake that image, forget the look of humiliation on his face.'

She waited for Liam to react, but he remained quiet, studying her, his only giveaway in the slight tightening of his mouth.

Hannah shrugged. He was obviously in writer mode.

She wandered into the room, emboldened by realising she could. That Mrs W couldn't hurt her.

There were two windows, one facing the bed, the other on the wall beside it, and from where she stood, she could see the pond where they had once swum and the fields where they had played. Her eyes fell on the garage, and again she remembered that day with Bill, when he had bullied her into dropping her underwear.

Breathe, Hannah. It all happened in the past.

Fuck Bill. Fuck Mrs W.

She moved to the second window, saw it had a clear view of the barn. It was the place where everything had unravelled and a familiar fear crept over her, as the unwanted memories of that summer came flooding back.

46

2002

After Mrs W had locked Hannah in the cupboard, Hannah had no intention of ever returning to the farm. She didn't care what the others said or did. Even if it meant spending the rest of the summer holiday alone, it would be preferable to ever going back there.

She had toyed briefly with trying to talk to her mother about what had happened but was terrified it might only make things worse. Mrs W had been so convincing when she had dropped Hannah off and she was regarded highly by all of the adults in the village. Telling tales on her might actually make things worse.

No, it was better for Hannah to keep her head down and stay out of the woman's way. It wouldn't be that difficult.

Or so she had thought.

After avoiding her friends over the next few days, choosing to stay home instead of meeting up with them and making up lame excuses when they knocked on the door wanting her to come out, Mrs W had come looking for her.

Hannah was in her bedroom reading when the doorbell rang, her mother outside hanging washing on the line, and assuming it was Tash or Rosie again, she reluctantly set her book to one side and went downstairs to answer it.

When she opened the door, she froze, her stomach dropping and nerves stealing her voice.

Her first thought was that Mrs W was here to get her in trouble or tell her off again. It didn't matter that she couldn't think of a reason why. Just the fact she was at the door was enough.

'Hello, Hannah.'

She was back to being all smiles and friendly, no sign of the angry woman who had terrified the life out of her. Hannah had seen behind this mask though and was still afraid.

'Hello, Mrs W.' She found her voice, but the words came out as a terrified squeak.

'I wanted to check up on you and make sure you are okay. You haven't stopped by the farm with your friends the last couple of days.'

'I... I... I haven't been feeling well.'

The hint of a frown made Hannah wish she hadn't lied.

'Really? The others didn't mention that.'

'I... um... I...'

'Well, as you haven't been there, you don't know we have something excited planned for tomorrow night.'

'You have?' Hannah wasn't interested, but she could see Mrs W was waiting for her to ask what.

'A camping night. We're going to cook hot dogs and burgers on the barbecue, then you kids can sleep out under the stars.'

'I don't know.' There was no way she wanted to go. 'My mum—'

'Your mother already knows and said yes. I saw her in the post office yesterday.'

No!

As Hannah's mouth flapped, Jane Lawrence came back into the

house, joining them in the hallway. 'This is exciting, isn't it, Hannah? And so kind of Eileen to do this for you kids.'

When Hannah didn't react to that, and was at a complete loss as to how she was going to get out of going, her mum gave her a nudge.

'Well, say thank you, Hannah.'

'Thank you, Mrs W.'

She wanted to cry as she listened to the pair of them make small talk, her mother so grateful for Mrs W's kindness.

'I don't want to go,' she said, as soon as the door shut.

'Why on earth not, Hannah?'

'I'm not feeling well.'

'Since when? You look fine to me.'

'I have a headache and a sore throat.'

'Really?' Her mother's look was sceptical. 'And when did that come on?'

'Earlier today.'

'Well, I'm sure you'll be fine by tomorrow night. Your stepfather has made arrangements for us to go away for the night, so I'm afraid you're going to have to go.'

'What?'

'We booked the hotel last night.' Jane sighed. 'Honestly, Hannah. Mrs Wickham is doing something nice for you kids and you should perhaps be a little more grateful.'

'Please don't make me go.'

'Don't be silly. I'm not going to let you ruin our one night away.' Jane gave her one of her 'mother knows best' looks. 'Besides, you've been cooped up in this house the last few days. It will do you good to get out and see your friends again.'

There was no more arguing with her, but it didn't stop one last protest the following day.

Not that it helped. If anything, it made her mother even more determined that Hannah would attend the sleepover.

'Honestly, what's got into you? You've been moping about, not wanting to see anyone. Go and enjoy yourself for goodness' sake.'

'But I don't want to go.'

'Sometimes in life you have to suck these things up and get on with it. I'm sure you'll have fun once you're there with the others. Now go get your things together and I'll find your sleeping bag.'

When Hannah pouted, not moving, her mother scolded her.

'I don't want you showing me up and embarrassing me. You're going to this camp night, young lady, so you'd better get used to the idea.'

As if to reinforce her point, Jane Lawrence insisted on driving her to the farm, not trusting Hannah to cycle there, and unfortunately by doing so, it meant Hannah was the first one of her friends to arrive.

Mrs W was all smiles as she opened the door, talking to her mother briefly as she wiped her hands on her apron, telling her about all the games and treats she had planned.

Hannah could smell the waft of frankfurter sausages and onions, but it only made her stomach churn with nausea.

'Don't you worry. Hannah will have a great time. I'll make sure she does.'

She turned to face Hannah as her mother drove away. The smile was still on her face, but it didn't quite reach her eyes, and Hannah's legs threatened to buckle, as she remembered her last visit.

'Come on inside and you can help me finish getting everything ready.' Mrs W's tone was easy-going, friendly even, but that could all be an act. Hannah could hardly refuse though.

'Okay.' She just wanted to get tonight out of the way, then never come back here.

The woman took her backpack, then made her wash her hands

before asking her to do a number of mundane tasks, such as putting crisps into bowls and sorting cutlery.

Bill didn't seem to be about, thankfully, and Hannah guessed he was outside somewhere doing his chores.

As they worked, Mrs W hummed an unfamiliar tune, pretty much ignoring her. Still, Hannah was careful with each job she was given, terrified of drawing attention to herself by accidentally dropping something or getting one of her tasks wrong.

When Rosie showed up, relief eased the knots of tension in her shoulders.

'Well, don't you look lovely in your pink jumper,' Mrs W was gushing as she welcomed Rosie inside, before saying goodbye to her dad.

'Can I help?' Rosie was more eager than Hannah, but then she would be. She hadn't seen Mrs W without her mask.

She was given the job of laying out the cookies, which she took very seriously as she lifted them from the tray where they had been cooling, arranging them prettily on the plate.

'What's that tune?' she asked, as Mrs W resumed her humming.

For a moment, the woman seemed distracted, as if she hadn't heard her, but then she smiled.

'It's from my music box.'

'What's a music box?'

Mrs W wiped her hands on her apron. 'You're doing a beautiful job with those biscuits,' she praised, looking at Rosie's plate. 'You finish laying them out and I'll go and get my music box to show you.'

She disappeared from the room and Rosie grinned at Hannah. 'She is so cool.'

'She's okay,' Hannah shrugged. She was busy organising bottles of ketchup, relish, and mustard on the worktop, and feeling the weight of Rosie's stare, refused to make eye contact.

'Just okay? She's the best, Hannah. No other mums would let us have this much fun.' Rosie fell silent for a moment. 'How come you haven't come out with us the last couple of days? Do you not like it here?'

Tears pricked at the backs of Hannah's eyes. She couldn't let them fall. If Mrs W caught her...

'You can tell me, Hannah. I promise it's okay.'

She wanted to tell someone. She wanted to, so badly. Rosie was one of her best friends, but would she even believe her?

'Out of the way, girls.'

The moment was lost as Mrs W returned to the room. She cleared a space on the worktop before carefully setting down a varnished box with an intrinsic floral pattern carved into the woodwork.

'What's in there?'

'This, young Rosie, is my music box.'

'Does it really play music?'

'It does.'

Mrs W undid the clasp at the front, raising the lid, and a tiny figurine ballerina appeared. She twisted a key at the back of the box and a sweet melody began to play as the ballerina started spinning.

Hannah recognised the tune as the one she had been humming.

Inside the box were brooches and beads and other pieces of jewellery, and Rosie was staring in wonderment. 'This is like a magic box of treasure,' she breathed.

'My husband gave this to me.'

'It's beautiful.'

'It really is.' Mrs W spared a glance in Hannah's direction. Apparently she had drawn attention to herself by staying quiet. 'What do you think, Hannah? Has the cat got your tongue?'

She was using a different tone to the one she reserved for Rosie. It was cooler.

'I... um... I think it's lovely,' Hannah stammered, scared to look at the woman.

As Rosie reached for the box, wound it up again, her curious fingers touching the jewellery, Mrs W's eyes hovered on Hannah.

'I nearly forgot my special pickled sauce. Hannah, would you mind fetching it for me?'

'Yes, of course.' Hannah quickly nodded, glancing round at the cupboards. 'Where is it?'

When Mrs W didn't immediately answer, she made the mistake of making eye contact with her, saw the sly smile cross the woman's face as her glance slid to the closed cellar door.

'It's just down in the cellar. Bottom of the stairs. Shelf on the left.'

Hannah froze. 'You want me to go down *there*?'

'It's not a problem, is it?'

'I don't know... I don't think...'

Rosie was looking at her now, wondering what was going on. 'What's wrong, Hannah? Are you scared of Mr Bennett? He's just a silly story.'

She wasn't. At least she hadn't been until she had been locked down in the cellar. But, of course, she couldn't tell Rosie that.

'Come on, Hannah. It's just a silly cellar. I'd go myself, but my knees play me up. We can't have the barbecue without my special pickled sauce.'

'I'll go,' Rosie offered.

'No, I need you to help me lay the table. You do such a lovely job. Hannah will go and get the sauce, won't you, Hannah?'

Mrs W's tone was firm. There would be no arguing with her, and Hannah was actually more fearful of any consequences than she was of the cellar. She wouldn't get locked down there this time. Not while Rosie was here. Mrs W wouldn't dare, would she? Not in front of witnesses.

'I'll go.'

Her legs were jelly as she descended the stairs, the familiar dank dusty air threatening to paralyse her. With each step she took, the more light-headed she felt, and she was scared she was going to pass out, topple down the stairs.

She clung on to the banister.

Breathe, Hannah.

The only light came from the open door, Mrs W telling her that the bulb in the cellar was broken, and as she neared the bottom, she glanced frantically at the shelves.

'Can you see it?'

Mrs W's voice sounded so far above, but she heard the goading tone.

Hannah saw jars, but couldn't make out what was written on them. 'It's too dark. I can't read the labels.'

'Give it a moment. Your eyes will adjust.'

She didn't want to wait. She just wanted to find the jar and get out of the cellar.

'I'll go help her look.'

'No, Rosie. I need you to start taking things outside. Can you do that for me?'

'Yes, Mrs W.'

No, don't go, Rosie.

Hannah glanced back up the stairs, could see Mrs W standing in the doorway watching her.

'I can't find it. Please let me come back up now.'

'It's just a jar, Hannah. For goodness' sake. Do you *really* want me to have to come down these stairs?'

There was that edge to her voice now, that suggested Hannah was annoying her. She didn't want to make her angry.

'I'm trying to find it.' She could hear the panic in her voice and tried to keep calm.

She pulled down a jar to read the wording, blinking and trying to make her eyes adjust. She managed to make out the words blackberry jam. No, that wasn't it.

As she put the jar back, there was a shuffling sound behind her.

Please don't be Mr Bennett. Please don't be Mr Bennett.

She didn't dare turn around and look.

'Have you found it yet?' Mrs W sounded impatient. 'Try the bottom shelf.'

Hannah reached down for one of the jars. Pickled sauce. She had it.

Gripping it tightly in her clammy hand, she charged back up the stairs.

Mrs W still stood blocking the doorway. She glanced past Hannah into the darkness, her eyes widening. 'What's that behind you? Oh no. Mr Bennett? Is that you?'

In her panic to get out of the cellar, Hannah tripped on the last step, going down heavily on her knees, the jar of pickled sauce slipping from her grip. The sound as it fell down the stairs, the glass smashing as it hit the bottom, echoed loudly.

Ignoring her throbbing knees, Hannah glanced up at Mrs W, fear clogging her throat. 'I... I'm sorry.'

Mrs W's mouth twisted into a cruel smile and while she looked angry, she also seemed to be enjoying herself. 'You're going to pay for that.'

47

No longer here. Can't hurt you.

Hannah repeated the mantra as she strode around the bedroom, determined that she was in charge now and reminding herself that Mrs W no longer had any power over her.

The memory of what had happened next would stay with her forever, but she refused to let it control her, and she was angry now that it had done for so long.

With Liam and Tank in tow, she insisted on exploring every bit of the farmhouse.

The hardest moment was standing at the top of the stone steps trying to build up courage to go down into the cellar. She remembered the rush of fear that Mr Bennett was lurking, the sound of the pickle jar breaking, and look of hatred on Mrs W's face as she stood trapped on the stairs. Forcing herself to push through it, she used the torch on her phone to lead the way, showing Liam the cupboard where Mrs W had locked her inside.

He frowned as he looked at her, the shadowy light making his handsome face appear almost dangerous. It wasn't him though. It was this place and the evil that she associated it with. The evil that had once lurked inside.

'I'm sorry she put you through that.'

Hannah nodded, trying to keep the emotional side of her detached. It was easier that way.

Besides, they both knew that the cupboard wasn't the worst of it.

'I want to go out to the barn.' She fought to give the tremor out of her voice.

'Are you sure about that?'

'I'm sure. I need to deal with this once and for all. When I leave here today, I want it to be over.' This was it. After today, she wouldn't be coming back.

Liam shrugged and let her lead the way back up the stairs, out of the house.

They crossed to the barn in silence, Tank making plenty of noise as he panted, straining against his lead, eager to get there.

He was the only eager one, though Hannah pushed on, determined in her quest.

Inside the barn, it was cool, shadowy, and quiet, her footsteps against the dirt floor disturbing that silence. She headed over to where the hole had been, surprised to find her memory had it slightly wrong. In her mind, she remembered it being more central, but truth was, the area she was looking for was further back, deeper into the shadows.

The hole was still there and that surprised her. For some reason, she had thought it would have been covered up. Of course it was empty. The box gone. It would have no doubt been used in the trial; the police having combed it for evidence. Still, she stared down, remembering.

48

2002

She had been the first, that awful night when they had camped at the farm.

Mrs W had said she would pay for dropping the jar, and boy did she pay.

She recalled how she had been on edge all night, sticking close to the others, waiting for something to happen, but they had eaten hot dogs and burgers, played games, and told ghost stories as they sat around the campfire that Mrs W had built.

If Hannah could have wiped those memories of her previous visit and what had happened in the cellar, it would have been perfect.

Of course she couldn't though and she had finally crawled into her sleeping bag wondering if it was her, if she was perhaps overreacting. Maybe Mrs W had been justified in her actions and Hannah really had deserved the punishment. Her own mother would never do anything like it, but perhaps Mrs W was just stricter.

She had fallen asleep under a sky of stars, so it confused her when she awoke to darkness.

This wasn't her bedroom and when she remembered she was

on the camp night, she realised it wasn't the field where she was supposed to be sleeping beside her friends either.

So where was she?

As she sat up, a bright light flashed in her face and she put her hand up to shield her eyes.

'Who's there?' Her voice was shaky, but she was frightened, and with good reason.

There was no response, but she heard the shuffle of footsteps and then the hush of whispering, telling her there was more than one person with her.

Were her friends playing some kind of prank?

'Tash? Lauren? Is that you?'

Still no reply, but this time she heard the low rumble of laughter, fear clawing at her as she recognised it.

Bill.

Her heart was thumping wildly. 'Where am I? I want to go back to my friends.'

The light dropped suddenly and Hannah blinked, trying to focus as two pairs of legs came into her vision.

Bill. And with him was Mrs W.

They were higher up than her, their feet at her eye level, and it took her a moment to realise why. She was still inside her sleeping bag, but it was no longer in the field. She was inside somewhere. One of the barns, she realised, seeing the bales of straw stacked high, blocking her view of the door. And she was in a hole in the ground.

Panicking, she started to scramble out of the sleeping bag.

'Stop that right now,' Mrs W demanded and the sharp tone of her voice had Hannah freezing. 'Don't you dare move.'

'Please let me go.' Shame heated her cheeks as she started to sob.

'You broke my jar. Ruined my special pickled sauce.'

'It... was... an... accident.'

'You're a clumsy girl. You need to be taught a lesson. How to be more respectful of other people's things.' There was a malice to Mrs W's voice. A cruelty Hannah recognised from the day she had disturbed her with Bill in the bedroom.

'Please... I'm sorry.'

'I'm going to give you something to be sorry about. Now stop your crying, girl. You're thirteen, not five. You take the punishment you deserve.'

What was Mrs W planning to do to her? Hannah didn't understand. She knew enough to be afraid, having already experienced one of the woman's punishments. And the nasty grin on Bill's face suggested he was looking forward to whatever was coming.

She glanced around frantically, seeing through her tears that there was a box in the hole and she was sitting inside it.

Why had they put her in a box?

'Lie back down, Hannah.'

'What... what are you going to do to me?'

'LIE BACK DOWN!'

Hannah jumped at the tone, but didn't comply. 'Please,' she begged.

Mrs W sighed deeply; her tone disappointed when she spoke. 'Listen to me, young lady. This is going to be a whole lot worse for you if you don't start doing what you're told.'

'Please let me go!'

'Boohoo. *Please let me go*,' Bill mimicked, pretending to wipe tears from his eyes.

'I'm adding another half an hour to your punishment for insolence. If you don't lie down by the time I count to five, I'll make it an hour.'

What were they going to do?

'One.'

Could she run for it?

'Two.'

She would have to get out of the sleeping bag and the hole without them catching her.

'Three.'

And she couldn't see the door. What if it was locked?

'Four.'

If she tried to escape, Mrs W would make her punishment worse. It was no good.

She scurried down in her sleeping bag, pulling it up to her chin just as the woman counted, 'Five.'

As Hannah stared up at them through her tears, she saw that Mrs W was leaning over her and Bill now held a shovel. Her teeth started to chatter in fear.

Why did he have that?

Oh my God. They're going to bury me.

Hannah started to sit up again, but she wasn't quick enough. Mrs W pushed something over her, trapping her in the hole. As it clicked into place, Hannah realised it was a clear plastic lid. She could see them through it, but she was now trapped in the box and could only raise her head by just a few inches.

Frantically, she tried to wriggle her arms free of the sleeping bag, though it was difficult with so little room. She finally got one hand free and pushed against the lid. It was jammed shut and there was no way she could open it.

'Please let me out. Please don't do this.'

Her breath was steaming up the plastic and she couldn't see them clearly, though she heard the peal of Bill's laughter again. It sounded distorted and far away, as did Mrs W's voice when she spoke.

'None of your friends know you're in here, so I suggest you take your punishment like a good girl. If not, I might not let you out, then you'll be down here all alone for ever.'

Hannah was crying harder now. She couldn't help it. And when she didn't think things could get worse, something heavy thumped on top of the plastic lid.

It took her a second to realise it was a shovel full of dirt. Followed by another, then another.

They were... they were burying her.

That was when she started screaming.

49

No longer here. Can't hurt you.

It was just a hole in the ground, and yes, she was remembering, but truthfully, she had never forgotten that awful night.

As a kid she had been terrified. Frightened that Mrs W would leave her, scared that she would run out of air. Of course, she was too young to realise that a tube had been fed into the box so she could breathe.

They had kept her buried in the ground for what felt like hours, though it was actually much less time than that. It was still dark when they had let her out and Mrs W escorted her back to her friends. They were still asleep, though Tash had woken as Mrs W put Hannah's sleeping bag back on the ground. Of course Mrs W had a story ready, claiming Hannah had needed the loo and become disorientated. She had always been prepared and Hannah knew better than to call her out.

Liam had told her he had been to the farm before while researching for his book, still he waited patiently, allowing her to take all of the time she needed, while Tank sniffed around the barn, interested in all the new smells.

A rustling noise from outside caught his attention and he let out a bark.

Hannah and Liam both glanced up as a rabbit scampered past the open door. Seeing it, Tank's tail thumped and he bolted after it.

'Tank! Get back here.'

Hannah knew the dog wouldn't listen, but it didn't stop Liam calling him again as he headed to the door.

'I need to go get him.'

'I'll catch you up in a minute.'

Liam glanced back at her; his eyebrows raised. 'Are you sure?'

'I'm fine. I just want another minute or two.' When he hesitated, she told him, 'Go!'

She wasn't lying. She really was fine. This place that had terrified her for so many years no longer had any power.

She kicked a stone into the hole. 'Fuck you, Mrs W.'

And fuck Bill too. He might have only been fifteen and under Mrs W's influence, but he had been just as bad.

Her phone vibrated in her pocket. A reminder of the call she had earlier ignored from Josh. He had left her a message, but she hadn't listened to it.

She saw she had a missed call from Tash too, though Tash hadn't left a message.

Hannah dialled her voicemail. As she waited for Josh's message to play, she wandered back to the doorway of the barn. In the distance, she could see Liam still trying to catch up to Tank and it made her smile. She should really go and help him, though it was quite entertaining watching him chasing after the dog, a colourful list of swear words turning the air blue.

Josh's voice cut in and Hannah continued to watch Liam and Tank as her ex-husband spoke.

'Han, it's me, Josh. I need you to call me urgently. It's about Liam Quinn. Don't shoot me, but I did some digging.'

What? Hannah's shoulders tensed in anger. What the hell was Josh playing at? How dare he take it upon himself to investigate Liam? She was going to call him back right now and tell him he was bang out of order, but then she heard his next words and everything inside her turned cold.

'You need to stay away from him. He's not who he says he is.'

The message ended and shaken, she clicked to save it before slipping the phone back in her pocket.

In the distance, Liam finally had the leash on Tank and was heading back towards the barn.

Stay away.

He's not who he says he is.

What the hell did Josh mean? Just what had he found out about Liam and who the hell was he?

She wanted to call Josh back and ask him, but there wasn't time.

It was the *stay away* bit that unnerved her and the request for her to call Josh urgently. Was he intimating that she was in danger?

'Is everything okay?' Liam was a little breathless, his grip on Tank's lead tight. His blue eyes were narrowed as he studied Hannah's face. 'You're looking at me weirdly.'

'Am I?'

For fuck's sake, act normal, Hannah.

'I'm fine. Just processing everything.'

There, that was better. And she must have sounded convincing, because Liam just shrugged.

'So where do you want to look next?'

'Actually, I think I've seen enough. Let's walk back to the car.' She glanced at the sky, relieved to see the sun had disappeared behind ominous dark clouds, giving her a decent excuse. 'It looks like rain is on the way and we don't want to get caught in it.'

Liam nodded, but he didn't say anything, letting her lead the way back towards the farmhouse.

She didn't like that he was behind her, her belly jittery with nerves. Josh's message had changed everything. She had come here with Liam and had trusted him completely. Now she just wanted to get away from him, at least until she had found out what the hell Josh was talking about.

No one knew they were out here at the farm, and they were all alone, no houses for at least a mile or two in any direction. Even the lane where they had left the car was seldom used, with motorists preferring the new carriageway that circled around the village.

Hannah tried to rationalise with herself. If Liam was dangerous, he'd had ample opportunity to attack her. They had been in the farmhouse and then in the cellar, as well as the barn. If he wanted to hurt her, surely he would have done so in one of those places.

And it had been her idea to come out here to the farm. He hadn't forced her.

Josh was wrong. He had to be. Either that or he was over-reacting.

She knew Liam. She had slept with him.

You didn't know him before he showed up on your doorstep.

And he was a celebrated author. She had read about him online and seen videos. Of course he was who he said he was. Though she realised he had never told her much at all.

'Wait up a minute.'

Hannah glanced back at him. 'What's wrong?'

'I meant to take some more photos while I was here. You don't mind if we go back in the farmhouse, do you?'

Yes. Yes, I do.

'I was hoping we could head back now. I don't want to get home too late.'

'Just five minutes.'

'Why didn't you take them when we were inside before?'

'I forgot. I was distracted by you, making sure you weren't going to freak out.' Liam's tone had turned a little agitated. 'What's the big deal, Hannah? It's just a few more minutes.'

She was sounding unreasonable and she didn't want to make him suspicious.

'Okay, it's fine. I'm going to wait outside. I've seen enough.'

He stared at her and she thought he was going to say something, try to pressure her into going back inside, but instead he nodded curtly.

She wondered if he was going to hand Tank's lead over to her, but he seemed happy for the dog to accompany him, heading up the path to the front door and stepping inside without another word to her.

Hannah's heart thumped. Should she try to get away? It would probably take her five minutes to get back to the car if she ran. Liam was inside and hopefully wouldn't see that she had gone.

She felt a stab of guilt at the idea of leaving him behind. They had brought her car and he would be stuck here. If she had this wrong...

No. Screw him. Josh had warned her to stay away.

She patted her pocket for her keys. Panicking when she couldn't find them.

And then she remembered.

Liam had taken them.

Fuck!

Okay. Stay calm, Hannah. Think.

She could try to hide. But where? And would it really do her any good?

No, she was better to sit tight, drive back to Norwich, and act as normal as possible, until she had spoken to Josh and until she knew what the hell was going on.

In fact, she could call him now. Liam wouldn't overhear. At least then she would know whether she was in danger or not.

She dialled Josh's number, listened to it ring, willing him to pick up. It clicked into voicemail and she left a terse whispered message. 'I'm in Hixton and I'm with Liam. You need to call me back and tell me what the hell is going on, Josh.'

As she hung up, she wondered if she should call the police. But how could she do that? Liam hadn't attacked her and until Josh got back to her about his stupid cryptic voicemail, she couldn't accuse him of anything.

Instead she turned to Google. Typing in Liam's name again and looking through the search results. What was it she had missed?

Liam James Quinn. Thirty-five years old. Son of James and Jennifer Quinn. One younger sister, Ashley, and there was quite an age gap between them.

In one of the articles, Ashley was referred to as his half-sister. So who were her parents?

Hannah searched for James Quinn alongside Liam Quinn. He had met Jennifer twenty-two years ago, so how could she be Liam's mother?

The first spit of rain hit the back of her hand. Another, moments later, landed on her phone screen.

What was it he had said about his mother as they were walking down to the farm?

She's been absent for a lot of my life

That made no sense. There were photos of Liam with Jennifer. They seemed close, which was at odds with what he had told Hannah.

So if Jennifer was actually his stepmother, who was his real mum?

I don't have the easiest relationship with my mother.

She's back in my life now.

No. Hannah's stomach dropped. it wasn't possible. Liam wasn't Eileen Wickham's son.

Hannah would know. She would recognise him, surely?

Besides, Mrs W's son was called Bill, so why the different name?

Bill Wickham. William Wickham. Wil... Liam.

Fuck. It wasn't possible. How could she not have known? He looked nothing like the kid she remembered, but then it had been so long and people changed. At least in their appearance. They didn't change fundamentally.

'Hannah?'

She swung around at the sound of her name, the phone dropping from her hand, smashing as it hit the ground, and she immediately thought she was going to be sick.

Liam Quinn stood in the doorway of the farmhouse, his face sinister in shadows and his expression difficult to read, and in his hand he held a knife.

50

It was mid-afternoon and Hannah wasn't home yet, which surprised Rosie, as she knew Hannah wouldn't want to stay in Hixton any longer than possible.

So where was she?

As each minute ticked by, Rosie's anxiety increased.

Was Hannah okay? What if something had happened to her?

She tried to calm herself as she paced Hannah's flat, but her overactive imagination was giving way to all sorts of dubious scenarios. Had Mrs W followed her back to Hixton or had she sent Bill?

No, Rosie. Don't think like that. Mrs W didn't know she was going there.

But if she was stalking them.

Think, Rosie. Think.

She tried to be productive. First calling Hannah's mum, Jane, and trying her best to hold her shit together, knowing Jane would want to have a good old catch-up.

'Rosie, what a lovely surprise to hear from you. I was sorry you couldn't make it back for the party.'

'Did you have a good time?' She had to ask. Knew it would be rude not to. Still, she gritted her teeth as Jane started telling her all about it, as if they had all the time in the world.

'Is Hannah still there?' she asked eventually when Jane stopped for a breath.

'No, they left after breakfast.'

'Sorry. They?'

They? Who the fuck was they?

'She brought that nice young man of hers.'

What man? Had Hannah taken Josh?

'Liam,' Jane said, before she could ask.

'She's with Liam?' Rosie failed to hide the incredulous note in her voice. Why the hell was Liam Quinn with her?

'Have you met him? I'm so glad she's finally found someone to settle down with.'

'Yes, I know him.'

What the hell was Hannah playing at? She had taken Quinn to her mother's anniversary party and introduced him as her boyfriend? Either she had gone mad or she was keeping a lot of secrets from Rosie. The betrayal had her reeling.

She managed to bluff her way through the rest of the conversation, not letting on how shocked she was, and getting off the phone as quickly as she could.

'You'll have to come visit, love,' Jane told her.

Rosie made the right noises in response, but knew there was no way on hell's earth she was ever going back to Hixton.

After ending the call, she hunted all over Hannah's flat, looking for the card Quinn had given Hannah. It was possible she had it on her or had slung it out, but Rosie hoped not. If Hannah was ignoring her, then maybe Quinn would answer.

She found the card in one of the kitchen drawers and immediately dialled Quinn's number.

It went to voicemail and Rosie hung up.

She noticed there was a scribbled address on the card. It must be where Quinn was staying. Maybe he and Hannah had gone back there.

She pocketed the card, then tried Josh's number. This went to voicemail too.

Damn it? Why wasn't anyone answering their phone?

Did Josh know Hannah was with Quinn?

Deciding that she was wasting her time waiting around in the flat, she slipped on her jacket and grabbed her car keys. It was a twenty-minute ride to Josh's. If he wouldn't answer his phone, she was going to show up on his doorstep, and she didn't intend to leave until she had some answers.

51

'Are you okay?'

Hannah's eyes had widened and her face had drained of colour. 'What are you doing with that?'

She was looking at Liam's hand. The one he realised held the knife.

'I found it under the bed in one of the rooms upstairs. No idea who it belongs to. Someone probably left it here.'

'Shouldn't you put it back?'

'And risk it falling into the wrong hands? Knife crime is a real issue, you know.'

'So you're just going to carry it back to the car like that?'

Liam shrugged. 'That's the plan. I'll hand it in to the police.' He narrowed his eyes. 'What's up with you? You're behaving really strangely.'

She had been jittery and seemed suspicious before he had gone back in the house and right now she looked like she was going to throw up. Something had happened to spook her; he was certain of it.

He moved towards her and she immediately took a step back,

and he realised that it wasn't this house she was afraid of. It was him.

'Hannah?'

'I'm fine. Can we go now, please?'

She bent down and picked up her phone, looking dismayed as she stared at the cracked screen.

'Is it broken?'

Hannah glanced at him, quickly pocketing the phone. 'Let's just go.'

Yeah, she was definitely wary of him, keeping her distance as they started walking back to the lane and he was wracking his brain trying to figure out what might have instigated her change in attitude towards him.

She had been fine in the house and then in the barn, her earlier fear morphing into a much more productive anger. Had something happened when he had left her in the barn alone? Maybe she had experienced a flashback or being in there alone had been too much for her.

He was certain it was him she was jittery of though, and not this place.

It briefly crossed his mind that perhaps she had worked out who he was, but he quickly dismissed the thought. After all, how would she find out?

That didn't stop him keeping a close eye on her as they made their way back to the car, both of them picking up pace as the rain started to fall harder. And he kept hold of the keys when she asked for them, not handing them over until both he and Tank were sat inside. She was too skittish and he didn't trust her not to drive off without them.

'Can you put that knife away please?'

It was the first time she had spoken to him apart from asking for the keys.

He shrugged, opened the glovebox and slipped it inside. 'Happy?'

She nodded and started the engine; the tension rippling off her. It was starting to piss him off and he considered having it out with her, but then a pheasant ran out in front of the car and she swerved so sharply, almost running them off the road, that he reconsidered.

'Jesus, Hannah!'

'Sorry,' she apologised, flustered. 'I didn't see it.'

'Do you want me to drive?'

'No!' She snapped the word out.

'Okay, well can you at least concentrate please? I'd like to make it back in one piece.'

She mumbled something under her breath.

'Sorry?'

'Nothing.' She glared at him, but didn't say anything else, turning her attention back to the road and he understood this wasn't going to be a comfortable journey.

They managed to make it back to Wells speaking about six words between them, most of the noise coming from the scrape of the windscreen wipers and the rain that pounded against the car roof, and when Hannah pulled up outside the Airbnb, she didn't even kill the engine, instead just giving him a pointed look. One that clearly said, *get out*.

Liam had no intention of inviting her inside, but he wasn't going without one last attempt to figure out what was going on.

'So are you going to tell me what's up?'

The briefest hesitation told him she was debating how best to answer his question, while the shifting of her eyes and the pursing of her lips suggested she had decided against the truth. 'Nothing's up. It's been a stressful weekend and I'm tired.'

'You've barely spoken to me since leaving the barn.'

'I've had a lot of my mind to deal with. Going back to the farm, to where it happened, wasn't easy. It's not you.' She raised her hand to her face, rubbing her thumb along her jawline as her gaze sloped away. She was definitely lying.

He decided to push a little further. 'Okay. So do you want to catch up tomorrow?'

'I don't know. I have a busy week with the dogs. I'll check my schedule.'

Non-committal, cool, and lying again. He would get to the bottom of what was going on, but right now wasn't the time. If he pushed too hard, she would likely shut him out completely, and he didn't want to risk that. He had made too much progress to throw it all away.

'Fine. I'll leave it with you.' He took the knife from the glovebox, let Tank out of the rear seat, and grabbed his bag. 'I'll catch up with you later.'

He didn't look back as he headed towards the house, but knew she lingered for a moment watching him, before turning the car around and driving away.

Once inside, he shook the rain from his hair and turned on the radio, welcoming the music that cut through the silence. There had been too much of that over the last hour. He checked his phone; saw he had a couple of missed calls. One from his mother, the other from a number he didn't recognise. Deciding to ignore both, he fed Tank and was about to fire up his MacBook when the song that was playing ended and the radio station cut to the news headlines.

'The body of a woman who was found on Friday has been identified as Lauren Bell.'

Liam stilled, aware of the tension building in his shoulders as the word 'suspicious' was said, before the newscaster went on to explain that police wanted to speak with a man in connection.

His mind worked overtime as he processed the news and its implications.

Lauren's body had been found.

He had been planning on catching up with work, but his focus was broken and he knew he wouldn't be able to concentrate. Did Hannah know? He needed to go after her.

A knock at the door had him looking up. Was she back?

He hadn't given the address out to many people, so couldn't think who else it would be.

The knock came again. Whoever it was sounded impatient.

'Okay! I'm coming.'

Liam pushed his chair back and went to the door, throwing it open.

It wasn't Hannah and he glanced down in surprise at the tiny bundle of angry energy on the front step.

'Rosie?' Her dark hair was plastered to her head and the rain was soaking through the blouse she wore, but she didn't seem to notice.

'Where the hell is Hannah?'

'Hello to you too.'

She ignored his sarcastic response. 'I know you've been with her. I tried to call you. Where is she?'

So it was Rosie who had called? Liam hadn't even realised she had his number.

Or address. What was she doing here? Was she really just after Hannah?

'I have no idea where she is. Probably back home by now.'

'Really?'

From Rosie's tone, he suspected she didn't believe him. Well. Tough. That wasn't his problem. And while he could do with talking to Rosie at some point, he really wasn't in the mood for her right now.

'If you don't mind, I'm working.'

He started to close the door, annoyed when she stuck her foot out to block him.

'Actually I do mind.' Temper flared in her eyes. 'You and I need to have a talk.'

Liam looked at her in surprise. 'We do?'

Behind him, Tank was on his feet. He started barking.

'I've just come from Josh's house,' Rosie told him, undeterred by the dog. 'You remember him, don't you? Hannah's ex-husband. I've known from the start that there is something off about you and I asked him to help me figure out what it was. He's just told me everything.'

She had done what? His temper cranked up a notch.

'What are you talking about, Rosie?' He had tried for affable, needing to find out exactly what she knew, but failed to disguise the steel behind his words.

It didn't deter her. Rosie Emerson seemed to be a woman on a mission and that could be a problem.

'Hannah has no idea who you really are, does she? You have a lot of fucking explaining to do, Liam Quinn.'

52

This ends tonight.

Everything I have worked for, everything that is important. It's gone.

At first, that left me empty, but now the anger is back. White-hot and burning for revenge.

I messed up by going to Lauren Bell's house and it will only be a matter of time now before the police figure it out. Before they come for me. Lauren is dead and an eyewitness can put me at her house at the time it happened. There is no getting away from that.

There is no longer anything here for me. I have lost everything.

And now I realise that, I know I have nothing to lose.

This ends tonight, but I intend to go out on a high. To take the one thing I crave.

I will at long last get my revenge on Hannah Freemont.

Hannah Freemont, or Cole as she is now known, has always been at the centre of this for me, ever since that day in the farmhouse. She witnessed my humiliation and I have been hellbent on trying to put us on an even keel.

I despise her, I lust for her, I am obsessed with her. All of these years, I have denied myself, but she has never been far from my thoughts and since I started playing these little games, my control has gradually been slipping.

This ends tonight. I plan to go down in flames and I intend to take Hannah with me.

53

Hannah was exhausted by the time she arrived home, a cocktail of emotions draining her.

After kicking Liam out of her car, she had turned on the radio for company as she drove back to her flat. The news that started playing moments after she tuned in had floored her.

Lauren was dead.

The shock was so sudden, the grief overwhelming, a fist clenching her throat and making it difficult to breathe, and she had swerved to the side of the road, pulling the car to an abrupt halt as she wept for her friend.

It wasn't until that initial shock had subsided and she had finally pulled herself together to safely drive home that the thought occurred to her.

Was Liam responsible? She recalled how he had shown up suddenly on Friday after going AWOL for days. Is that where he had disappeared to? Had he gone to Kent and murdered Lauren?

While she was relieved to get away from him, she still couldn't shake the rush of sadness for something that didn't actually exist. He had tricked her into falling for him, concealing his true identity, and for what reason? Was this all part of some sick way to try to get back at her for what had happened to his mother?

Josh's words echoed around her head.

You need to stay away from him.

He's not who he says he is

Liam was obviously behind it all. The flowers she had received, the car that had followed her to his house. It would explain why he hadn't been home. And Rosie's break-in? Had he orchestrated that as well? It all made sense now, how he would disappear and she wouldn't hear from him for a few days. And was he behind Jill's death too? Had he pushed her down the stairs?

How could she have been so stupid not to realise?

The idea that she had fallen for Mrs W's son, that she had slept with him, trusted him, made her want to vomit. What was worse was that she still couldn't separate Liam Quinn from Bill Wickham. Some depraved part of her still lusted for Liam. Even though it had never been real.

Once home, she let herself into her flat and pulled out her phone. The screen was dead and she tried to restart it, groaning in frustration when she realised it was definitely broken. How was she supposed to speak to Josh now?

And she needed to. Tired as she was and keen to get out of her damp clothes, Hannah knew she wouldn't settle until she found out whether her suspicions were right.

She should have driven to Josh's instead of coming home.

Damn it. She was going to have to go out again; she wouldn't feel safe in her flat until she knew the truth about Liam.

She had wanted to act normal on the ride from Suffolk, but her emotions had got the better of her. It had been obvious she was mad at him. Frightened too. Would it really be that difficult for him to piece it together and work out why? And when he did, when he realised she knew. What then? What if Liam came after her?

If he had murdered her friends, then he was surely planning to kill her at some point too.

She had been alone with him on so many occasions these last couple of weeks, had trusted him completely. How could she have been so foolish?

She would go to Josh, get confirmation of her suspicions, then they could call the police and tell them exactly what Liam... no, Bill, had been up to.

She grabbed her keys, threw open the door, almost tripping over the music box that was sitting on her doorstep.

A chill crept up her spine as she stared at the box, even after all these years recognising the ornate pattern carved into the wood-work. She didn't need to open it to know the ballerina would pop up, and the tune that would play was already in her head.

She glanced warily around the landing. Was Liam here? Had he followed her? Left it there to scare her?

If he had done, it was working.

She hesitated, unsure what to do. Barricade herself inside the flat or make a run for it and go to Josh?

The creak of a door opening had her tensing and her head shot round in time to see the figure step out of the maintenance room, blocking her path to the stairs.

Twenty years had passed, but she recognised him immediately. The glacial blue of the eyes, the cruel curve of his mouth. His face just a shade too hard to be handsome. And in that moment, she realised she had made a terrible mistake.

54

2000 – 2002

Liam Quinn had been almost thirteen years old when his mother disappeared.

Although Von Quinn was a self-absorbed woman and even at a young age he had picked up on vibes that she found him an inconvenience, it still came as a shock.

He had thought his parents were happy. They lived in a nice house, close to the coast in South Devon, and okay, so his dad worked away a lot and his mum mostly left him to his own devices, but as a family unit, he had believed they were okay.

She vanished one day while Liam was at school and his father was on a business trip. Liam had returned to an empty house and a brief note telling him and his father that she couldn't do this any more and to take care of each other. Knowing Liam would be home alone for a few days, she had left a ten-pound note and made sure there was food in the fridge. Something she no doubt thought was considerate.

His first reactions had been confusion and panic, and when he was unable to get in touch with her, he called his father.

Over the next few months, his life was upended. James Quinn did his best at single parenting, taking time off from work to look after Liam, but he was reeling too. Like Liam, he hadn't suspected anything was wrong, so he was shocked by Von's actions and had his own emotions to deal with when divorce papers arrived.

It was through a friend that they learned Von had met someone else. A widower with two young children. He was a doctor at a private hospital in Plymouth where she had gone for treatment. She remarried almost immediately after her divorce came through.

Yet, it wasn't just James she wanted to sever ties with; it was Liam too. She had a new ready-made family and wanted to move on.

How could she abandon her own child?

Liam heard those words many times in the period after his mother left and for a long while it messed with his head. Was there something wrong with him? Was he not worthy of a mother's love?

Learning his mother had moved to Plymouth, he wrote letter after letter, begging her to come home. Wanting to know what he had done wrong and promising he would be the perfect son if she gave him another chance.

They all went unanswered.

Desperation turned into obsession. He tried to find out everything he could about her new family, wanting to know what was so much better about them. Needing to know why she loved them more.

They were American, her new family, and Liam found out that Von no longer liked to go by her shortened name. To her new friends, she was the much posher sounding Veronica. Wife of Doctor Grant Goldberg.

Her new children were Jill and Miles.

Liam had never met the Goldbergs, but already he couldn't stand them. How dare they take his mother from him?

His father tried his best to make things up to him and his aunts and cousins rallied around, but life had changed and in that blink of an eye, his childhood was over.

It was over two years later when Von eventually reached out to her son, and he had just turned fifteen. Von had recently moved to Suffolk and at first she had contacted him by telephone.

By that point, he had stopped writing to her and was trying his best to get on with his life. His grades had been slipping and for a while he had been hanging out with the wrong crowd, but thanks to close supervision from his father and old friends who were there for him even when he had turned his back on them, he was gradually getting back on track. His dad had also met someone. A lady called Jennifer, and while Liam was initially wary of her, over time the pair of them had become friends.

When he was told Von was on the phone, he refused to speak with her.

The woman who had given birth to him was now dead to him, and he didn't want anything more to do with her.

But then she had travelled to Devon, showing up at the house and blindsiding him.

She was different now. Her hair shorter and lighter, her clothes neat and smart, and her face more heavily made up. She looked like his mother, but an imposter version, and he shied away from her touch when she tried to hug him.

That was a mistake as it started the waterworks. Tears dripped from her eyes and she daintily wiped at her nose with a handkerchief, as she begged for his forgiveness.

She hadn't meant to hurt him, she just needed to find herself. Now she was much better and stable and she wanted him to come and meet her new family.

The idea filled Liam with dread, though part of him was still curious. He talked it over with his dad and Jennifer, not knowing what to do. He was worried he would be betraying his father by going, but James was quick to allay his fear, telling Liam he would support whatever decision he made.

Initially he said no, but his mother knew how to manipulate him and her parting words were all about family, blood ties, love, and forgiveness. The guilt had gnawed away over the following days, eventually becoming too great a burden to bear, and he had conceded, agreeing to visit the Goldbergs at their new home in the village of Hixton in Suffolk.

Nerves had jittered in his belly during the train journey, the conversation with his mother, when she came to pick him up from the station, false and uncomfortable. He wasn't even at her house and already he felt he had made a huge mistake in coming. It wasn't even like he could ask his dad to come and get him as he lived hours away and the return train tickets weren't until Sunday night. He had a whole weekend stuck with these people, these strangers.

He had already decided he was going to hate the Goldbergs and his first impression of them grated on him. Grant struck him as cheesy and false, while Jill was too perky and self-assured for his liking, especially as she was two years younger than him. Both of them seemed to have a different way about them, which probably had a lot to do with their accent, and they were confident, bordering on arrogant, not afraid to speak their mind. They were all so neat and picture-perfect and that made Liam feel even more out of place, with his scruffy mop of hair and his ripped jeans. The other kid, Miles, was a complete dork, all blond curls and big glasses. At eleven years old, he was four years younger than Liam and barely spoke a word to him. Miles irritated him on sight.

Although the house had five bedrooms, one was used as a study, while another had been converted into a gym. That meant Liam had to bunk in with Miles, much to his annoyance.

He had laid in bed that first night, listening to Miles each time he puffed on his inhaler and wondering why his mother preferred these kids to him and what it was he had done wrong for her to reject him.

Okay, she was making out now that she wanted him in her life, but he wasn't stupid. He had seen how she had acted around Jill and Miles, simpering after them.

The weekend passed by painfully slowly. Jill and Miles had asked Liam if he wanted to hang out with them and their friends, but honestly, Liam could think of nothing worse than playing with a bunch of thirteen-year-olds. Instead he stuck close to the house, making painful conversation with his mother and Grant. He was made to help Grant paint the garden fence, then had to endure a visit from his mother's friend, a woman called Kathy Finch, and her daughter, Nicola.

Nicola was about Liam's age and looked as thrilled to be there as he did, perched awkwardly on the sofa beside her mother, sipping at a cup of tea as the two older women gossiped and tried to outbrag each other.

At first, Liam thought Nicola was another dork like Miles, but then she caught his eye, rolling her own in mock amusement as the conversation dragged on and he had to stifle a grin. The rest of the visit was made more bearable as the pair of them pulled grimacing faces and tried to make each other laugh behind their mothers' backs.

It was as Nicola and Kathy were leaving that Jill and Miles returned home, their friends in tow.

They were all girls, he noted. Probably all Jill's friends, which suggested Miles hung around with them by default. Did he not have any friends of his own?

One girl, her hair tied back in a blonde ponytail, kept glancing shyly in his direction. She was taller than her friends and pretty too. Not that he was interested in thirteen-year-olds. It did have him wondering if he should have accepted the offer to hang out with them, however. He wasn't sure if he could stomach another day stuck with his mother and Grant.

Later that night, as they were getting ready for bed, he tried talking to Miles. It was difficult feigning an interest while trying not to come across as too keen.

'So what is there to do around here?'

When Miles shrugged and muttered that there wasn't much, he pushed a little harder.

'You were out with your friends all day. You must do something.'

'We just hang out. We ride around on our bikes and go the woods or the railway bridge.'

'Is it just girls?'

The younger boy nodded, blushing. 'Yeah, but they're cool girls. Especially Tash. She's good at building dens and she says her mum and dad are going to buy her a BMX so she can do jumps. She's pretty cool.'

'Tash? Was she the blonde one with the ponytail?'

Smoothly done, Liam.

He gave himself a mental pat on the back.

'No, Tash has short hair. The blonde one is Hannah. She is nice too.'

Hannah. Liam considered her name as he climbed into bed. It suited her.

Across the room, Miles was taking off his glasses. He folded them up carefully and put them on the bedside table.

'How come you hang out with your sister's friends and not your own?'

If he was offended by the question, Miles didn't show it, but he did drop his head in shame. 'I don't have any.'

'Friends? Why not?'

'We only moved here recently and the other boys make fun of me.'

Liam rested his head back on the pillow as he considered that. He had been jealous of Jill and Miles for so long, he had never considered that their lives might be anything short of perfect. He had always had friends. A tight group who had been his saving grace after his mother had left. He couldn't imagine not having any.

While he still thought Miles was a dorky little kid, he couldn't help but thaw towards him a little.

The conversation continued long after they had turned the light out, Miles telling him about his life back home in Florida. His mother had passed away and he really missed her; he had struggled to cope with the big changes in his life.

Liam realised they had common ground after all and he started to feel sorry for Miles when he spoke about how difficult he had found it adjusting to life in a new country. Smaller than the other kids, they tended to tease him over his accent and his glasses, calling him names and whispering behind his back. He was too shy to retaliate, which only seemed to make it worse.

Liam had really wanted to hate the kid, but now knowing the challenges Miles had faced, it played on his mind much of the night.

The following day, he had a proposal for the younger kid.

Instead of hanging out with the girls. Miles could show Liam around the village and they could go to all of the places Miles was afraid to go, scared he would run into the bullies.

Liam didn't relish spending the day babysitting an eleven-year-old, and it would mean foregoing his chance to get to speak to Hannah, but the kid deserved a break. He found himself wanting to do this one little thing for him.

They actually ended up having a lot of fun. It was a warm day and they explored the woods, swam in the river, Liam introduced Miles to British football, and Miles in turn told him all about what it was like at Disney World.

On the way back into the village, they stopped at the garage and Liam went inside for cold cans of Coke. As he was paying, he glanced out of the window and spotted a group of boys surrounding Miles. Anger surged inside him as one of the boys knocked Miles's inhaler to the ground.

'Are you ready to go, Miles?' he asked, leaving the garage shop.

All eyes looked in his direction. Miles's were wide and fearful behind his glasses, while the four boys surrounding him looked a little unsure, though made no attempt to move.

Liam wasn't afraid of them. They were all at least a year or two younger than he was.

He strode over to the group, casting his gaze over each of them, a disdainful sneer on his face.

'Who are you?' the one who was standing directly in front of Miles asked. He was an overweight kid with a skinhead and although he had gone for bolshy, Liam could hear the hesitancy in his tone.

'Liam's my stepbrother.' Miles sounded proud, a grin spreading across his face. 'And he does karate.'

What? Where had that come from? Liam had told Miles he would like to learn karate, but he had never actually done it. And stepbrother? He had never thought about it like that, but yes, he supposed he was.

He realised what Miles was trying to do and it seemed to work, the fat kid backing off a bit.

'You really this squirt's brother?'

Liam nodded and took a step towards him. 'I am. He tells me you've been picking on him.'

Now all four of the bullies looked worried.

'Come on, George, we should go,' the one at the back said.

'Look, mate. We don't want any trouble,' George agreed.

'Is that why you were all standing here surrounding him?' he asked, warming to this new, still unfamiliar, role.

'We were just talking.'

'It didn't look like it.'

'We're gonna go now. Like I just said, we don't want any trouble.'

'Wait!' Liam told them as they started to walk away. 'You never apologised.'

'For what?'

'For calling Miles a squirt.'

'I...' George looked at his mates. 'It was just teasing. Just a silly nickname.'

'You should apologise.'

'What? Don't be silly.'

'Do you want me to come after you and make you?'

It was a threat he hadn't really thought through, but George looked worried now. He shook his head.

'Then apologise.'

It took a moment, the apology seeming to catch in his throat as he kicked at the ground, unable to look at Miles. 'Look, mate. I'm sorry. No hard feelings, all right?'

'And pick up his inhaler. Give it back to him.'

Again a pause before George did as asked, his cheeks flaming. Then he and his friends scarpered.

Miles's expression was pure glee. 'That was awesome. So, so cool.'

Liam shrugged as it was no big deal, but inside he was buzzing. Helping this little kid, making him smile like this, it gave him a real kick. He tried on the stepbrother tag again, found he liked it. He had a little brother.

Relations with his mother were still frosty, but he had found a positive in the situation: Miles. And before he left that weekend, he promised the kid he would be back again and he would make sure the bullies stopped harassing him for good.

It was a promise he never got to keep, as by the end of that summer, Miles was dead.

55

'What the hell difference does it make if Miles was my stepbrother? It's nobody's bloody business.'

'Yes, it is, because it means it's personal,' Rosie fumed. 'And I bet you never told Hannah about the connection.'

'No, I didn't, because it's irrelevant.'

'I bet she doesn't see it that way?'

'Doesn't? So you've told her then?' Liam was furious. What the fuck kind of right did Josh Cole and Rosie Emerson have, poking into his life, then going to Hannah behind his back?

It had been bothering him that Hannah might have worked out who he was. He didn't want anyone knowing of his connection to this story. If it became about him, then it made everything messy. This was for Miles. It was the story Liam had always wanted to tell.

He had feared that Nicola Finch might have figured it out. She had recognised him last night, though fortunately couldn't quite place how she knew him. A lot of years had passed since that day they had been forced to endure afternoon tea with their mothers and he had never returned to Hixton as a child.

Rosie seemed a little taken aback by the anger in his words.

'Josh told her. And rightly so. He's just looking out for her. Unlike you.'

'You don't know anything about me.'

'I know I don't trust you!'

'Why's that, Rosie? Because you're jealous?'

His gibe hit close to the mark because her pretty face flushed with rage.

'What the hell is that supposed to mean?'

'It means you like having Hannah as your crutch, to pick up the pieces each time you fuck your life up. It's all about the Rosie show, isn't it? God forbid Hannah dare have a life of her own.'

He was perhaps being a little too blunt, but damn it, she had made him so angry. Not just because of the snooping, but because she had turned Hannah against him. That bothered him more than he cared to admit.

He had tried his best not to mislead Hannah, knowing he would be walking out of her life eventually and hoping they could part on good terms, but Rosie had destroyed that.

And besides, everything he was saying, it was all true. Yes, she might care about Hannah, but over the years Rosie had begun to manipulate their friendship. Was she really so wrapped up in herself that she couldn't see that?

She looked furious and he actually thought for a moment that she was going to fly for him, but then she shocked him, her face crumpling as she burst into tears.

Fuck! Liam hadn't expected this reaction.

He had mothers and a sister, plus a string of ex-girlfriends he'd had to let down gently over the years, so he had plenty of experience with tears. Problem was, he didn't really have the time or the inclination to comfort Rosie. This was just another one of her games, wasn't it?

But then she sank down onto the sofa, shaking her head as she swiped them away.

'I love Hannah. She's so important to me. She's my best friend. I don't mean to use her.'

Was that an admission? He let her continue.

'She's the only one who completely gets me, who understands why sometimes I react the way I do. I guess I get so wrapped up with it all, I forget she deserves a life too. I want her to be happy. I really do.'

'Then we have a common goal,' Liam told her, his tone softening. 'Because I want her to be happy too.'

Rosie studied him carefully. She seemed much calmer now. Rational.

'Do you love her?'

'I care about her a lot.' It was the best he could offer. He wasn't going to lie to Rosie, not at this point. 'Hannah knows the score. I'm here to write a story, but I made a friend along the way. At least I had made a friend.'

The barb hit and he saw Rosie wince.

'So you're *just* friends then?'

Liam nodded.

Not quite the truth. What he felt for Hannah ran much deeper. It couldn't go anywhere, though, so there was no point in saying it out loud, but two of her friends were dead and he planned on sticking around at least until he knew she was safe.

He reached for his keys. 'Look. I hate to be a dick, Rosie, but you have to leave now. I need to go and try to fix this.'

She looked up and there was a flash of something in her dark eyes. At first, he thought it was temper, but then he realised it was fear.

Not of him. At least he hoped it wasn't. But of losing Hannah.

He had a huge amount of sympathy for everything Rosie

Emerson had gone through as a child, but it was time for her to let it go.

That's when she surprised him for the second time since showing up at his door, nodding as she got up from the sofa. 'Okay. I want to come with you.'

56

She recognises me the second she sees me and the fear in her eyes as they widen is everything I have dreamt of.

I had hoped to toy with her for much longer, but my plans have been forced to change. Hannah is dessert and if everything has to end today, there is no way I am leaving without my dessert.

This moment is finally happening and she is reacting exactly how I want her to.

'Bill?'

She looks so shocked to see me, for a moment I don't think she can move. She recovers quickly though, running back into her flat and, turning, she tries to slam the door in my face. I am quicker than her, my foot already moving to block the door and my fist shooting out, connecting with her jaw. It makes her teeth snap together in a satisfying crunch that sends her flying backwards, landing in a heap on the floor.

Have I hurt her? I fucking hope so.

There will be no subtlety where Hannah is concerned. I intend to experience every moment of her fear and of her pain. This bitch was the catalyst for it all and she has a lot to pay for. She humiliated me and destroyed my childhood, and still it seems that isn't enough for her.

After Mum's incarceration, I tried to follow the right path, to keep the fantasy of this moment in my head, staying away from Hannah and her friends. Even though the anger and resentment has always bubbled away, I worked hard to move on.

But then I understood it wasn't over. That even though Mum has been released from prison, those who judge her will never forgive. And she has been so disappointed that I haven't exacted revenge on her behalf. She had dropped hints when I had visited her, but now she was out, she made it clear she expected my help.

It was unfair, she told me, that the Hixton Five got to go on leading normal happy lives while hers was in ruins.

I was already getting twitchy, hating that I had disappointed her, when Hannah sent that writer friend of hers to harass us, trying to dredge up the past. It was lucky I had followed Liam Quinn back to Norfolk, otherwise I wouldn't have realised her involvement.

I was planning on giving him a warning to stay the hell away from Mum and was shocked when I realised he was cosy with Hannah Freemont, or Cole as the bitch is now known. I have been keeping tabs on the pair of them, following Hannah, understanding that she is involved with Quinn, and seething as I realise she can't let it drop. That she will never leave it alone.

And little Rosie Emerson. I saw her too. Understood she was probably scheming with them.

I knew I had to show them. If they wanted to go down this route, I could play games too.

The problem is the more I have played, the more obsessed I have become with Hannah again.

She was gangly and self-conscious as a kid, but I have always been drawn to her. Adulthood has smoothed out the awkwardness of adolescence and although she is still guarded and definitely more jaded, she has blossomed, filling out curves, her breasts still pert and perky, and her eyes that startling jewel green that sucks the breath right out of me even though I want to throttle her. I think back to that afternoon in the barn, when I bullied her into dropping her pants. The memory never fails to make me hard. And now I have her again.

Quinn is a lucky bastard. Or should I rephrase that as 'was' a lucky bastard. Because he won't be getting her back. Hannah has interfered one too many times and her actions have consequences. I will have my fun with her, because after everything she has put me through, everything she has taken from me, I deserve that at the very least, but she won't be walking away from this. I will make certain of that.

By the time I am finished with her, she will never be able to stick her meddling nose in anyone's business ever again.

I slam the door shut, then grabbing a fistful of her hair, I yank her backwards, knocking her off balance again. As she lands on her bum, I start dragging her by her hair towards her bedroom.

I have already familiarised myself with the layout of her flat during a previous visit while she was staying the night at Quinn's, aware after my visit to Lauren Bell's house that pre-planning leads to less fuck-ups. I will not be denied this moment.

I know where everything is and that she has no neighbours on this level, the attic space split between her flat and a maintenance room where I was hiding until the moment I took her by surprise. I also know that the flats on the floor below her are empty. One resident on holiday, the other property currently up for rent.

Hannah has spent the weekend with Quinn in Hixton and she has dropped him off at the house he is renting. She is all alone, which means I can take my time. Savour it.

She is screaming and yelling at me now, her initial shock giving way to panic, and she is trying to free her hair from my grip. I need to get her subdued and quickly.

Into the bedroom and onto the bed, dropping the bag I have brought onto the mattress. I climb on top of her, trying to keep her still with one hand, while the other rummages inside the bag for my rope.

The bitch is going nuts now, kicking and squealing as she tries to fight me off. Her knees are hitting into my back and she manages to pull one of her arms free. It is like wrestling a bloody octopus and despite all of my planning, I am wondering if I have underestimated her.

She is stronger than she looks, her free hand now on my face, pushing and poking, making it difficult for me to concentrate.

'Will you just calm the fuck down?'

It is probably a stupid thing to say because we are on her bed, which means she knows exactly what I am planning to do to her. I am angry and not thinking straight, especially when she manages to sink her teeth into my arm. The pain has me screaming and, without thinking, I release her other wrist as I try to pull my arm free from her mouth.

Somehow that gives her the momentum, because suddenly she is shoving at me and I am falling backwards. I land with a thump on the floor, take a moment to gather myself.

By the time I am back on my feet, Hannah has bolted.

57

Hannah was barely a second ahead of him and knew what he planned to do to her if he caught her again, so she didn't allow herself time to consider how wrong she had been about Liam, jumping to conclusions over a cryptic voicemail and a similar name.

There had been no mistaking Bill Wickham when she had seen him. Over twenty years had passed but she had recognised him straight away. She was no longer a vulnerable little girl, but she also understood that he was bigger than her and physically stronger. She had to get away.

As she fumbled with the front door, his arm clamped around her, squeezing and lifting her off the ground.

Hannah kicked out, heard a grunt as she caught bone. She struggled frantically, using her elbows, head, and legs. Any part of her that he didn't have hold of. As her skull smacked back against his face, she heard a crack, followed by a string of expletives, and she tried to ignore the stab of pain in her head. She stepped hard on his foot, thrashing against him, and finally succeeding in getting him to loosen his grip.

Running into the kitchen, she grabbed the frying pan from the hob, smacking it clean into his face. He stumbled, but it wasn't hard enough to stun him or knock him out, and he now looked mad as hell.

'You fucking bitch!'

He rushed at her before she could react, punching her hard in the stomach, and Hannah doubled over in agony, heaving and gasping for breath, as her diaphragm spasmed violently.

'Not quite so smart now, are you?'

He dragged her up by her hair, pressing her against the wall, and as she cried out in pain, she realised just how much trouble she was in.

'I've been looking forward to getting my hands on you, so how about we have ourselves some fun?'

She didn't even see his fist the next time, but heard the sickening crack as it landed against her nose, then felt the burning pain. Moments later, her world turned black.

* * *

She had probably only been unconscious for a couple of minutes, if that, and the first thing she was aware of was the pain. Her head and face throbbed and an intense searing sensation was cramping her stomach. She could taste something metallic. Was it blood? And there was a horrible whimpering sound. It took her a moment to realise it was coming from her.

All she wanted to do was curl up in a ball, but something heavy was pinning her down.

Where was she?

She forced her eyes open. They were watering badly and she struggled to see through the blur. Blinking, she tried to clear them, and as she did, the fog lifted.

Bill.

She could see him now, realised she was on her bed, flat on her back, and that he was sitting on top of her. He was leaning forward so she only had a view of his torso and for a moment she wondered what he was doing. Then she realised she couldn't move her hands. Her arms were pulled above her head, rope tightening around her wrists as he lashed them to the headboard.

Panic kicked in and she started thrashing beneath him. He held her down easily, appearing amused at her efforts.

'Glad to see you're awake. I don't want you to miss any of this.'

This couldn't be happening.

A fresh wave of cramps hit, turning to nausea. She needed to sit up, needed to get to the bathroom, but the rope and his weight on top of her prevented her from doing so.

'Please... I'm going to be sick.'

His face was close to hers now, his hot putrid breath intensifying her need to vomit.

'Did you ever show any mercy to my mother? No, you didn't. So why the fuck should I show any to you? She served her time, but you just couldn't leave her be.'

What?

'All she wanted was to live the rest of her life out in peace. You had to keep at her though. Pick, pick, pick.'

'I don't know what... I don't know what you mean.'

A hard slap across her cheek distracted her momentarily from her cramping belly.

'Liar! Do you think I'm bloody stupid? I know exactly what you and your boyfriend have been up to.'

Who was he talking about? Did he mean Liam?

His weight shifted as he climbed off the bed and she watched as he left the room without saying another word.

Groaning in pain, she tried to turn onto her side, pulling her knees up into a foetal position. She needed the cramps to subside so she could think straight, because right now she didn't understand what she was supposed to have done. She hadn't seen Mrs W since her release.

Was he upset because they had gone back to the farm? How did he even know about that? Had he followed them? It just didn't make sense. It didn't give him a reason to attack her, and it didn't explain why he had gone after Jill or Lauren.

Oh God. Jill and Lauren. They were both dead, and now he was going to kill her too.

She yanked hard on the rope, pulling herself closer to the headboard so her fingers could reach the knots. She had to get free.

Twisting her face into her arm, she tried to clear her eyes so she could focus. Her head was thumping, her nose throbbing from where he had punched her, and her gut painfully sore. She tried to swallow, her mouth dry and what little saliva she had was tinged with the taste of blood.

Her hands shook as she worked at the knots and she ordered herself to focus. It was going to get a whole lot worse if she didn't get free. Her fingers were trembling badly and she kept losing her grip.

'Would this help?'

Hannah jumped at the voice. She hadn't heard Bill come back into the room.

She stilled when she saw the knife he was holding out to her. It was one from the drawer in the kitchen and she knew how sharp it was.

'Please, no.' She tried to scoot across the bed as he approached, a sob escaping. She knew he was enjoying her fear and she shouldn't give it to him, but she couldn't help it. She was so frightened.

Maybe he just had the knife to scare her. If that was the case, it was working.

She watched him carefully as he put the blade down on the bedside table. What was he going to do to her?

Reasoning with him didn't seem to work, but if she could get him talking somehow, keep his attention from using the knife, she might be able to buy herself some time. She scrambled her brain for something to say.

'Why Jill and Lauren? What did they do to you?'

Perhaps not the best question to ask, given that they were both dead, but she had panicked and was still struggling to think clearly.

It was a valid question, though. Yes, both girls had been part of the Hixton Five and they had spoken with the police, but they had never suffered like the rest of them.

She saw the frown pass over his face. 'I know what you're doing.'

'I'm not trying to do anything, I swear.'

'You're trying to confuse me and distract me. Your games aren't going to work this time, Hannah.' He gave a humourless laugh. 'I've got you exactly where I want you. Remember that day out in the barn?' He leered at her. 'We can finish what we started. No one is here to stop us this time.'

Shit.

She reached again for the knot, but then he had hold of her ankles and was yanking her down the bed, and she cried out in pain as her arms were stretched above her.

He was back on top of her now and she bucked and writhed, trying to throw him off, screaming again when she felt his fingers unbuttoning her jeans.

'No, please.'

Her heart was thumping as she fought against him. She would not make this easy for him.

He tried to hold her down, breathing heavily and cursing her, as he warned her to stay still.

Suddenly there was a thwack and she saw his eyes go wide. One moment he was looking down at her, his expression stunned, the next he had collapsed on top of her.

Behind him stood Rosie with Hannah's heavy frying pan in her hand, the one Hannah had dropped, and she continued to smack it hard against Bill's head, even after he had fallen.

'Get off of her! Leave her alone.'

'Rosie?'

Thwack, thwack, thwack.

With each hit, Bill's face mashed against Hannah's breasts.

'Rosie. He's unconscious. Can you please get him off me and untie me?'

Rosie wasn't listening. Her sole focus on Bill.

Thwack, thwack, thwack.

'Rosie! Please stop.' Hannah was crying now. She just wanted this to be over.

Thwack, thwack, thwack.

Why wasn't she listening to her?

'Rosie!' Another voice.

Hannah saw Liam enter the room, his eyes widening as he took in the scene before him.

He rushed over to the bed, one arm wrapping around Rosie, his free hand catching hold of hers and easing the pan from her grip. 'It's okay. You got him,' he told her, easing her back.

'He was attacking Hannah. I had to stop him.' Rosie seemed dazed,

'You did. He won't hurt her again.'

'I'm okay, Rosie,' Hannah assured her. It was a lie. She felt anything but okay and was struggling to hold herself together.

'We need to call the police, and an ambulance. Can you do that for me?' Liam was easing Rosie onto the stool in front of the dressing table now.

She nodded compliantly, taking his phone, and he watched her just long enough to make sure she was calling the number before going back to Hannah. He pushed Bill off the bed, before using the kitchen knife to slice through the rope binding her wrists.

Hannah tried to roll over, crying out in pain.

'He did this to you.' Liam's face was dark with rage, his tone fierce, and for a moment Hannah thought he was going to pick up the frying pan and take over where Rosie had left off.

'I'll be okay. It just... it hurts.' She winced as she tried to sit up.

'Try not to move too much, okay? Here, I've got you.'

He slipped his arms carefully around her and Hannah eased into his embrace. Resting her head against his shoulder, she wept.

58

The next few days were a competition. Liam versus Rosie.

The uneasy truce they had formed still held, but they were definitely in a game against one another, and Hannah was the prize, both of them vying for her attention.

Part of her wanted to be annoyed with them, but they were taking care of her, and if she was completely honest, she needed to lean on them right now.

Initially she had been embarrassed, aware she had let her guard down and they had seen her vulnerability. Hannah had always been the tough one, the one who supported others, but Bill Wickham had exposed the chink in her armour.

He had reminded her of how it felt to be afraid, to be weak, and in doing so had stolen her confidence. His attack had proven that it was always possible for the monster to get to her and she was painfully aware that if Rosie and Liam hadn't shown up when they did, she would most likely be dead.

Instead, she had walked away with bruised ribs, two black eyes and a sore and bloody nose.

The wounds Bill had inflicted would in time heal, but Hannah feared the trauma of his attack would linger. It had been five days and she was terrified of being alone in her flat, and an anxious mess on the occasions she dared to venture out.

She would get over it, she was determined to, but it would take time.

Just as it would take time to adjust to the truth about Liam.

He had lied to her.

Josh had warned her that Liam wasn't who he said he was, and she had jumped to all kinds of conclusions, but never would she have guessed the truth.

She had asked him if this story was personal to him and he had said no, failing to mention his connection to Jill and Miles.

Would it have made a difference if he had introduced himself as their stepbrother? Would she have talked to him about the past, let him into her home and her bed?

Honestly? The answer was probably yes. If anything, she would have felt more empathy towards him, knowing he had wanted to tell the story of a sweet and often lonely little boy, who had met such a terrible end. It bothered her that he hadn't trusted her with his secret and it was one more shock to deal with.

When Liam had first confessed who he was, she had asked him to leave, and to be fair he had, but only for an hour or so. The stubborn man had returned with his dog and an overnight bag, promising he would stay out of her way, but insisting on being close by in case she needed him.

Perhaps Hannah should have told him no, but truth was, it was comforting knowing he was in the next room and it made her feel safer. He had started out on the sofa, but her nightmares had brought him into her bed on the second night, and now they didn't bother with the pretence. It wasn't about sex – she was still too sore and traumatised for that. It was just about comfort. Besides, she was still learning to forgive him and didn't know what the future held for them.

He hadn't made any further comments about leaving Wells. Hannah guessed it would happen eventually, but for now they seemed to live from day to day. Anything further into the future was too far off to worry about.

While he took nights, Rosie insisted on being there for the days. Her frenzied attack on Bill had been a shock to Hannah at the time and as a result, the police had been interested in talking to her, but they had quickly agreed that years of pent-up frustration at the Wickhams had taken their toll.

Hannah was the most important person in Rosie's life and seeing Bill hurting her friend had triggered something in her brain. She was remorseful for the intensity of the attack, but defiant that Bill had deserved it.

As for Bill. He was still unconscious in hospital. The police were hopeful he would recover, knowing he was a vital link to telling them where Mrs W was. She hadn't been seen now in over two weeks. Given that Bill himself had been fairly elusive before attacking Hannah, it was assumed he had been with his mother.

They were also keen to speak with him about the murder of Lauren Bell. An eyewitness having placed him at the scene.

Both Lauren's and Jill's deaths were something that seemed to bother Liam.

'His pattern with you was so completely different.'

They were in bed and facing each other, deep in conversation, which seemed to be a routine over the last few nights. Hannah seeking comfort in talking until she fell asleep.

'You mean compared to how he killed Jill and Lauren?'

'Yeah. Jill fell, or was pushed, down the stairs and Lauren was suffocated. There was nothing to suggest he tortured them beforehand. Why suddenly change things for you? You saw what was in his bag.'

'I did and can we not talk about it please?' Hannah shuddered, remembering.

Rosie had peeked inside the bag before the police arrived and it was clear Bill had come prepared for a long night. Just the thought of what he had planned to do to her before ending her life made her want to throw up.

'I'm sorry.' Liam ran his fingertips up and down her arm in a soothing gesture. 'He can't hurt you now, remember that. If he does wake up, the police have him on attempted murder, and two other counts of murder potentially. He'll be looking at a prison sentence.'

Hannah did know that, but it brought little comfort. Bill had killed two of her friends. She knew Jill's death had been caused by him, even if the police couldn't prove it. And the timing of Bill's attacks, coinciding with Mrs W's release and disappearance, suggested that she was involved too.

Bill would go to prison, but what about his mother?

Would Hannah and Rosie and Tash always be looking over their shoulder?

59

Liam had dropped the subject of the differing patterns, but it continued to play on his mind.

Two days later, Bill woke up and when questioned, he took everyone by surprise, confessing to the attack on Hannah, but claiming he didn't know where his mother was and insisting he had nothing to do with what had happened to Lauren or Jill.

An eyewitness had put him at Lauren's home in the early hours of the morning after her murder and he was charged, but still it bothered Liam. Bill had confessed to stalking Hannah and Rosie, so why so vehemently deny being involved in Lauren and Jill's deaths?

As Hannah pointed out, the charge he was admitting to was attempted murder, whereas if he confessed to the others, it would mean a more severe sentence, but even still, Liam's gut told him something was off and he had learnt to trust it over the years. That was why he decided to head south and do a bit of investigating himself. He was going to have to do it at some point for the book. He was just escalating the timeline.

Deciding it was best if Hannah didn't know anything about the trip, he came up with the ruse of having to go see his mother. Von

Goldberg lived just a short distance from Jill, but he had no intention of calling in to see her. This visit was all about keeping Hannah safe.

He still hadn't addressed his feelings for her and how they had changed since her attack. He wasn't a person who committed. Hell, he was happy with his nomadic lifestyle, just him and Tank, plus he had only known her for a few weeks. That was way too soon to develop real feelings for someone, and certainly too early to decide whether they played an important role in your life.

On the other hand, there was no getting away from the fact that Hannah would be dead if he and Rosie hadn't shown up at her flat, and his head was a little fucked up from trying to deal with that. If the worst-case scenario had happened and he had lost her, he wasn't quite sure how he would have handled it. And that scared the hell out of him.

Unsure how to proceed and unwilling to leave her alone for any length of time, fearful something could happen again, he had stuck close, convincing himself that she needed him, all of the while denying the fact that he needed her right back.

He and Rosie had settled into an uneasy alliance, both sharing a common goal: help Hannah get over what had happened. That was why he went to Rosie now. If he needed to disappear overnight, then Rosie would have to stay with Hannah. She was the only one he trusted. Well, Rosie and Josh. Liam knew the ex-husband meant well, but he hadn't yet quite forgiven him for digging into his past.

As he suspected, Rosie was more than willing to take over the night shift. Liam had seen a different side to Hannah following the attack. A vulnerability that either hadn't been there before or that she had kept well hidden, and he didn't want to leave her alone.

'I can stay for a few days if you like. Give you a break.'

'Just Saturday night is fine. I'll be back on Sunday.'

'Well, the offer is there. I'm sure your mum will be pleased to see you.'

Liam hadn't told her where he was really going. He might trust her to look after Hannah, but he was quite aware she would still like to get him out of the picture. If he told Rosie the truth, he suspected she would intentionally let it slip.

The less the pair of them knew, the better.

He left Saturday morning, once Rosie had arrived.

'Are you sure you're going to be okay?' he asked Hannah as they said goodbye.

'I'll be fine,' Hannah's tone was casual as she slipped into his arms, but he knew it was early days. Her physical injuries were only just beginning to heal. And she might make jokes about having panda eyes, but he knew the mental scars ran deep.

Anger still choked him whenever he thought about how Bill Wickham had hurt her and he understood Rosie's frenzied attack. Had he been the one with the frying pan, Wickham would probably be dead now.

He held Hannah close, careful not to hurt her ribs, and breathed in the scent of her shampoo. He could feel the tension in her body as she hugged him back, and knew she was reluctant to let go.

Eventually, she eased away, forcing a bright smile.

'Go!' she told him.

Tank was staying with them. He wasn't a guard dog by any stretch, but he would be a comforting presence for Hannah and a deterrent to anyone who might try to harm her.

As Liam left her flat, he quashed down his guilt at leaving her and decided on a plan of action. He was going to Jill and Lauren's hometowns to satisfy his own curiosity and to try to find answers, but it would be a flying visit as he was anxious not to leave Hannah for too long.

Croydon was the sensible place to start. His stepsister had been the first to die.

He had never been close to Jill. In fact, he had barely known her. That weekend he had visited Hixton, she hadn't paid him much attention, too busy wrapped up in her friends. And after Miles had died, Liam had seen her at the funeral, but then his mother had pushed him away again. He had never really had the opportunity to get to know her properly.

He met her husband, Adrian, a few days after Jill's body had been found. Veronica had been hysterical at the news, even though she and Jill barely spoke these days, and Liam had been left with no choice but to go to her. They had both been at Adrian and Jill's house in Croydon when Lauren Bell had shown up to pay her condolences and for a brief moment, Liam had wondered if he had slipped up. Had Hannah mentioned him to Lauren at all?

Thankfully, she hadn't reacted when Adrian introduced them.

At least he had an opening in Croydon. Adrian knew him, so would talk to him. Lauren would be trickier, as he had no connection to anyone in Sevenoaks, but he would figure it out. He had always been good at getting answers out of people.

Giving one final glance up at Hannah's flat, telling himself she would be okay, he climbed into his car. Time to try to figure out what the hell was going on.

60

When she thought about how close she had come to losing Hannah, it made Rosie hyperventilate. The idea of what would have happened if she and Liam hadn't shown up scared the shit out of her and it had been such a shock to the system, it had her reassessing everything.

Hannah had always been the strong one. The one Rosie could rely on. She was always there to pick up the pieces or bail Rosie out whenever anything went wrong.

Bill had broken her, though, and now their roles had reversed.

Liam Quinn was doing his bit, she guessed, although it irritated her how he had inserted himself into Hannah's life. Okay, so she and Liam had reached an agreement of sorts, but she was still annoyed at his deceitfulness. And, in her opinion, Hannah had forgiven him too easily.

In a way, she understood why she had. It was the trauma. It had made her weak. But Hannah didn't need him. He had deceived her once and he would do it again. It had always been Hannah and Rosie against the world. And Hannah would come to realise that it still was.

The danger was still out there. The police might have arrested Bill, but he hadn't confessed to where his mother was, saying he didn't know. He was playing games with them. Of course he knew. Mrs W was behind all of this. Why else would Bill have waited until she was released from prison before waging his campaign of terror?

He wasn't telling them because Mrs W wanted to finish what he had started. There were three of them left and Tash, Rosie, and Hannah needed to watch their backs because Mrs W wasn't done with them by a long shot.

And it sounded mean, because Rosie was genuinely fond of her, but Tash was on her own now. Rosie wanted to help her, but she couldn't split herself in two. Besides, Tash had Sam. Right now, Rosie needed to look after herself and Hannah.

She glanced over at her best friend now, curled up on the sofa watching romcoms, Tank at her feet, and her heart swelled with love. Hannah was so important to her and Rosie would do anything to protect her. Had Liam not pulled her off Bill, she would have killed him, and perhaps, in truth, she wouldn't have regretted it.

It was a day of treats, Rosie had declared. A special day of all of Hannah's favourite things. The foods she liked, her choice of movies, plus some other goodies. Rosie had brought spa masks and her poshest bubble bath, plus two bottles of Hannah's favourite wine.

Her plan seemed to be working and Hannah actually looked relaxed for the first time since the attack. Every now and again, though, she would get this faraway look in her eyes and Rosie knew she was reliving it all.

She wanted so badly to ease her suffering, knowing exactly what the pain felt like. She had been living with her own for the last twenty years.

Hannah was a good person and she didn't deserve what had

happened to her. It was Rosie's job now to fix it and make sure Bill and Eileen Wickham could never hurt her again.

Rosie had noticed the change in Hannah's personality. She looked sad all the time and was reluctant to go to the Wickham farm, but Rosie was too young to really question why. She assumed Hannah was tiring of hanging out with them and even got a little snotty about it at one point. Was she finding them boring?

Mrs W was the coolest and she spoilt them rotten. Even Rosie's mum and dad were impressed with how she looked out for their daughter, which is why when they had to go away for the weekend for Rosie's great-aunt's birthday, she ended up staying at the farm.

Initially, she was supposed to go with her parents, but her aunt was turning eighty and Rosie couldn't think of anything more boring. She mentioned it in conversation to Mrs W one day and was excited when the woman offered to look after her.

The Emersons said no at first. Rosie was to go with them, but she begged and pleaded, eventually guilting them into agreeing.

They were away for two nights and the first night's sleepover was so much fun. Rosie had never been at the farm without the others, but she didn't really miss them, lapping up the attention as Mrs W spoilt her rotten, brushing her hair, allowing her to play with her music box and letting her have all of her favourite food treats. She helped Mrs W feed the chickens, and even Bill, who could sometimes be a bit of a grump at times, was okay to her, agreeing – at his mother's request – to take Rosie for a ride on his quadbike around the farm. Rosie decided this was the best weekend ever, and when she saw Miles the following day, she told him all about it, keen to brag about how cool it was.

As she expected, he was green with envy.

'I wish I could stay over. My dad's away with Jill and I'm stuck at home with the step-monster.' He pulled a yuck face. 'I bet she'll make me go to bed early because she has her friends coming over for some make-up party.'

'That's rubbish.'

'I know. It sucks. You're so lucky. Mrs W is really nice.'

Rosie had an idea. 'Why don't you stay over too?'

Mile's eyes widened behind his glasses, but then his shoulders slumped. 'She might not want me to. My dad says it's rude to impose.'

'We could ask her. I bet your stepmother would agree so she can have the house to herself.'

'Do you think we should?'

'I'll do it.'

Rosie knew she was Mrs W's favourite, so she had no issue with asking the question.

Mrs W pulled a face as though considering it, but it didn't take much to get her to agree.

Once Miles had the go-ahead, they cycled over to his house and put the idea to Veronica, who, as Rosie suspected, was on board straightaway. She didn't even seem that bothered about where Miles was staying, more interested in rearranging furniture for her party guests.

Rosie helped Miles pack an overnight bag and they headed back up to the farmhouse.

This was going to be so much fun.

* * *

Mrs W put Miles in the bedroom next to Rosie, which was just across the landing from her own room, but after dinner, instead of letting them stay up late as she had done with Rosie the previous night, she insisted they go to bed early.

Rosie had been so disappointed and argued a little, but Mrs W was firm in her decision.

It wasn't until she looked back through adult eyes that she realised how different things had been that second night. Mrs W had still been friendly, but there had been shared glances with Bill, like they were keeping a secret, and she kept reminding Rosie and Miles to respect her rules.

What rules? There had been no warnings the previous night and Mrs W was far too cool for rules.

After telling them to go straight to sleep, she had pulled Rosie to one side.

'You know, part of the fun of a sleepover, is trying to sneak around without getting caught by the adults. But you're not going to do that, are you, Rosie?' She had winked then, her face breaking into a grin, and Rosie realised she was joking. Mrs W was encouraging them to have fun.

That's what she told Miles when she snuck into his room ten minutes after the lights were turned out. She had Mrs W's music box with her, having been allowed to sleep with it in her room.

Miles sat up in bed, reaching for his glasses. 'Are you sure she won't mind? She told us to go to sleep. And she has been good to us.'

'Of course she won't. I promise, she wants us to have fun.'

'Well, if you're sure.' Miles didn't sound particularly sure, but he was much less confident than Rosie.

'I'm sure. I promise.'

Miles's eyes went bug wide the moment before Rosie heard the voice.

'What are you both doing?'

She spun around, caught off guard, having not heard the door open.

'Mrs W. I was just showing Miles the music box.'

'What did I tell you about going straight to sleep?'

It was a joke, right?

Rosie hesitated. Mrs W sounded angry and her face was stern. All red and scrunched up, like Mr Frost the maths teacher at school, when he caught someone talking in his class.

'GET BACK TO BED, NOW!'

Rosie was so shocked at the yelling, the music box slipped out of her hand, crashing to the floor.

For the longest moment, no one reacted. Miles frozen still, while Rosie and Mrs W stared at each other, Rosie trying to process what was happening. Was this part of a game?

Except Mrs W looked really, really cross. Like really mad cross, and for the first time since she had been coming to the farm, Rosie was scared.

Her chin wobbled and big fat tears spilled from her eyes. 'I'm sorry. It was an accident.'

Mrs W continued to stare at her, her expression mean, though she didn't react to Rosie's apology. Instead, she called for Bill. 'Can you come here, please?'

Moments later, he wandered into the room, glancing briefly at Rosie and Miles, then at his mother. 'What's up?'

'We have two very naughty children here. They are going to need to be punished.'

Rosie gasped, her legs trembling in fear. 'I said I was sorry,' she mumbled, fresh tears rolling down her cheeks. Beside her, Miles started sobbing quietly.

Mrs W smiled at them both. It wasn't one of her friendly smiles though. It made her face look scary. 'You wait. I'm going to give you both something to cry about.'

* * *

The box was barely big enough for the two of them and Rosie screamed and sobbed as Bill and Mrs W forced her and Miles inside. They were out in the barn and she was terrified.

What was Mrs W going to do to them? She wanted her mum and dad. Wished she had never come to stay here.

Then the lid closed and they were trapped inside. Rosie was hysterical, begging to be let out, while Miles cried quietly. She banged on the plastic lid, looking at Mrs W, pleading with her and apologising again and again. She hadn't meant to break the rules. She had dropped the music box by accident.

Why were they in this box in the ground? Mrs W couldn't just leave them here.

'Bury them.'

At first, Rosie thought she had misheard. The plastic lid made it difficult to hear properly. But then the first shovelful of dirt landed on the box.

She screamed harder, clung on to Miles.

Soon they were completely in the dark and there was no light filtering through from the lantern Mrs W had brought into the barn with her.

Eventually, Rosie's voice was hoarse from the screaming and she sobbed along with Miles, who was gulping for air as he cried. Seconds ticked into minutes and although there was no way of telling how long they had been down there, minutes turned into hours.

What if she is going to leave us down here?

The thought filled Rosie with dread, had her crying out again.

Somehow they fell asleep, but the box was cramped and the air was stale and there didn't seem much of it. Rosie woke again and felt like she was suffocating.

'Miles?'

Her voice was croaky and she was desperate for water.

'Miles?'

She could feel him against her, and he was no longer trembling. He was really cold and when she found his hand, threaded her fingers through it, it was stiff and cool, and he didn't squeeze back. Was he still asleep?

She wanted him to wake up. Hated feeling all alone in this nightmare.

A fresh bout of tears hit. This had all been her fault. She had promised him it wouldn't matter if they broke Mrs W's rules.

'I'm sorry,' she whispered.

Her words seemed to suck up more of the air and it was already difficult to breathe, so she didn't speak again. Instead she lay in the box, clinging on to Miles's cold hand, growing more and more sleepy. When the darkness tried to pull her under, she didn't fight it.

* * *

She was still sleeping when the box was opened, didn't even realise she was outside and on the ground until she heard Mrs W and Bill talking. They sounded panicked and Rosie struggled to wake herself properly, surprised to see it was almost daylight. Her body shuddered as she recalled the events of the previous night. How Mrs W had turned nasty and locked her and Miles in the box.

Where was Miles?

She pulled herself to her feet, peered inside the doorway, looking over to where Mrs W and Bill stood over his body. He was completely still.

No, no, no. He was just sleeping, right?

But then she picked up on words of their conversation.

He's dead.

I only meant to scare them.

We can't explain this away like the pond.

The girl has seen.

We need to deal with her.

Rosie's hand went to her mouth to cover the scream that threatened to escape.

What were they going to do to her?

She backed away from the barn door, her eyes wide with terror, understanding that she needed to run and fast.

They never heard her go and she cut through the woods, scared in case they realised and came after her. The woods had plenty of places where she could hide.

Eventually, she made it back to the village and to Hannah's house, which was the closest. When Hannah opened the door, Rosie burst into tears.

It took forever to manage to calm herself down and explain what had happened. Hannah's face going from shocked to serious.

When she finally spoke, her tone was grave. 'We need to call the police.'

62

Miles had suffered an asthma attack. Rosie had found that out much later, just as she had learnt they weren't the only victims of the box. Hannah had been trapped in there too, when they had been on the camp night.

After the Wickhams were arrested, there was an air of shock reverberating around the village. This was a place where everyone knew each other and where it was safe to raise young families. Neighbours were friends and they could be trusted. Eileen Wickham had been trusted.

Journalists and television crews descended from all over the country and villagers who had lived in the area for years were suddenly regarding each other with wariness. Parents wanted to know where their children were at all times and everyone stayed away from the farmhouse.

Eventually, things quietened and a sense of normality returned, the newsmen and women drawn away by newer dramas, and the village closed ranks. Eileen and Bill were in custody now. Rosie had been too young to understand fully what that meant, but her parents promised her neither of them could harm her again. It wasn't easy though to forget or to feel safe.

The Goldbergs were barely seen, hiding away behind their big front wall. They put their house on the market just months after Miles's death.

When Rosie eventually returned to school, she was labelled 'the girl in the box' and she felt like a freak show, under the constant gaze of fellow pupils, some of them viewing her with open curiosity, while others whispered behind her back. Tash, Lauren and Hannah had stuck close by, but in truth, Hannah was the only one Rosie felt a true allegiance with. Only she understood how it felt to be trapped in the box.

The village was back in the limelight when Eileen Wickham went to trial. She had pleaded not guilty, but luckily the jury had decided she was. She was sent away to prison, while Bill had to spend time in a young offender's institute for his part in the crimes.

It was over. Rosie was told that repeatedly. But how could it be when she still woke up most nights screaming in terror at the nightmares, scared she was back in the makeshift coffin.

She struggled to accept Miles was gone and when she eventually did, the guilt overwhelmed her. She had been the one who had broken the rules and she had promised Miles it was okay to do so.

Years of therapy had followed. Had it helped? She wasn't sure. These days, she preferred to self-medicate. Pills, booze, sex. It worked for her and sod anyone who argued otherwise. They weren't her and they had no idea how it had felt being locked in a box and buried alive. To know she had clung on to a dead boy's hand, wondering if anyone was coming back for her.

The counsellors she had seen had encouraged her not to blame herself. Eileen Wickham was looking to find fault, wanting an excuse to use her crudely made coffin. It was easier said than done and Rosie couldn't help thinking that if she had made different choices that night, Miles might still be alive.

She thought about him often. Talked to him too. Telling him how sorry she was and begging for his forgiveness.

Rosie and Hannah had always been close, but that bond strengthened when they learnt they had both been through the same ordeal. They tried to deal with the trauma Mrs W had put them through by sticking together, and it was why Hannah would always be Rosie's best friend and why Rosie would do anything to protect her. They understood each other.

Mrs W was evil and so was her son. Rosie had already slipped up once, letting Bill get to Hannah. She wouldn't make the same mistake again.

As dusk settled, she moved to the living-room window to draw the curtains, taking a moment to survey the street below. Mrs W was out there somewhere and they couldn't afford to let their guard down.

Earlier, Rosie had persuaded Hannah to come with her as she took Tank for a walk. Although Hannah had been reluctant, the fresh air had done her good, her eyes hidden behind dark sunglasses to avoid unwelcome stares.

Now they were cocooned back inside the flat, the door bolted and the windows locked.

She would make Hannah her favourite dinner and open a bottle of the wine, and for a short while they could pretend that everything was okay, that they were safe.

* * *

Croydon had been a waste of time. Liam had called in on Adrian Peters, this time taking flowers and a condolence card. Adrian had seemed grateful for the company and the opportunity to talk about his late wife, and it had been easy to guide the questions and piece together what happened the day of Jill's death, which was unfortunately very little.

The last time anyone had seen her had been on the Tuesday afternoon. She had called in sick on the Wednesday, which was the day she had fallen or been pushed down the stairs.

Jill's death still wasn't being ruled as anything other than an accident, and sensing he was wasting his time, Liam had offered his sympathies to Adrian again, thanked him for the coffee, and decided to move on to Kent and the village where Lauren Bell had lived, just outside of the town of Sevenoaks.

It was still late afternoon and if he made progress with Lauren, he could hopefully be back in Norfolk early tomorrow.

As he suspected, her house was locked up, and knowing she didn't have any relatives or friends close by, he headed to the local pub, where he ordered a sandwich and a coffee, and got chatting with the barmaid and a couple of locals, working the conversation around to Lauren.

None of them knew her well, but they were all aware of her murder and were nosey enough to gossip.

'She never really came in here,' Robin, the barmaid, told him. 'Maybe on the odd occasion. She mostly kept to herself.'

'Lived in that cottage all alone. No husband or boyfriend,' the old, bearded chap, who was propping up the bar, chipped in. 'Never saw her with any friends. She didn't even have a dog.'

He seemed shocked by that and Liam glanced at the pretty spaniel on the floor beside him. The dog had been his way to get chatting to them. He had stopped to make a fuss of her and the conversation had moved on from there.

'That's not strictly true,' Robin pointed out. 'Young Andy who delivers for Tesco said she had company the day before it happened.'

Liam's ears pricked up. 'She did?'

'A woman was there when he dropped off her shopping. He remembers hearing them arguing.'

Liam's mind was racing. 'Did Andy give a description of this person?'

'You'd need to ask him that.'

'Do you know where I could find him?'

Robin looked at Liam. 'Are you a journalist or something?' she asked, her tone suddenly suspicious.

He held her gaze for a moment, sussing her out. 'Friend of the family,' he decided.

That was easier. He suspected the villagers would be wary of reporters.

She relaxed a little. 'You should have said. Andy will be working, but you might be able to speak with him. I think you'll be wasting your time. The police have already arrested the man who killed her.'

* * *

Forty minutes later, Liam was heading back to Croydon.

He had tracked Andy down, an eighteen-year-old who had been difficult to miss with his shock of bright red hair.

The kid had been more than happy to talk to him, especially when Liam discreetly slipped him twenty quid, and what he had to say turned out to be worth every penny.

Lauren hadn't been alone when her shopping had been delivered and she had been agitated. There was someone else in the house with her, though Andy only heard the woman's voice, never actually saw her.

Lauren and the mystery woman had been arguing when he was unloading the carts and it was clear she was trying to get her to leave.

'She didn't seem scared?' Liam had asked.

Andy had shaken his head. 'No, she wasn't afraid. More like angry. I did wonder if it was a lovers' tiff.'

'Was there a second car there?'

'No, just Miss Bell's.'

'Have you told the police about this?'

'I didn't think it was important. Should I?' Andy had looked worried. 'It was the evening before. Everyone knows that guy broke in during the night and killed her. That's right, isn't it?'

Liam had nodded, though didn't say anything to confirm or deny. Instead he'd thanked the kid and left.

On the way back to Adrian's, he called Hannah to check on her, a little irritated when Rosie answered her phone.

'Is everything okay?'

'We're having a great time,' Rosie told him smugly. 'This is exactly what Hannah needed. A girls' day.'

'Where is she? Can you put her on?'

'She's soaking in the tub. I ran her a bath with my favourite oil.'

'Nice.' Liam had tried for enthusiastic, but the word came out a little sarcastic. He wasn't really in the mood for discussing bubble bath with Rosie. 'So can I speak to her?'

'I'd rather not disturb her. She's relaxing while I cook dinner.'

Liam bit down on his irritation, reminded himself that Rosie was doing him a favour. 'Okay, well, will you ask her to call me please?'

'I can pass on a message.'

'There's no message. I'd just like to talk to her. Tell her to call me.'

He ended the call, a little annoyed.

Unsure if she would pass on the message, he decided he would leave it an hour and, if he hadn't heard from Hannah, he would try her again.

63

While she gave Hannah her alone time, Rosie busied herself in the kitchen. She had just finished tossing the salad when Tash rang.

'How's Hannah doing?'

'Better today,' Rosie told her. 'We had a pamper session and I'm cooking her dinner.'

'Is Liam not with her?'

'No, he's gone to see his mother.'

And even while he was away, he couldn't leave them alone. His phone call had annoyed her. This was Rosie's time with Hannah. Why couldn't he just piss off for a bit?

'Where are you both?' Tash wanted to know. 'Are you at Hannah's?'

'Yes, I'm staying with her tonight.'

'How about I come over? Sam is on nights.'

Rosie didn't like that idea and she tried to quash down the guilt, knowing Tash was in danger too. Yes, it was selfish, but she wanted to have Hannah to herself tonight.

'We're having dinner. And Hannah's really tired. She'll probably want to go to bed early.'

Again another silence.

'Okay,' Tash said eventually.

Was Rosie mistaken or did she sound put out?

She mused over the conversation as she took the moussaka out of the oven.

'You've been chatty,' Hannah commented when she came through moments later.

'It was just Tash.' Rosie didn't mention that Tash had wanted to come over. Hannah didn't need to know that.

'I thought I heard my phone ring a short while ago too.'

Shit. Had she?

'Oh, yes. That was Liam.' Rosie kept her tone blasé, as if it was no big deal.

'I should call him back.'

'You can't.'

'I can't? Why not?'

'He said he won't be able to answer for the rest of the evening.'

'Oh, really?' Hannah looked disappointed.

'Apparently he's in an area with no signal,' Rosie told her. It was just a tiny lie and for Hannah's own good. She was fed up with him interfering.

She studied her friend. Having her hair wrapped up in a towel only served to emphasise the black eyes, which made Rosie rage inside and wish she had twatted Bill even harder with that frying pan.

'I'm going to dish out the dinner so go and dry your hair and get your PJs on.'

Hannah nodded, managed a smile. 'You're such a good friend. Thank you for this, Rosie.'

As she disappeared through to the bedroom, Rosie wandered over to the window and eased back the curtain, peering out again. It was completely dark outside now, the road below illuminated by a single street lamp. Was Mrs W lurking in the shadows, watching the flat?

The thought made her shudder.

She kept telling them all that the woman was still dangerous. There was no way that Bill had acted alone. She just wished they would believe her.

* * *

Liam didn't waste any time when he got back to Adrian's. He told Jill's husband where he had been and admitted he was involved with Hannah. He stopped short of using the word boyfriend. They weren't in a relationship. Involved could mean a number of things and wasn't really a lie.

He had expected Adrian to be annoyed at his earlier deception, but the man was so good-natured and eager to get to the bottom of his wife's death, he brushed it off.

'What do you need to know?'

'You said Jill had had called in sick at work. Did she give any indication why?'

'She told the receptionist she wasn't feeling great, but didn't go into specifics. I did try to call her late morning, but there was no answer.'

'Is it possible she might have had someone here with her?'

The man's eyes widened at that. 'You think she was having an affair?'

'No, no, I don't mean that. Lauren was arguing with whoever was in her home and trying to get them to leave. I'm wondering if Jill had an unwelcome visitor too.'

'I'm sorry. You've lost me. You think someone was here and made her call in sick?'

Liam picked his words carefully. 'Bill's attack on Hannah was fuelled by rage. He beat her up and would have likely raped her before he killed her. Lauren was suffocated and Jill fell down the stairs. Both completely different to Hannah's attack.'

'So you don't think he killed Lauren?'

'I don't.'

'And you don't think Jill's death was an accident?' Adrian's voice wobbled as he asked the question.

'No. If I'm right, I think a woman attacked Lauren and your wife.'

Adrian seemed a little shocked by the idea, but didn't altogether dismiss it. 'You think it was her, don't you? That Wickham woman?'

Liam knew Eileen's name had already been mentioned at the time of his wife's death, but he ignored the question. Instead he asked, 'Can I look around?'

'The police have already been here. And I haven't seen anything out of place, but I guess if you think it would help.'

Adrian hovered close while Liam poked around. He had no idea what he was looking for and knew it was likely he would find nothing, but he owed it to Hannah, Rosie, and Tash to at least try.

Fifteen minutes passed and he sensed Adrian was getting a little frustrated, though good manners stopped him from asking Liam to leave. He could have pushed it, but he didn't want to take advantage of a grieving man. He was getting ready to call it quits when he spotted the friendship bracelet sitting in a trinket dish in the spare room. He recognised it immediately, having seen Hannah's.

'Oh, that was Jill's,' Adrian told him as he picked it up. 'I found it on the floor. It must have fallen off while she was cleaning. I didn't think she wore it any more.'

Liam twisted the bracelet between his fingers, saw the frayed cord had snapped.

All of the kids had one. Tash had made them for each member of the Hixton Five. Friendship bracelets. Each piece of string was extendable and had a friendship symbol charm and a tiny initial bead. Hannah's had a H and Jill's a J. He looked at it now and blinked, everything inside him going cold.

It was the wrong letter.

'Does Jill have a jewellery box?'

'In the bedroom. Why?'

'Can I see it? Please.'

Adrian shrugged, but led the way.

Jill's bracelet lay amongst her other jewellery inside the box.

As Liam picked it up, Adrian looked confused. 'I didn't realise she had two the same.'

'She didn't.'

Liam ran his thumb over the J charm, and pulled his phone from his pocket. He tried Hannah, then Rosie, but both phones went to voicemail.

This wasn't good. He left messages for them asking that they call him back, knew he needed to get back to Wells urgently.

He understood now, everything starting to make sense.

Bill hadn't killed Jill or Lauren.

If he was right, the danger came from within the Hixton Five.

64

Rosie was right. Today had been good for Hannah.

She was still missing Liam, but Rosie had gone above and beyond to make today special for her. When she had first suggested a pamper day, Hannah hadn't really been interested. The attack had numbed her and she could think of little else. All she wanted was to retreat into her shell and wallow.

Rosie hadn't allowed her to do that, though, and Hannah was glad. Wallowing was not the way forward and they had spent a lovely day just chatting, watching movies, enjoying pamper treatments, and she was starting to appreciate the little things again. Even taking Tank for a walk hadn't been too traumatic. She felt safe with him by her side and knew he would look after her, and it was good practice for her, getting out and about. She had been forced to let her doggy charges down again and knew she needed to get back to work as soon as possible, scared her clients might look for someone more reliable.

For now, she silently praised herself for managing to have a good day. One that Rosie was finishing off by cooking Hannah's favourite meal. Moussaka.

How she wished she had an appetite. Truth was, she had struggled to eat over the last few days, managing just what was necessary. Rosie had gone to so much effort for her though and so she gamely picked her way through the meal.

'Here, have some more wine. I bought your favourite.'

Hannah didn't really want any more, could already feel the glass she had drunk had gone to her head, but Rosie was topping up her glass. Hannah noticed her hand was shaking a little.

'Are you okay?'

Hannah was familiar with Rosie's brave smile and that was what she was getting now. When her friend's eyes filled with tears, guilt stabbed at her. She had been so self-absorbed with the attack; she had forgotten that Rosie was suffering too.

'What's wrong?'

'It's nothing. I just can't stop thinking about Mrs W. I know she's still out there, Hannah, and she's going to come after us. I'm scared.'

Had Mrs W been working with Bill? Hannah honestly didn't know and she was trying her best not to think about the woman too much. The police had Bill. He was surely the bigger threat. Could Mrs W hurt them without his help?

'We're going to be okay. We're here together and we have each other, right?'

Rosie nodded.

'The front door is locked and we won't let anyone in who we don't trust. We're safe here, I promise.' Hannah wasn't sure she believed her own words, but they were what Rosie needed to hear, and the tension in her shoulders eased a little when Rosie gave her a watery smile.

She needed Rosie to be strong, knowing she couldn't carry her right now.

'I'm sorry, Hannah. It's okay. I've got you.'

After clearing away the dishes, Rosie insisted they watch

another movie. Hannah was exhausted, but agreed to stay up a little later. She really didn't fancy the rest of her wine though, pouring the contents of the still nearly full glass down the sink while Rosie was in the loo. She dozed off on the sofa before the film was even halfway through.

'Come on, sleepyhead. Let's get you into bed.'

She came to, realised the credits were rolling, and took a moment to remember where she was.

She was so tired, her limbs heavy as Rosie helped her into the bedroom. It was too much effort to go and clean her teeth and she fell onto the bed, let Rosie pull the duvet over her.

* * *

It was Tank's barking that woke her.

At first, she thought Liam was holding her, but then she remembered Rosie was staying. Her friend had wrapped her arms around her and was stroking Hannah's hair.

'You're awake again. I'm sorry. I thought I'd given you more.'

'More what?'

It was then that Hannah smelt the burning.

'Rosie, did you leave the oven on?'

The words came out, but they were groggy and slurred. Her voice sounded alien, even to her own ears. She tried to sit up, but it was too much effort.

Rosie didn't answer her, continuing to stroke her hair in a slow methodical action. 'It's going to be okay, Hannah. I'm making sure she can never hurt us again.'

The smell was getting strong. Tank sounding more frantic.

'Rosie...'

'Go to sleep, Hannah. It's just the two of us, like always'

Something wasn't right.

What had Rosie done?

* * *

It wasn't supposed to be like this. Hannah was meant to stay asleep.

This was the easiest way. The kindest way. Mrs W would never be able to hurt them again.

Rosie still felt guilty about how things had ended with Jill. She hadn't meant to push her.

She had been in London, was drunk and an emotional mess. Jill hadn't been happy when she had called her at 3.30 a.m., but she had reluctantly agreed to put her up for the night. When Rosie had surfaced the next day, Jill was angry and blaming her for her lack of sleep, saying she had been forced to call in sick at work as she was so tired.

It was then that she told Rosie how Hannah had messaged and was trying to reach her.

'Please don't tell her I'm here.'

'Why not? She's worried about you. Look at you, Rosie. You're a joke. You need to get yourself back to Norwich and sort yourself the hell out.'

She had kicked Rosie out and told her not to come back.

Rosie had stood outside the house debating what to do. Jill's cruel words ringing in her ears.

They had all once been so close. What had happened?

As she often did when she sought comfort, she had reached to tug on her bracelet, the one Tash had given them all as kids. Rosie never removed it, so when she realised it wasn't on her wrist, she had panicked. She couldn't lose it. That bracelet meant something. It was the thread that kept them all connected.

Had she lost it in the club? No, she was certain she was wearing it when she arrived at Jill's last night.

She had knocked on the door and Jill had let her back in, but she hadn't been happy, following Rosie upstairs as she hunted for it in the bedroom where she had spent the night. She said so many spiteful things, still furious with Rosie, and when Rosie couldn't find the bracelet, Jill demanded she leave. Rosie was panic-stricken.

'I can't. Not without my bracelet. I know it's here somewhere. I just have to find it.'

'You can see it's not here. You must have left it somewhere else. I need you to leave, Rosie. Now.'

'Please, just a few more minutes.'

Jill had rolled her eyes. 'I'm messaging Hannah. I don't need this crap.'

'No, you promised.'

'I never promised anything.'

Jill had her phone out, typing as she had turned to walk away, and desperate, Rosie had reached out to stop her. The next thing she knew, Jill was at the foot of the stairs, her head twisted at an unnatural angle, and Rosie knew before she checked that her old friend didn't have a pulse.

Initially, she had panicked, knew she had to call the police. It had been an accident. She hadn't meant it to happen. But what if they didn't believe her? What if they arrested her? Rosie couldn't go to prison. She would never cope. Inside were hundreds of Mrs Ws waiting to prey on her. The very thought terrified her.

She had stumbled around Jill's house, wiping over the surfaces she remembered touching, taking Jill's phone with her when she left. Although she had called her the previous night on Snapchat and the history shouldn't show, she was too paranoid to risk it. Instead she dropped the phone in the river that ran through the park close to where Jill lived.

She had sat on the grassy bank for a while, numb with shock as she tried to come to terms with what had happened. She had no idea where she went from here. Did she head back to Norwich and try to pretend none of this had happened?

Not sure she was ready to face that yet, certain her actions would be written all over her face, she had tried to lose herself in shopping, knowing that buying clothes always made her feel better.

This time it didn't work.

When she had bumped into her ex, Gavin, it had been an easy decision to go with him.

She needed something that would make her feel again. Sex with Gav usually did the trick.

The whole time, Jill's voice was ringing in her ears, reminding her that she was a screw-up and she needed to get her life back on track.

Jill had no idea.

In fact, maybe she had done her a favour, Rosie reasoned when later that day she made her way back to Norwich. Jill had no idea of the danger she had been in and in death she had looked so peaceful.

Mrs W was still coming for the rest of them. If only they could all escape.

That idea had stayed with her, though of course she had no plan to act on it. Then Lauren had hired her private investigator, ready to confront Mrs W and Bill.

Hannah had told her not to go to Lauren's, but Rosie was worried. Lauren had no idea of the danger she was putting them all in. She needed to be stopped.

Rosie was down in London for her audition and Sevenoaks wasn't far. She would go and see Lauren, try to reason with her. She went prepared, just in case, her dealer handing over the bag of ketamine, no questions asked. It was easy to buy anything if you had money.

Rosie had tried to talk her round, but Lauren was dead set on doing things her way, so there had been no other choice. She had barely been conscious when Rosie put the pillow over her face.

She would have shown the same kindness to Tash, but Sam had unexpectedly come home, and Rosie had been forced to ditch her plan. Tash had her girlfriend and Rosie trusted Sam to look after her.

The decision to help Hannah was the easiest one Rosie had made. Bill's attack had changed things and now she understood how vulnerable Hannah was. Rosie couldn't go on without her, so they would go to sleep together. She would plan the best day for Hannah, involving all of her favourite things, then slip the drug into their wine. Hannah's first, so Rosie could make sure she was comfortable in bed. She didn't want her friend to suffer when the flat started to burn.

She had fucked up though, as Hannah had woken up. Rosie obviously hadn't given her enough and now it was too late. Holding Hannah tightly, and fighting her own fatigue, she whispered that it would be okay and prayed it would soon be over.

* * *

The room was getting hotter, the air making her choke. Hannah tried again to sit up. They had to get out. She had to find Tank.

She struggled to lift her head, saw smoke billowing around the door frame, could hear flames the other side, and panic skittered through her. She was really awake now, though everything was still blurry and distorted, her limbs too heavy.

Rosie clung to her, seeming unbothered by the fire. She started to cry.

'I'm sorry... you wouldn't wake.' Her voice was really slurry. 'Sleep... be easier.'

'What have you done?'

Had she drugged them both?

Why?

And had she set the fire?

It seemed implausible. Rosie was her best friend. Why would she do this?

Was it some kind of suicide pact?

Hannah didn't want to die. She couldn't let this happen.

Rosie's grip had weakened now. Was she still conscious? Gathering all her energy, Hannah managed to roll towards the edge of the bed.

She hit the ground with a heavy thud, aware of how thick the smoke was now, the sound of the building flames intense.

Tank was still the other side of the door, barking and scratching and going nuts. Hannah pulled herself across the bedroom floor towards the sound.

She eventually reached the door, managed to pull down on the handle and open it. Tank was with her then and she could feel the dog's nose nudging at her as he whined.

She couldn't see through the smoke. How were they going to make it out of the flat?

She was so tired and didn't think she could move any more.

Tank kept barking and pulling at her, but he would have to wait. She needed to rest. Just for a few seconds.

* * *

At first, she wasn't aware of the arms lifting her, carrying her out of the flat, then, when she realised, she was still so out of it she could barely focus on the firefighter's face. 'Rosie... you have to help her. She's still inside.'

She didn't hear his response, lost consciousness again, waking when she was outside and cold air hit her face. She was on a stretcher now and being loaded into an ambulance. Liam was with her, had her hand in his.

'You're going to be okay.'

'Tank and Rosie...'

'Tank's here. He's fine.'

'And Rosie?'

'They're trying to get to her.'

Liam squeezed her hand.

'Please help her,' she managed again, and then her eyelids fluttered shut.

EPILOGUE

And then there were two.

They had been known as the Hixton Five for so long. Some of them had only witnessed moments of Eileen Wickham's true nature. Others in the group had suffered unimaginable cruelty at her hands, but all of them had provided evidence that led to her incarceration.

It had started with the death of Miles Goldberg and ended with Rosie Emerson taking her own life. The children in the box. The two youngest victims.

Because, despite what she had done, Rosie was a victim. The families of Jill and Lauren might still be struggling with that, but it was true. Like a ripple effect of a stone dropping into water, the repercussions of Eileen's actions had continued to spread.

If she hadn't abused the children, Rosie could have blossomed, Jill and Lauren would still be alive, and Liam wouldn't have been compelled to write a book in memory of his stepbrother. By approaching the Wickhams, he had triggered Bill's suspicion, and after following Liam back to Norfolk and seeing him with Hannah,

Bill had assumed she had orchestrated the visit. This had only added to the cocktail of simmering emotions he was experiencing following his mother's release, and was very likely the catalyst that finally pushed him over the edge.

In turn, one of the ripples had worked out positively. It had brought Liam into Hannah's life, and Bill's attack had pushed the pair of them closer together. Liam had been her rock in recent weeks as he supported her through her recovery.

She had encountered Veronica Goldberg at Jill's funeral, an awkward moment for them both. Hannah couldn't help but remember her as Jill and Miles's step-monster, and got the impression that Veronica wasn't entirely happy that her son was involved with someone who would always be a reminder of Hixton and the events that led to Miles's death.

Veronica's reaction had Hannah nervous about meeting the rest of Liam's family, and her stomach churned with nerves as he drove her down to Devon a few weekends later.

She had tried to get out of the trip, telling him she was too busy. It was actually true. The fire had destroyed her flat and she was forced to start afresh, having lost everything. She had managed to rent a place further inland, but rebuilding her home and her life was going to take time.

Liam had been insistent they go, convinced the break would do her good, and given how things were progressing between them, she had eventually agreed.

It was still early days in their relationship, but he was already looking at property in North Norfolk and talking about relocating. Hannah didn't push him, continuing to focus on her own plans, understanding that things would work out in their own way and in their own time. This trip to see his parents and sister was just another step that proved they were heading in the right direction.

Her physical scars had mostly healed, so at least she didn't have to worry about meeting them while she was covered in bruises. The psychological ones would take longer and she was dealing with them one day at a time.

At least Bill had finally confessed to knowing where his mother was and Hannah had been shocked and relieved to learn she was dead.

After leaving prison and moving into the terrace house Bill had rented in Sudbury, Eileen had been subjected to a campaign of hate. She wasn't welcome and as word spread, things became worse for her. It wasn't the fresh start Bill had hoped to give her, so when he managed to get the keys to a remote cottage in Lincolnshire, he had moved her, hoping the vigilante mob would finally leave her in peace. The cottage had belonged to the father of a friend of his and was standing empty after the old man had passed away. Bill had struck a deal with his friend. Let his mother stay there until it went on the market and Bill would fix the place up for free.

Unfortunately for Eileen, that decision hadn't worked out for the best as she had suffered a stroke while out in the garden and had been unable to get back inside to phone for help. Bill had found her days later.

He was convinced the stress had been brought on by the Hixton Five, and by Hannah sending Liam Quinn to see her. And it made his need for retribution all the stronger.

He claimed he had buried his mother in an unmarked grave in a wood close to the property, determined that her final resting place would not be tainted by vandals. Police were still trying to get the location from him to verify his story was true.

Regardless, he would be facing trial for attacking Hannah, and it was likely he would be serving his own prison sentence.

She pushed thoughts of the Wickhams to one side as Liam

pulled off the coastal road and up a long driveway to a modest bungalow that Hannah was sure had stunning views over the sea.

The front door was open before the car had stopped, an attractive woman with a dark bob rushing out to greet them.

Hannah self-consciously brushed a hand through her hair as she got out of the car. The icy wind blowing in off the sea taking her breath away.

'Liam.' The woman threw her arms around him the second he was out of the car and he squeezed her back as Tank ran circles around them, barking his delight as he realised where they were.

'Hey, Jen.'

So this was his stepmother.

As they parted and Jennifer's gaze shifted, Hannah shuffled uncomfortably.

'You must be Hannah. I'm Jennifer. I'm so glad you're here.'

There were no formalities in this house, Hannah soon discovered, as Jennifer hugged her tightly, then moments later when she met Liam's dad, James, she received another warm embrace.

Later, as they chatted over dinner, Liam's younger sister, Ashley, having joined them, Hannah realised Liam had been right to insist she come. The Quinns were warm, welcoming people and they didn't judge her. Only happy that she and Liam had found one another.

With her circle decreasing, it was good to have the strength and support of new relationships. It would help steady her during the days she struggled to cope. Of course, she still had Josh, and her mum was trying to make the effort, though Hannah wasn't sure Jane would ever fully understand the trauma she had experienced. And she still had Tash. The pair of them were in regular contact, seeking comfort from each other as they tried to come to terms with Rosie's actions and her death.

They would never forget her, preferring to remember her as the sweet and excitable little girl she had been before Mrs W had tainted her. And as they clung on to the older happier memories, Hannah tried to visualise the six of them together, out on their bikes, building dens in the woods, playing on the train track, or wandering down country lanes. Rosie and Miles always at the back. Always lagging as they chattered away, their laughter bubbling in the air.

But now when Hannah turned to tell them to hurry up, the lane was empty.

* * *

For a commitment-phobe, it had taken almost losing Hannah twice to understand how important she had become to him. Liam knew Hannah still had her own demons to face. And Rosie's death had only added to her anguish. Knowing that her best friend had tried to kill her and had taken her own life, feeling guilty that she hadn't realised quite how dark a place Rosie was in, was a lot for her to deal with. He would help her come to terms with everything, but understood it wouldn't be an easy fix, and he vowed to himself that he wouldn't let anyone ever hurt her again. It was who he was. He protected those he cared for.

The woman he was falling in love with and the little boy he had once loved.

Miles had always been at the heart of Liam's book. The shy but big-hearted kid with his huge glasses and impish grin. Had Liam had the chance, he would have been the best big brother to him. Eileen Wickham had stolen the chance, and he would never forgive her for that.

Before he had travelled to Norfolk, before he had met Hannah and Rosie, he had visited Eileen, knowing that she was a necessary part of the story but eager to get her interview over with. Bill had been at the house at the time and he had kicked Liam out. The Wickhams weren't interested in listening to anything he had to say.

After going to Sudbury with Hannah and learning that Eileen had fled, he had contacted a private investigator friend, calling in a favour. The police were already looking for her, so he didn't hold out much hope of finding her first. Bill Wickham was insistent he didn't know where his mother had gone to, but the PI placed a tracker on his car anyway. Eventually it had paid off.

Liam had been at Hannah's, having just agreed to go back to Hixton with her to her mother's anniversary party, when the PI tried to call him and he had quickly found an excuse to leave. The following day he had gone to the house in Lincolnshire, finding Eileen in the garden.

She had been hanging out washing and looked surprised when she spotted him.

'What the hell are you doing here?'

'I just want to talk.' Liam had kept his tone reasonable, though everything inside him seethed. This was the woman who had stolen Miles from him and he hated her with every fibre of his being.

'I already told you to piss off. Get out of here or I'll call Bill.'

The conversation had continued. Liam trying to talk her round, Eileen becoming more worked up. He wasn't going to leave until she spoke to him and he told her that, threatening to make a call of his own and let everyone know where she was.

She had stared at him then, her mouth twisting cruelly. 'Those little bastards deserved it,' she had taunted. 'You should have heard them beg.'

For the briefest moment, she seemed to struggle with her balance, the anger that had been twisting her features dropping away to resemble something that looked like confusion.

Then she had collapsed.

Looking back, he supposed he had spotted the signs. The drooping of her face, the slurring of her speech moments before it happened. As she lay on the ground, she tried to reach a hand out to him. Her words when they came out were a weak whisper. 'Please... help me.'

He could have called for an ambulance, but instead he remembered the frightened little boy who had been locked inside a box and buried alive in the ground.

Had Eileen ever experienced terror like that?

He had stayed with her for ten minutes, told her all about his little brother, savouring the shock on her face when she realised who he was, and then he asked her if he should forgive her.

Eileen didn't answer him. Her eyes had filled with bitterness and hatred, and, he thought, self-pity, as a single tear had escaped.

'I didn't think so,' he'd told her.

Giving her one final glance, he had turned away from her and headed to his car.

From there, he drove back to Norfolk and to the Airbnb he had hired in the pretty town of Wells-next-the-Sea, where he took a few days to process his actions.

Should he have called an ambulance?

He had thought of Miles. The boy he had been, the man he would have become if given a chance. Then he had considered Hannah and the scars she carried, afraid to return to her childhood home for a party. Eileen had shown zero remorse and appeared to still be tormenting the Hixton Five.

Finally, at peace with his decision, he had gone back to Hannah.

She had been annoyed with him at first for disappearing on her, but he couldn't tell her the truth of where he had been. Eventually she forgave him and he went to Hixton with her to help her fight her demons.

To this day, he hadn't told anyone he had gone to Lincolnshire and it was a secret he intended to take to the grave. It was easier that way. Hannah was safe and justice had been served for Miles. Liam took comfort in knowing that Eileen Wickham could never hurt anyone ever again.

ACKNOWLEDGMENTS

My first novel for Boldwood Books and a huge thank you to the lovely team for their very warm welcome. I might write the stories, but I know it takes many people to polish them to a publishable standard and then make them shine, and I believe Boldwood have the very best people to do this.

I must single out my editor, Caroline Ridding. I am so excited to finally be working with her and she has undoubtedly made my book so much better than when I first presented it to her. We never stop learning and evolving, and I love that she is pushing me to be a better writer. My thanks also to Jade Craddock, who did a fantastic copy edit and came up with some brilliant suggestions, and also Emily and Sue who helped polish the final version.

To my family. Thank you for putting up with me when I am grumpy and on deadline.

There are so many supportive folk in the writing world and I hate mentioning names, because I always forget people, so I am going to do a collective shout-out to the brilliant gang at Team Beev, who always have my back with all things bookish. I appreciate you all more than you know.

To Lexi Hartman and Nicola Finch. Competition winners to have their names mentioned in the book. Thank you, ladies. And also, to two of the most supportive book groups on Facebook – Bitchy Bookworms and Book Swap Central. Thank you to all of the lovely readers and admin for buying and spreading word of my books.

A mention next to a very special young man, Will Hagg. One of the coolest kids I know. Thank you for my crash course on Snapchat.

To Paula Armes, who gave me the kick I needed when I had given up on my dream of being published. I will forever be grateful to you. And to Josephine Bilton, who has supported me right from the start. Thank you both.

Then finally to the Teletubbies – Trish Dixon, Nathan Moss, and Heather Fitt. Every writer needs a writing support network and these guys are my Musketeers (how we arrived at Teletubbies I can't quite remember). Thank you for being there to talk to and for making me smile every day.

I must single out Trish, as we read for each other as we write, as well as brainstorm together and work through any plot issues. This business can be lonely at times, so I count myself as very lucky to have found my writing soulmate.

As always, the places I write about are real. All except Hixton. In my head it is located close to Sudbury in Suffolk, and there are many sleepy villages like it. But this one you won't ever find on a map.

MORE FROM KERI BEEVIS

We hope you enjoyed reading *The Sleepover*. If you did, please leave a review.

If you'd like to gift a copy, this book is also available as an ebook, digital audio download and audiobook CD.

Sign up to Keri Beevis' mailing list for news, competitions and updates on future books.

https://bit.ly/KeriBeevisnews

ABOUT THE AUTHOR

Keri Beevis is the internationally bestselling author of several psychological thrillers and romantic suspense mysteries, including the very successful Dying to Tell, published by Bloodhound. She sets many of her books in the county of Norfolk, where she was born and still lives and which provides much of her inspiration.

Visit Keri's website: http://www.keribeevis.com/

Follow Keri on social media:

twitter.com/keribeevis
facebook.com/allaboutbeev
instagram.com/keri.beevis

Boldw⬤⬤d

Boldwood Books is an award-winning fiction publishing company seeking out the best stories from around the world.

Find out more at www.boldwoodbooks.com

Join our reader community for brilliant books, competitions and offers!

Follow us
@BoldwoodBooks
@BookandTonic

Sign up to our weekly deals newsletter

https://bit.ly/BoldwoodBNewsletter

Printed in Great Britain
by Amazon